THE SAVING CLAUSE

Books by " SAPPER "

HODDER & STOUGHTON LTD.,
WARWICK SQUARE,
LONDON, E.C.4

THE
SAVING CLAUSE

BY

"SAPPER"

HODDER AND STOUGHTON
LIMITED   LONDON

01009960

First Printed . . . . March, 1927
Fourteenth Edition . . . May, 1934

*Made and Printed in Great Britain for Hodder & Stoughton, Limited,
by C. Tinling & Co., Ltd., Liverpool, London and Prescot.*

CONTENTS

I GUESS I don't hold with missionaries. I've been in most corners of this globe, and I reckon that the harm they do easily outweighs the good. Stands to reason, don't it, that we can't all have the same religion, same as we can't all have the same shaped nose ? So what in thunder is the good of trying to put my nose on to your face, where it won't fit ? And it sort of riles me to see these good earnest people labouring and sweating to do to others what they would only describe as damned impertinence if those others tried to do it to them. Yet, as I see it, there's no reason why the others shouldn't. 'Tisn't as if any particular bunch had a complete corner in truth, is it ?

But there are exceptions, same as to most things. And for the past twenty years whenever I've said I don't hold with missionaries, I've always added a saving clause in my mind. Care to hear what that saving clause is ? Right : mine's the same as before.

It was just after the Boer War that it happened. I'd come home : got a job of sorts in London. Thought a few years of the quiet life would do me good, and an old uncle of mine wangled me into the office of a pal of his. Funny old thing my boss was, with a stomach like a balloon. And I give you my word that he was the last man in London whom you'd

7

have expected to meet at the Empire on a Saturday night. It was sheer bad luck, though I don't suppose I could have stood that job, anyway, for long.

I'd met a pal there, you see, and I suppose we'd started to hit it a bit. Anyway a darned great chucker-out came and intimated that he thought the moment had come when we'd better sample the cool night air of Leicester Square.

Well, I don't say I was right : strictly speaking, I suppose I should have accepted his remark in the spirit in which it was intended. But the fact remains that I didn't like his face or his frock coat—and we had words. And finally the chucker-out sampled the cool night air—not me. The only trouble was that just as he went down the stairs, my boss was coming up with wife and family complete. And that chucker-out was a big man : I guess it was rather like being hit by a steam roller. Anyway the whole blessed family turned head over heels, and landed on the pavement simultaneously with the chucker-out on top.

Again strictly speaking, I suppose I should have gone and picked them up with suitable words of regret. But I just couldn't do it : I was laughing too much. In fact I didn't stop laughing till I began to run—the police were heaving in sight. Still you boys know what the Empire was like in those days : so I'll pass on to Monday morning.

Not that there's much to say about Monday morning, except that it closed my connection with the firm. The old man had a black eye where the chucker-out had trodden on his face, and the hell of a liver. And he utterly failed to see the humorous side of the episode. As far as I could make out his wife had smashed her false teeth in the mêlée, and was as wild as a civet cat ; and only the fact that his own firm would be involved had prevented him giving my name to the police. My own private opinion was that it wasn't so much the firm he was worrying about as himself. Still, that's neither here nor there : all that matters is that my job in London terminated that morning.

Maybe you're wondering what the dickens all this has to do with missionaries and my saving clause, but I'm coming to that part soon. And I want you to realize the frame of mind I was in when I found myself propping up the Criterion bar just before lunch on that Monday. It may seem strange to you that a bloke like me could ever have stomached quill driving in a City office, but the fact remains that at the time I was almighty sick with myself at having got the sack. And as luck would have it, I hadn't been in that bar more than five minutes when a bunch of four of the boys blew in, whom I'd last seen in South Africa. They were the lads all right, I give you my word : four of the toughest propositions you're ever likely to meet in your life. There was Bill Merton who had graduated in the Kimberley diamond rush : Andy Fraser who had left Australia hurriedly, and it didn't do to ask why : Tom Jerrold with a five-inch scar on

A*

his face that he'd picked up in Chicago : and last but not least Pete O'Farrell.

Gad ! he was a character, was Pete. A great big hulking fellow of about six feet three, with muscles like an ox, and a pair of blue eyes that went clean through you and came out the other side. I once saw him tackle four policemen in Sydney, and get away with it. So did one policeman who ran for his life : the other three went to hospital.

As soon as they saw me Pete let out a bellow like a bull, and led the charge.

" If it isn't old Mac," he shouted. " Gee—boy, but it's great to see you, even if your face is like a wet street. What's stung you ? "

" I've lost my job, Pete," I said. " Upset the boss and all his belongings into Leicester Square on Saturday night and got the boot."

" You mean you're at a loose-end," he said, and he looked at the other three. " What about it, boys ? "

" Sure thing," said Andy, " if he'll come."

" Of course he'll come," cried Pete. " Bring your poison into this corner, Mac, and we'll put you wise."

So we went and sat down in a corner, and they told me the scheme. It doesn't much matter what it was : it's got nothing to do with the yarn. But it appeared they were sailing for South America the following Friday, and they wanted to know if I'd go with them. Something to do with a revolution in some bally little state, and Pete swore we'd all make our fortunes.

Well, I guess if I hadn't been feeling so sick with

myself I shouldn't have gone. I ain't no lizard lounger myself, but from past experience I knew that hunting with that bunch meant a pretty fast pace. Particularly Pete. He was a darned good fellow, but if he got a bit of liquor inside him, it was well not to contradict him. I will say, to do him justice, it took more than a bottle of whisky to get him into that condition, but whisky was only four bob in those days.

At any rate I did go. And on Friday morning we sailed in a tin-can sort of effect from Liverpool. She was really a cargo boat that took a few passengers, and she just suited our pockets. Moreover she was going to call at some obscure spot, where none of the big lines touched, and which, according to Pete, was the exact place from which we could best start our operations.

We ran into bad weather right away, and by Jove! that old tub could roll.

Mercifully we were all good sailors, and it wasn't until we went below for dinner that we realized there was another passenger. She only accommodated six, and up till then we had thought we were one short. But there were six places laid at the table, with a seat at the end for the skipper, who was on the bridge and had sent down word for us to start without him.

The cabins led off the dining-saloon, and suddenly during a slight lull in the ship's movement, Pete began to laugh.

" Holy Smoke ! boys," he cried, " listen. Steward, who is the occupant of the sixth seat, whom I hear enjoying himself in his cabin ? "

The steward grinned.

" Gent by the name of Todmarsh, sir," he answered. " Ain't never been to sea before. 'E's in a hawful condition."

" Well, I hope he doesn't make that row all night," said Pete. " I'm in the next cabin. Good-evening, skipper. We've taken you at your word and started."

" Quite right," said the captain, hanging up his oilskin. " We're in for a bad forty-eight hours, I'm afraid."

" You've got the brass band all complete, any-way," grinned Andy. " Who is Mr. Todmarsh, skipper ? "

For a moment or two he didn't answer. From under a pair of great bushy eyebrows he took us all in : then he chuckled.

" Well, gentlemen," he said, " I've had some pretty strangely assorted bunches in this saloon during my time but I'll stake my oath that mixing you five and Mr. Todmarsh will constitute a record."

It was Andy Fraser who turned pale.

" Don't say," he gasped, " that he's a parson."

" That's just what I do say," howled the skipper delightedly. " At least he's a missionary."

" Steward—a double whisky," said Pete feebly. " Skipper—it ain't fair. You ought to have had a notice hung over the side. Where's he going to ? "

" Same place as you," answered the other. " Then
he's going up into the interior. So you'll be able to look
after him when he lands. It's the first time he's left
England."

Well, gentlemen, I don't want to tread on anybody's corns. I have always had the highest respect
for the Church myself, but I think you'll agree with
me that what the skipper said about ill-assorted
bunches was right. The trouble was that the ship
was so small—at least the passenger part of it—that
you couldn't get away from one another. And the
prospect of three weeks cooped up with a devil-dodger
was a bit of a staggerer.

It was three days before we saw him, and then the
staggerer became a knock-out. I found Pete and
Andy holding one another's heads on the deck, and
asked 'em what the trouble was. Personally I hadn't
seen him yet, and it was just as they began to sob in
unison that Mr. Todmarsh appeared from below.
Gosh ! I've never thought of such an extraordinary-
looking little bird in my life. Boys—that man had
to be seen to be believed. Making all due allowances
for the fact that he had been sick for three days
without cessation, Todmarsh won the freak stakes in
a canter.

His face was pasty, and his eyes behind his spectacles
were weak and watery. He can't have stood more
than five feet three, and his physique was that of a
stunted child.

" Good morning, Mr. Todmarsh," said Pete gravely.
" Hope you're feeling better."

" I thank you, yes," he answered, and at that
moment Bill Merton and Tom Jerrold hove in sight.
Then they disappeared again quickly and I saw 'em
a minute or two later w th their foreheads pressed
against something cold.

It was Pete who called a council of war, which was
duly held in the saloon over the forenoon bracer.
Todmarsh, enveloped in a rug, was up on deck, and
we knew we shouldn't be disturbed.

" Look here, boys," said Pete, " that little guy is
worse than anything I could have believed possible.
I reckon that the temptation to pull his leg is going
to be almost more than we can bear. But it seems
to me that since there are five of us and only one of
him, it's up to us to give the poor beggar a sporting
chance. He must have a certain amount of guts
presumably to start off on his own, when he's made
that way. So I votes we play the game by him and
treat him square. Anyway no monkeying about
with religion—that's his affair, not ours."

Well, we did our best. Pete only blasphemed twice
at lunch, and Andy darned near choked in biting off
a story half-way through, that he'd suddenly
remembered was unprintable. But that guy was
difficult. He didn't *say* anything on the subject of
alcohol—but he looked a lot. Still we could have
stood that, and the general cramped style of the conversation, if he hadn't come butting in after dinner.

We were playing poker, when in he comes from a stroll on deck. I'll admit his arrival coincided with Pete's remarks on the subject of a full house aces while Tom had fours, and for a moment or two we didn't see him. But the next instant, blowed if he hadn't advanced to the table and snatched up the pack of cards.

Well, I suppose, looking back on it now, that it showed a certain amount of pluck. But at the moment it struck us as an unwarrantable piece of impertinence.

" Look here, little man," said Pete ominously, " if that's your idea of fun and laughter it isn't mine. Put back those cards on the table."

" Never," cried Mr. Todmarsh. " These are the devil's counters ! "

" Devil's grandmother," said Pete getting up, and putting his hand on the little man's shoulder. " See here, Mr. Todmarsh—you're a missionary. I and my pals are not : it takes all sorts to make a world, you know. But there's no reason why we shouldn't all live quite happily together on board this ship, if you'll mind your business same as we're going to mind ours."

" This *is* my business," answered the other. " To play cards for money is one step down the road to Hell."

" Well, I'm afraid we're too darned near the bottom of the hill to worry about that," said Pete quietly. " Put back those cards on the table."

" I will not," said Todmarsh defiantly.

For just a moment I thought Pete was going to lose

his temper, and Heaven alone knows what would have happened to the little blighter if Pete had hit him. He'd have burst. However he didn't : he took both Mr. Todmarsh's wrists in one of his hands and took the pack out of his pocket with the other.

" Don't do it again," he said gently. " You're a stupid little man, and you've got a lot to learn. But now you've lodged your complaint, and salved your conscience : so, all I say to you is—don't do it again. Next time I might hurt you."

And it wasn't until we were having our final nightcap that anyone alluded to it again.

" You know," said Andy as he put down his glass, " he's mad and all that, but for a thing of that size to do what he did to five fellows like us—well, it's not too bad."

And that, I think, is what we all felt until the following day, when a thing happened that changed the whole atmosphere. In the bucketing we'd had, a lot of the cargo had got shifted, and the men were straightening things up under the first officer. As a matter of fact Pete and I for want of a bit of exercise were lending a hand ourselves, and the job was almost done when a heavy case suddenly toppled over and caught one of the sailors underneath.

My God ! but it was a nasty sight. The poor devil had the lower part of his body pretty well squashed flat : the mess was something frightful. There he was screaming fit to beat the band, though it was obvious to all of us that he was a goner. As I say—still, I'll draw a veil over the details.

" Get the missionary, Mac," shouted Pete to me.

I raced off, and found him on deck.

" Accident, Mr. Todmarsh," I said. " Man dying. No hope."

I'd got him by the arm and was hurrying him along.

" You can say a prayer or something, can't you ? It's a matter of seconds."

It was : the poor chap's groans were getting feebler. A bunch of his pals were round him, while Pete was holding up his head. They made room for us as we came, and I heard Pete mutter—" Hurry : hurry."

And then I looked round : there was no missionary. He was being sick in the corner : he was still being sick when the groans ceased. And it was left to Pete to say—" God rest your soul, old chap."

Then he got up, and I can't say I blame him. He lifted Mr. Todmarsh some five feet in the air with his boot, and left him where he lay.

" And if the little swab complains to the Captain, Mac," he said to me grimly, " I'll do it again."

But he didn't complain : he shut himself into his cabin for twenty-four hours. He didn't even come on deck when we sewed up in some canvas what was left of the poor devil who had been crushed, and buried him overboard.

" Ashamed to show his face," remarked Pete. " And that's the wretched little coward who had the gall to speak about devil's counters."

It was about three o'clock next afternoon that he suddenly appeared again. We were lounging about on deck—it was beginning to get almighty hot—and he went straight up to Pete.

" I want to thank you, Mr. O'Farrell," he said, " for kicking me."

Pete stared at him.

" Are you trying to be sarcastic ? " he said curtly.

" Far from it," answered the other. " The fact that you did what you did is as nothing to the mental torture I've been suffering since it happened. I failed that poor chap, and my only prayer is that I may have a chance of atoning. It's no excuse to say that it was the first time I'd ever seen an accident, and that the sight of it made me physically sick. I failed him, and there's no more to be said. I realize that I was just a rotten coward. And that's why I'm glad you kicked me, because it's part of my punishment that I should realize the contempt you rightly feel for me."

With that he was gone, leaving Pete staring after him speechlessly.

" Well, I'm damned," he muttered at length. " I reckon that little cove has me beat."

He filled his pipe thoughtfully, and then he looked at me.

" What do you make of him, Mac ? "

" Well, it *was* a nasty sight, Pete," I answered. ' And they say that medical students often faint at

their first operation. But for all that if you hadn't
kicked him yesterday, I should."

" I reckon I just felt wild at the moment," he said.
" But now—somehow or other—I wish I hadn't."

And for the next two or three days I often noticed
a puzzled frown on his face. He seemed to be trying
to size the little man up. He used to peer at him,
when he wasn't looking, as if he was some strange
specimen, until we started pulling his leg about it.

" Can't help it," he grinned. " The blighter sort
of fascinates me. I've never met anybody like him
before. But what for the life of me I can't make out
is what good he thinks he's going to do. I was leaning
over the side this morning talking to him. And there
were a couple of sharks in the water. So I told him
a pretty lurid story of what I'd once seen happen to a
fellow bathing at Durban, when a shark got him. I
give you my word, boys, he was the colour of putty
and shaking like a leaf when I'd finished. Well,
what I want to get at is what earthly use a freak with
nerves like that is going to be. Told me he always
suffered from a vivid imagination ever since he could
remember : told me—hullo ! what on earth has
bitten the skipper ? "

The captain was coming along the deck towards us,
and his face was white.

" I've got the most appalling ncws, gentlemen," he
said gravely. " There's a case of plague on board."

" Good God ! " Pete sat up staring at him.
" Plague ! "

" Yes. I'm sorry to say there's no doubt about it whatever. We've got, as you know, no doctor on board, but I've seen plague before. And the symptoms are absolutely unmistakable."

It was then that for the first time I noticed Todmarsh. His eyes were fixed on the skipper's face, with a look in them of such terror as I have never seen before or since. His lips were moving as if he was trying to speak, but no words came.

" There is only one thing to be done," went on the captain, " and that is to try not to think about it. I shall segregate the case completely, but in a boat of this size it's very difficult. And since I've been in contact with it I shall take my meals in future by myself. But I thought it was only fair to warn you at once, gentlemen, as to what has happened. I'll get every ounce I can out of her, but we can't make land in under eleven days at the earliest."

" Plague ! " Tony Jerrold got up suddenly. " I was in Canton in '94. We had a hundred thousand deaths. Hell ! "

He moved over to the side as the skipper left us— and I noticed that Todmarsh had gone too.

" This is a proper lucky trip, boys," said Pete. " First a man crushed to death, and now plague. The tame freak is a mascot all right."

He laughed, but it didn't ring quite true.

" Where is the little blighter ? " he went on. " This will put the wind up him."

" Probably gone below to pray," sneered Andy.

" Plague ! What the hell did we come in this rank tub for ? "

" Go to blazes," snarled Pete. " Sorry, Andy." He pulled himself together. " No good quarrelling. I guess we're all in the same boat, literally as well as metaphorically."

The breeze blew over, but it showed which way the wind had already begun to set. I don't know if any of you gentlemen have ever had a similar experience ; if not I hope for your sake that you never will. Hot as blazes : a dead flat calm : a small cargo boat with no doctor—and plague. Men's tempers become a bit ragged : they get apt to see insults where none are intended. And, what is worse still, you begin to watch your next-door neighbour when you think he isn't looking. You see, there's nothing to do : it's the inaction that frays one's nerves—and the fear. You can banish it for a bit : you can forget it for a while with the help of some whisky—but back it comes gnawing at you sooner or later. Are you going to be the next victim ?

The first afternoon it wasn't so bad. After all there was only one case : with luck it might not spread. Besides we had something to amuse us— Todmarsh. It was Andy who discovered him, sitting in a deserted corner reading a medical book. And it was Andy who, of the whole bunch of us, took the show hardest from the very beginning. Outwardly, at least. It seemed to bring out all his worst points.

" Hullo ! missionary," he said harshly, "reading

about the plague, are you ? You don't need to read, my lad : I'll tell you."

And he did for five minutes, till Pete growled at him to shut up, and Todmarsh sweated and shook like a man bereft of his senses.

" Don't worry, little man," said Tom Jerrold, " you'll be all right out in the open here. As long as you keep away from infection."

" Is it terribly infectious ? " quavered the other.

" To blazes with you," cried Pete angrily. " You haven't got the courage of a louse. Why don't you draw a circle round yourself, and stop inside it ? We'll throw you your food."

It was the following morning that the first man died, and we had him overboard almost before the life was out of his body. And that afternoon there were two more cases. If possible it was hotter—the sea more oily. There wasn't a breath of wind : the deck was like a burning plate. And still ten days to go. But what finished us was that Todmarsh seemed to have taken Pete literally. He hadn't actually drawn a circle round himself, but when he wasn't below in his cabin he was sitting as far away from us as possible. He used to eat his grub on deck, and after he'd finished it he'd disappear for hours on end.

And we baited him—baited him brutally. I make no excuses for it : I was as bad as the others. We used to form a ring round him, and rag him cruel. This second exhibition of cowardice had put the tin-hat on. We were none of us too happy ourselves :

only, you see, you don't show that sort of thing.

But it had no effect : he just stood there and sweated, and backed away if any of us came close to him. It was the day that three men went down with it, I remember, that Andy suddenly lost control of himself. He made a sudden dart for the little man and shook him like a rat. And Todmarsh screamed like a wounded hare.

" Stand away ! Don't touch me ! "

We pulled Andy off : he was mad for the moment and in another instant he'd have flung him over the side.

" Quit it, Andy," growled Pete. " Leave the little swab to his own devices."

And then came the worst thing of the lot : the saloon steward, William, got it. That was when there were still five days to go, and he was the tenth case. We found him groaning in the pantry when we went down for lunch. And I guess it didn't improve our appetites. Poor devil—his was a pretty rapid case : he was dead next morning.

And so we went on through that dead calm sea. Save for the fact that we were now short-handed, even a gale would have been welcome—except that it would have meant less speed. We never saw the skipper : he regarded himself as being in quarantine. And there was nothing we could do to help him. Pete and I shouted to him once—he was up on the bridge—to know if we could assist. But he shook his head.

" I've got all the help I want," he answered.   " And there have been no fresh cases for two days—so perhaps we're through."

It was in the middle of that night that Pete came into my cabin and woke me up.

" Mac," he said gravely, " the missionary is ill. Listen."

Through the open door you could hear him groaning, and we looked at one another with the same thought in each of our minds.   Illness in that ship meant only one thing.

" We'll have to go to him, Pete," I said.

So we went.

" Don't come near me," he croaked at us as soon as we appeared.   " I'm not feeling well."

" Look here, Todmarsh," said Pete, staring at him, " there's no good beating about the bush.   I'm afraid your isolation tactics haven't succeeded. You've got it."

" I know I have," he said hoarsely, and turned his face away.

He was delirious in a couple of hours, and all through another interminable day we could hear him shouting about atonement and cowardice.   And there was nothing to be done except to listen and to wait for the end.

" I'm sorry for the poor little devil," said Andy. " I'm sorry I baited and ragged him.   But, by Jove ! you fellows, if ever there was a case of cold feet getting punished this is it."   Which is, I think, what we all felt.

He only spoke one coherent word before he died, and that was to Pete and me.

" I have atoned, haven't I ? "

" Of course you have, my dear fellow," said Pete awkwardly. " And we're deuced sorry and . . ."

He shrugged his shoulders hopelessly : the missionary was rambling again. He was back once more in his childhood, and for a while we listened to hopes and aspirations which sounded too pathetic for words coming as they did from such a miserable specimen of humanity. To do something big and great—that was his ambition : to be a leader of lost causes—a man whom men would follow. This little undeveloped, undersized creature.

And then suddenly he spoke one intelligent sentence.

" It will be all right, William. Quite all right on the other side."

For a moment he sat bolt upright, and his eyes behind his spectacles were shining with a strange look of exaltation. Then he fell back : the eleventh case had gone the way of the others.

" A gallant little gentleman," said a voice behind us. The skipper was standing in the door. " I don't know what I'd have done without him."

We both stared at him speechlessly.

" And I'm glad you were with him to help him over the barrier, as he has helped all the others."

" What's that ? " stammered Pete.

" You knew, surely ? " said the skipper, looking at him in surprise. " ' It will be all right, William.

Quite all right on the other side.'   And he's said that
to every one of them.   He told me he was keeping
away from you for fear of infecting you."

And for the one and only time that he's ever done
such a thing in his life I should imagine, Pete O'Farrell
broke down and sobbed like a child.

Well—that's my saving clause.   I don't hold with
missionaries,   always   excepting   little   Todmarsh.
Another ?   Well—talking is dry work.

BILLIE FINDS THE ANSWER

I.

Now, as all the world knows, there are places in London where a beneficent County Council permits a man to leave his motor-car for a period of time which renders the concession absolutely futile. In fact, the number of people who have had the last act of a play ruined by the haunting fear of going to prison for over-staying the time-limit has never been accurately ascertained. But it must run the unemployed very close.

And it was in one of these places—to wit, St. James's Square—that a large man was standing at three o'clock on an afternoon in June, engaged in conversation with an obliging attendant.

" But," murmured the large man mildly, " it seems rather ridiculous."

The obliging attendant was understood to say that it was damned foolishness. Or words to that effect.

" I have lunched excellently," went on the large man, " and I now want to do some shopping. Close by here—in Jermyn Street. Yet, you tell me it is necessary for me to get solemnly into my car—drive it to Waterloo Place—and then walk all the way back."

" Two hours, sir," said the man in uniform. " Them's the regulations."

" And after two hours I must remove it from Waterloo Place and bring it back here ?   Well, well— I suppose it's another step on the road towards perfection."

He felt in his pocket for a coin.

" I am obliged to you for saving me from being shot at dawn," he remarked, and at that moment an electric horn delivered itself with a loud blast from a range of about one yard behind his back.

" Our celebrity returned," cried the driver.

The large man jumped : then a slow grin spread over his face.

" Confound you, Tubby ! " he said.   " But for the presence of ladies I would take you out and stand you on your head.   Monica—how are you ? "

He strolled to the side of the car and leaned over the door.

" When did you get back, Jim," cried Monica Marsham.

" Last night," answered the large man, suddenly becoming acutely aware of the third occupant of the car.

" Billie—this is Jim Strickland.   Miss Cartwright."

A pair of very blue eyes under the rim of a little pull-on hat. . . . A face, cool and faintly mocking. . . . A figure, slim and almost boyish. . . . Thorough- bred hands, faultlessly kept. . . . A pair of adorable silk-stockinged legs which a kindly fashion ordained should be seen. Especially when sitting in a motor-car.

" How d'you do ? " said Jim, gravely.

" But, Monica," said Billie, " I love the wrinkles round his eyes."

" Billie, you're the limit," remarked Tubby placidly. " Look here, people, I must put the bus away : we're blocking the entire gangway."

And then—struck by a sudden thought——

" Jim—what are you doing this week-end ? "

" Damn all," answered Jim. " Why ? "

" Then come down and stop with old Louisa Arkwright at Henley."

" Do," cried Monica.

" You'll probably have to sleep in the bathroom," murmured Billie. " But it's a very nice bath."

" Doubtless," remarked Jim. " The only drawback to your otherwise excellent suggestion is that old Louisa Arkwright doesn't know me from Adam."

" That doesn't matter a hoot, old lad," cried Tubby. " Her false teeth will chatter like castanets at the thought of getting you. I mean it, really, Jim. Look here, Monica can go and telephone through to her. Tell her we've met you, and that we're bringing you down. I *know* she'll be delighted to have you. Then you can motor down, and, incidentally take Billie if you don't mind. She can show you where the house is."

" I think I could bear it," murmured Jim gravely.

" Provided Miss Cartwright will trust herself to my driving."

" You'll come, then ? " cried Tubby.

Very blue eyes they were under the rim of that pull-on hat.

" If she'll have me, I'd like to," said Jim. " Where shall I meet you, Miss Cartwright ? According to the Powers that be, I have to take the car to Waterloo Place."

" I'll be there at five o'clock," she answered. " And we'll stop on the way down for a cocktail."

And because those eyes were astoundingly blue under that little pull-on hat, Jim Strickland, as he stepped into his Bentley, failed to see a foreign-looking man who dodged rapidly behind another car —a man whose teeth were bared in a snarl of satisfaction, a man who had heard every word of the conversation.

If he had seen him, strange things might have happened in St. James's Square on that sunny afternoon in June. As it was, life resumed the even tenor of its way. For man must buy shirts and ties to cover his nakedness, though God forbid that one should write of such a boring proceeding.

Of one thing, however, it is necessary to write, before coming to Waterloo Place at five o'clock. When a man has been hailed as a celebrity, something must be said to justify the word. Otherwise he might be a K.B.E. or an actor, or even an author—which would damn the whole show from the very beginning. Also it

conjures up visions of unwashed men signing auto-
graphs for flappers. . . .

Now it is safe to say that not one single flapper
had ever written to Jim Strickland for his autograph.
But then, except for two nieces who adored him, not
one single flapper had ever heard of his name. And
even they had to admit that his signature ranked
lower in the great scheme of things than that of the
French mistress's brother, who had once shaken
hands with Rudolph Valentino.

True—he was a V.C. But the war was a back
number. And when asked how he got it his reply was
unsatisfying to a degree.

" It was nothing, kids, nothing. I happened to be
there, that's all."

A few men there were, in High Places, who had been
heard to declare in strict confidence over the port that
twice since the war Jim Strickland had altered our
policy abroad—and altered it rightly. But policy
abroad is a tedious business—and, anyway, the remark
was made in strict confidence. And there were
swarthy hillsmen from over the Indian border who
placed him only a little after the Almighty : and
Bedouins who had told him strange stories under the
star-studded African night : and hard-bitten sailor-
men who had affirmed with oaths and curses that
they would sooner have Jim Strickland beside them in
a tight corner than any two other men.

But of all those things he never spoke, and even to
his nearest friends Jim Strickland remained a bit of

B

an enigma. That he disappeared for months on end
from the ken of man they knew, but where he went to
was a different matter. He would vanish abruptly
without a word to a soul ; only to reappear just as
suddenly—unchanged, save perhaps for a little more
brown on his face, a few more tiny wrinkles round his
eyes. And then for a space England would hold him
—Ascot, Cowes, Scotland ; with mothers angling in
vain and daughters running round in small circles.
But up to date Jim Strickland had shown no signs of
entering the holy paths of matrimony.

" What the deuce should I do with a wife, my dear
fellow ?" he was wont to observe. " I shouldn't see
the dear thing for more than two months a year, and
I'd have to pay for her for the other ten. Or someone
else would. I was nearly caught once, but, thank
God ! I had to go to Tibet suddenly. And she'd
married someone else by the time I got back.
I shall live and die a bachelor."

And after a while women of his acquaintance ceased
to prophesy that he was a liar, and began to believe
that he really would. True, they still dangled desirable
girls in his path, but it was more from habit than from
any real hope of success. And Jim Strickland, who
adored pretty girls, was only too delighted that they
should. The spreading of the net in the sight of the
wary old bird is always amusing—for the bird.

Wherefore, that being that, and descriptions being
at the best of times intolerably tedious, we can come
even as he did to Waterloo Place when the clock

still wanted five minutes to the hour of five.

He saw her at once curled up in the front seat of his car, smoking a cigarette.

" Punctual person," he remarked, sitting down beside her. " Are you certain you wouldn't like some tea before we start ? "

She shook her head.

" It's hot and stuffy here. Let's drive—fast."

" But certainly," he said, and glanced at her sideways. Just the tip of her nose and her firm little chin could he see : then he let in his clutch. And in silence they drove along Pall Mall.

The girl sat motionless, staring in front of her—her hands linked loosely in her lap. Evidently, she was in no mood for conversation, and suddenly the contrast struck him between her and other women who from time to time had driven in that same seat. No forced small talk—no banal platitudes. . . .

" How do you like travelling, Mr. Strickland ? " And : " Isn't your life very dangerous, Mr. Strickland ? "

Moreover, it seemed natural with this girl : she seemed so full of—he searched for the word—full of repose. No, that was wrong : reposc conjured up elderly ladies of aristocratic appearance, knitting.

Self-possession. That was nearer the mark. The right type of self-possession.

Once again he glanced at her sideways, and as he did so she turned and met his eye.

' Do you want me to talk ? " she said, quietly.

" I was just thinking how pleasant it was to sit beside someone and not feel it necessary to do anything of the sort," he answered. " It's rather a favourable sign, isn't it ? "

" It may be a very dangerous one," she remarked.

" Pointing to boredom," he said, lightly.

She gave a short laugh, and, leaning forward, lit a cigarette under cover of the wind-screen.

" I'm in a peculiar mood, Jim Strickland," she announced calmly. " I'm out of conceit with life— rather more so than usual. Met an old cat at my club."

He negotiated a lorry with care.

" I shouldn't have thought you were the type of person to be upset by old cats," he said non-committally.

They came to the new switch road, and she put her hand on his arm.

" Let her out—all out," she cried. " Seventy— eighty . . . Go on, Jim—she'll do eighty-five."

The wind roared past them : the needle quivered past eighty-five—stayed motionless at eighty-seven.

" Over ninety if she's tuned up," said Jim Strickland, slowing as they came to the main road.

" I felt like that," she said, lying back in her seat.

" The old cat was very cattish, was she ? "

" She insisted on giving me good advice," she answered.

" Nuff said," remarked Jim. " Men have died for less than that."

Once again she fell silent, a little frown puckering her forehead. And it was not until they were approaching that celebrated hotel by the river at Maidenhead that she spoke again.

" Mine is a Martini with an olive," she said. " And the point is, shall I marry him or shall I not ? "

For a moment Jim Strickland stared at her : then he burst out laughing.

" You really are an astounding person," he remarked.

" Why ? " she answered calmly, strolling across the lawn at his side. " You are just as capable of answering the question as my old cat at the club. And she said yes. In fact she said it so often that it sounded like bullets coming out of a machine-gun."

" Who is the fortunate individual ? " asked Jim politely.

" You'll see him. He's stopping at Henley. By the name of Trevor. George of that ilk. Stockbroker by trade. And full of money. Good-looking and dances divinely."

" One trifling detail," murmured Jim. " Do you love him ? "

She shrugged her shoulders.

" Can one afford to indulge in luxuries on the princely allowance of a hundred a year ? "

" Rotten," said Jim, curtly. " Cheap and rotten."

She stared at him, a hint of passionate anger in her eyes.

" It's easy for you to talk, Jim Strickland," she said,

in a low voice. " It's a problem that has never confronted you."

" True," he agreed. " Nor has a desire to commit forgery. But there are some things about which one can make up one's mind without actually encountering reality."

" And anyway," she went on, " what is love ? You seem to have escaped it yourself up to date ? "

" Maybe," he answered, quietly. " Or shall we say that it has escaped me ? Not quite the same thing. In any case, what has that to do with it ? The fact that I am not married—which I presume is what you mean—seems to me to be no adequate reason why you should do otherwise. I have never fallen in love : therefore I am not married. You, on your own showing, have never fallen in love : therefore you propose to get married. 'Tisn't sense."

" It's sense all right." She was sitting very still staring across the river. " Not the sense, perhaps, of romantic fiction : but common or garden horse sense, Jim Strickland."

" Then there's no more to be said," he answered shortly. " Incidentally I don't want to hurry you, but I think as the newcomer I ought to arrive before dinner."

" I suppose you think me a pretty average sweep," she remarked, in a low voice.

For a moment he did not answer ; then he spoke very deliberately.

" I think that, without exception, you are the most

attractive girl I have ever met. And I loathe to hear you talking as you have done. It's horrible : it's unnatural : it's not worthy of you. Shall we go ? "

And it was only when she made no movement to rise that he noticed that her eyes were swimming in tears.

" Sorry, Kid," he said gently. " No business of mine and all that. But—don't."

Impulsively he put his hand on her shoulder : felt her quiver under his touch. Then slowly his hand fell to his side, and, over her head, he stared with unseeing eyes at a passing steamer. For in that brief second of contact a new factor had entered into the situation. And because he was thirty-seven, and the thoughts and habits of a life-time are not easily broken, Jim Strickland shied away from that new factor like a frightened colt.

At last she rose, having furtively dabbed her eyes with a pocket handkerchief. The mocking smile had returned to her lips : the very blue eyes under the little pull-on hat seemed bluer than ever because of their mistiness.

" You're incorrigibly romantic, Jim," she announced calmly. " In fact, not at all the sort of person for an impressionable young girl to be alone with. But you're—rather a darling."

And then, abruptly, her eyes fell from his, and she began to fumble with her hand-bag.

" I think we'd better go," she said, a little unsteadily. " It would never do if you were late for dinner."

In silence he led the way to the car, wild, incoherent thoughts pounding through his brain. In silence she got in and sat down beside him. And that was the second time within the space of three hours that Jim Strickland, of whom it was said that he possessed not one but twenty pairs of eyes, failed to see a foreign-looking man, now reinforced by a companion, who watched the car as it drove off with barely concealed malevolence. If he had seen him, strange things might have happened in Maidenhead on that sunny afternoon in June.

II

There is a type of man whom women find " so amusing, you know," and men " quite a decent sort, but. . . ." And the " but " is left, as it were, high and dry. Nothing specific to follow the qualification ; nothing that can be put into so many words ; but— something. And to this type belonged George Trevor.

Immaculately groomed, sleek of head, good-looking and with charming manners, he was, undoubtedly, an acquisition to any house-party. Moreover, being a very shrewd business man not only had he prospered exceedingly on the Stock Exchange, but in addition he was able to impart valuable private tips to such of his friends as he desired. And the fact that those of his friends whom he desired to benefit were almost invariably pretty women, may possibly help to etch in his character.

He was standing in the hall performing rites with a cocktail shaker as Jim Strickland drove up, and the girl introduced them to one another.

" Mr. Strickland has just motored me down, George," she remarked. " And I won't have a cocktail as we stopped for one at Skindles."

With a little nod she turned and went upstairs, leaving the two men together.

" I presume," said Trevor easily, " that one is not your limit."

" No," said Jim, with a faint smile, " it is not. But it will have to be a quick one. I'm rather late."

To the outsider two very attractive men of totally dissimilar types, casually talking banalities over a drink and a cigarette : to a thought reader two utterly antagonistic personalities who disliked one another at the very first clash, but being men of the world con- cealed that dislike behind a discussion of Yorkshire's chances for the championship.

To Jim Strickland, accustomed as he was to forming instant judgment on his fellows, Trevor seemed all that he disliked most—a poseur of the worst descrip- tion. Which, to be just, was not quite fair.

To George Trevor, accustomed also to the quick summing up of character though in a very different school, Strickland appeared conceited and over- bearing. Which most certainly was not quite fair.

And so, when they went up to dress for dinner, they

B*

were each in the condition in which, for the benefit of all concerned, it would be better if they did not play bridge at the same table.

" The type of man," murmured Jim to his reflection as he shaved, " who plays little tricks with matches."

And then he broke off and stared thoughtfully out of the window : he was honest with himself always—was Jim Strickland. Was it entirely the clash of two mutually hostile men : or was it very largely the bitter instinctive rivalry of two male animals. Trevor was the man that Billie was thinking of marrying : except for that, would he have felt as he did ? And suddenly his hand began to shake a little : he was back at Skindles, and a girl with very blue eyes under a little pull-on hat was fumbling with her hand-bag. A girl whose voice was not quite steady. . . . A girl, who . . .

" Don't be a fool, Jim Strickland," he remarked firmly. " A man of your age doesn't fall in love with a girl whom he has known for an hour."

For a moment his eyes narrowed : wasn't there something moving on the other side of the lawn behind that bush ? He leaned out of the window to see better : then he gave a little laugh. Old habits die hard, but this was England, not his usual hunting grounds. England, where people kept gardeners—and a man could sleep with both eyes shut. . . .

The evening passed as such evenings do—bridge, a gramophone for dancing, drinks for the thirsty. And if Jim Strickland and George Trevor successfully avoided one another's society, only one other person was aware of the fact. And that one other person, because she was a hundred per cent. woman, secretly rather enjoyed it.

From the first moment that Billie had sat down to dinner next to Trevor she had sensed the hostility between the two men. Which was quite sufficient for any girl to start playing an age-old if somewhat dangerous game. Just once or twice she remembered the look blazing in Jim Strickland's eyes as they had stood together on the lawn at Skindles, and when she did her heart beat a little quicker, and she stole a glance at him over the table. Had he really meant it —that unmistakable message ? Or was it merely the passing feeling of a moment.

Somehow it struck her that Jim Strickland was not that sort. From George Trevor she would have expected it, and as the evening went on, more and more did the absolute contrast between the two men come home to her. And the result was not favourable to the stockbroker.

True he danced more divinely than usual, and that normally went a long way with her. But on this occasion. . . .

" What's the matter with you, Billie ? " he whispered half-way through their second. " You're as cold as be damned to-night."

" Am I ?" she answered. " You'd better go and dance with someone else."

It was at that moment that she saw Jim Strickland

standing in the door of the bridge-room staring at her. She smiled at him, but he turned away a little abruptly —and the smile turned to a frown.   When all was said and done he had not the faintest right to criticize her.

" That's better," said Trevor a moment later. " Now you're dancing more like yourself."

He, too, had seen Strickland in the door, and a faint smile flickered round his lips. He'd show the blighter the terms he was on with Billie. And because in modern dancing an exceedingly intimate, but wordless, conversation can be maintained between the dancers, he succeeded in reducing Strickland to a condition of silent fury which boded ill for someone. He also succeeded in working himself into a condition when the answer to his oft-put question to Billie could be waited for no longer.

" Billie darling," he said a little hoarsely, " come outside with me for a bit.   Can't you say yes, my dear : I'm simply mad about you."

And so the crux had come : it was now or never. Dimly came the advice of her female relative : dimly came worldly wisdom. Say—yes : say—yes. And then, clear as a trumpet call, came four words—" It's rotten : it's cheap."   Came also the vision of a clean-cut, sunburned face ; the feel of a strong hand on her shoulder. . . .

" I'm sorry, George," she said steadily, " but I made up my mind definitely to-day. I can't marry you."

" Why not," he demanded thickly. " I believe it's that damned fellow Strickland."

" Don't be offensive," she said coldly. " I met Mr. Strickland for the first time this afternoon. I can't marry you, because I don't love you."

And then George Trevor lost his head. He flung his arms round her, and before she could stop him he was kissing her on the lips, on her bare neck.

" Let me go, you brute," she said, furiously. " Let me go, or I'll hit you."

Sullenly he let her go, staring at her with smouldering eyes.

" I think," she said quietly, " that I hate you."

Without another word she walked back into the house, and up to her room. Her mind was seething : she felt she had to be alone. And after a while she undressed, and, turning out the light, sat down by the open window. She had burned her boats now all right. She had deliberately turned down the most eligible man of her acquaintance. But it wasn't that she was thinking of—it was that remark of his—" I believe it's that damned fellow Strickland."

Was it ? Had he hit the nail on the head ? And suddenly, with a little rush of colour to her face even in the darkness, she knew that if it had been Jim Strickland who had flung his arms round her and kissed her she would not have told him to let her go.

One by one the lights went out in the house : one by one bedroom doors shut as the house-party came to bed. And still she sat on by the open window.

Did things happen like that—suddenly, in an instant ? To her of all people—a girl who had asked what love was. Was she in love with this man whom she had only just met ? Was he in love with her ?

She stirred restlessly in her chair : had she been a fool ? Probably she would never see him again after this week-end ; he'd be away on one of these strange trips of his.   Not the marrying sort, as Tubby had said. And yet in spite of everything she knew that she was glad she had answered George Trevor as she had.

The bells rang out from the silent town across the river.   One o'clock.

Two hours had she been sitting there, and a little stiffly she got up, only to shrink back instantly behind the curtain.   Two dark shapes were stealing round the edge of the lawn coming towards the house.

Rigidly she watched them—burglars, of course. Saw them make a quick run over a little patch of open ground, and get into the shadow of the house.   Peered out cautiously : realized they were just under her window.   Heavens !   They'd probably come up through her room.

And then, suddenly, one of the dark shapes spoke in a low voice.   The night was still, and every word carried clear to the girl's ears.

" The third room from here.   I saw him shaving."

The third room ! The third room was Jim Strickland's.   These men weren't burglars : they were after Jim . . . And now her brain was ice-cold : the need for action was instant and imperative.   She

opened her door and tiptoed along the passage, to
pause for a moment outside Jim's room. No light
came through the keyhole : he was evidently in bed.
And without further hesitation she went in.

She could see him in the dim light asleep, one arm
flung loosely over the bedclothes. And the next
instant she was bending over him whispering his name.
Then she put her hand on his arm, and had to bite
back a scream as she found herself seized in a grip like
a steel vice—a grip which relaxed instantly.

" You," he muttered incredulously. " God ! girl
—what are you doing here ? "

" Jim," she whispered urgently, " there are two men
in the garden. And they're coming to your room. I
heard them talking under my window."

" You topper," he breathed, swinging out of bed.
" You absolute topper."

She heard the thrill of excitement in his voice—
realized that now she was seeing Jim Strickland in the
setting which was peculiarly his own.

" In that corner, Billie," he whispered. " I'm going
to catch 'em as they come in."

In his hand was the poker, and she laid her hand on
his arm.

' Listen, Jim. I'll get into the bed. Then they'll
think you're asleep. You hide by the curtain."

" You darling," he muttered. " You perfectly
priceless Kid."

And then, because she couldn't help it, she flung her
arms round his neck and kissed him on the lips.

" Slog the blighters," she whispered.

" Billie," he breathed. . . . " Billie, dear. . . . "

A faint noise outside brought him to his senses, and like a cat he crossed the room towards the window. The Jim Strickland of many a similar position was functioning automatically : but another Jim Strickland felt his senses rioting with the remembrance of warm young arms round his neck, warm young lips on his.

He stole a glance at the bed : she was curled up, apparently asleep. And then he had absolutely to force himself to attend to the business in hand.

Slowly, inch by inch, a head was appearing over the window-sill, but he bided his time. Then the body came, a leg was flung over—and still Jim waited. He wanted both of the men.

Came a sudden, sharp hiss, and with a furious curse Jim lunged and struck. Straight in the face he got him, and the man toppled over backwards without a sound, to crash in the flower-bed below. He had a glimpse of the other, running like a hare across the lawn ; then, sick with anxiety, he turned towards the bed. Fool—thrice damned fool that he was, not to have thought of a silent automatic. . . .

" Billie," he cried, and then—" Oh ! my God."

On the sheet an ominous red stain was already spreading.

" Jim," she whispered faintly, " my leg feels all funny."

" My darling," he muttered in an agony, " he's plugged you with a revolver."

" Did you get him, Jim ? "

Her voice tailed off, she had fainted. And for just once second did Jim Strickland hesitate : some things are a little bit difficult to explain. Then, with a feeling of contempt for his momentary indecision, he got to work. It was a nasty looking wound in the thigh, and the bullet was still inside—but the danger, as he well knew, was that it might prove septic.

" Expanding bullet," he muttered. " Curse the swine."

Into the wound went most of a bottle of iodine, and with a scream of pain the girl came to.

" Steady, darling," said Jim. " It hurts like hell, I know—but it's got to be done. Then we'll have a doctor here in no time and get the bullet out."

He ripped a towel in pieces and bound up the wound, whilst Billie, the bright colour flooding her face and neck, watched him.

" I'm going to tell them exactly what happened, dear," he went on quietly. " And I'm also going to tell them we are engaged. It may make things easier."

Already there were steps in the passage outside, and Lady Arkwright's voice : " Who was that who screamed ? "

" There, dear," said Jim, finishing the bandage. " Now leave it all to me."

He went to the door and opened it.

" Lady Arkwright," he called, " will you at once

telephone for a doctor ?   Tell him that there's a case of a bullet wound in the thigh, with the bullet still in. Say that the wound has already been dressed with iodine."

" But what's happened ? " cried his hostess.

" Explanations afterwards," said Jim, curtly. " Get the doctor." He saw Monica and Tubby. " Monica—will you remain in my room with Miss Cartwright ? "

" And now," he glanced round the row of amazed faces, " since every one in the house seems to be awake, I may as well explain what happened. Shall we go downstairs for a moment ?   And first of all we may as well see what has become of the gentleman in the flower-bed."

They thronged after him, too bewildered to speak, and pressed through the front door in a bunch. The man was lying where he had fallen, stone dead, his head almost split open ; and in his hand he still gripped the revolver.

" So," muttered Jim, half to himself, " it's Strabinoff at last. . . . That man, ladies and gentlemen, has been trying to kill me for four years. But for Miss Cartwright he would have succeeded to-night. However, the point is immaterial ; other far more important matters must be explained."

They followed him back into the house, and quite shortly he told them exactly what had happened.

" I may further add," he said when he had finished, " that only to-night Miss Cartwright did me the very

great honour of promising to become my wife."

A confused medley of congratulations broke out, interrupted suddenly by the arrival of the doctor.

" Gracious me," he exclaimed, " what's all this ? "

" Would you take the doctor up, Lady Arkwright ? " said Jim. " Once again, explanations after. By the way, it's an expanding bullet, doctor."

He strode to the telephone and rang up the police ; then, coming back, he sat down on the fender. And sitting down, became acutely aware of a man who, in the excitement he had forgotten all about—George Trevor. He was standing at the foot of the stairs, smoking a cigarette, with a cynical smile on his face.

" I congratulate you, Mr. Strickland," he said, with a slight sneer.

" On what ? " said Jim, curtly.

" Shall we call it—a ready imagination ? "

Jim Strickland rose slowly to his feet, and crossed the hall towards him. The rest of the party had dispersed : the two men were alone.

" You imply," he murmured politely, " that I lied."

" As anyone else would do," returned the other equally politely, " in similar circumstances."

" Will you come into the garden with me, Mr. Trevor ? " said Strickland gently. " You see, I'm going to break you up—and this is not my furniture."

And at that, full blast, the hatred of George Trevor blazed out.

" This isn't one of your savage countries," he snarled. " We don't do that sort of thing in

England. You can keep your breaking up and your seduction of girls for places where they belong."

" Indeed," murmured Jim, with a faint smile. " You are too kind."

Quite slowly his hands went out and fastened on George Trevor : quite slowly he walked George Trevor through the hall and into the garden : and then quite slowly he waded into George Trevor. He broke George Trevor up methodically and thoroughly till George Trevor could neither speak, nor hear, nor see ; and, having done so, he flung him into one of those trees that are known as monkey puzzles. And there he left George Trevor and returned to the house feeling better.

The police had arrived : but for the moment Jim Strickland was not concerned with the police. He was concerned with no one but the doctor, who was just coming downstairs.

" Quite all right," he cried cheerfully, as he saw Strickland. " We've got the bullet out, and she's going on capitally."

" Is she conscious ? " said Jim.

" Very much so," said the doctor, with a faint smile. " Would you like to go up and see her ? "

" Would I like," remarked Jim, taking the stairs three at a time.

He opened the door of his room, to find his hostess and Monica with Billie.

" Do you mind going ? " he said shamelessly.

And they went.

Very blue eyes they were, shining up at him from the pillows, and very dear and frank was the message in them.

" I thought," she said, " that when a man said he was engaged, he usually went through the formality of asking the girl."

And then there comes a slight discrepancy. Jim Strickland swears it was half a minute : the police-sergeant swears it was half an hour. Anyway, it is absurd to haggle over such a trifling difference. The fact remains that at the end of this doubtful interval a patient voice was heard on the other side of the door.

" Look 'ere, sir, there's a dead man in the flower-bed—and a 'orrible sight in the monkey puzzle—and can we get on with it ? "

Moreover, that pillar of the Henley constabulary swears that the only answer he got consisted of two words—

" We are."

THE RUBBER STRAP

Do you know that game called " Are you there? "
You may find it being played in mess on guest night after
dinner, and you will assuredly find it included in any
sports that may be held on an ocean-going liner.   Its
rules are simple : its charm immense—to the onlookers.
You lie down on the deck facing your opponent
grasping his left hand with your own.   Each of you
in his right hand holds a rolled-up copy of an
illustrated weekly, or some similar weapon.   A pillow
cover is then placed over each of your heads to
blindfold you.   At the word go, one of you says : " Are
you there? " The other answers " Yes," at the same
time moving his head into a position of safety.   Any
position may be chosen so long as his left elbow remains on the deck, and his left hand remains in yours.
You then lift your right hand and aim a heavy blow
with the weapon it contains at the place where you
imagine his head to be.   If you hit it you count
one, and then it's his turn.   You go on till one or other
of you is stunned.   In fact, a great game—for the
onlookers.

And my reason for this brief dissertation on one
pastime of the idle rich, is that it was directly responsible
for my hearing a very strange yarn.   I am aware that
when a teller of stories prefaces one of them with the
remark that it is true, the sophisticated reader prepares

himself resignedly for a worse lie than usual.   And so I won't say that this is true, but merely that it was told me by an American who claims to be a direct descendant of George Washington.

The game was over : the corpses had been laid out on the deck to cool.   Personally I had not competed : nor had the American.   On the subject of being but-chered for a Roman holiday our ideas coincided remarkably.   On other points too, there seemed no great divergence in our opinions.

" I've some fruit syrup in my cabin," he remarked, thoughtfully watching one of the corpses arise and stagger aft to die.   " Also some vermouth."

" I can supply gin and a shaker," I put in hopefully.

" Good," he said.   " Are we there ? Yes."

He mixed two of the best, and then he pulled out his cabin trunk and started rummaging through the contents.

" See that ? " he said.   " What do you think of it ? "

It was a piece of black india-rubber about fifteen inches long, an inch wide and half an inch thick.

" A rather good weapon for ' Are you there,' " I answered.

" I thought you'd say that," he grinned.   " And used for just one blow at a time it would be.   Used another way. . . . See here.   Put your leg up on that bunk."

I did so, and he raised the rubber thong in his hand.

"I'm not going to hit you hard," he said. "But just see how long you can stand it."

He started above my knee, and worked gradually up my thigh : then back again. And he didn't hit hard. He hit no harder than the smack you would give a naughty child, and a small child at that. Tap ; tap ; tap—that rubber thong wound itself round my leg in a different place each time. No one blow could even be said to hurt, and yet I only stood twenty-five of them. There's no good suffering agony for nothing. After about the tenth hit every single muscle and sinew in my leg started shrieking at the same moment : after the twenty-fifth I should have begun to shriek myself if I hadn't given in.

He smiled and mixed me another cocktail.

"A souvenir," he said, "of a very strange affair. That game this afternoon put me in mind of it."

"Having half-killed me," I said, "the talking is on you. Fire ahead."

"It took place in Paris after the war," he began. "Everything, including discipline, was a bit lax— same as it was in England. But the war was over and nobody minded very much as long as things were kept within reasonable bounds. I'd been in our Intelligence myself, and when my division went back overseas I got leave to stop on in France for a while.

"I was sitting in my hotel one morning, when in walked a man I knew fairly intimately. His name was John Thripley, and he was in charge of one of our big military stores. Not ordnance, but commissariat :

tobacco, ham, tinned beef, all that sort of stuff. I'd been over it once while the fighting was on, and there was enough there to have fed all the belligerent armies for a year.

" I gave him a hail, and he came over and sat down.

" ' Morning, John,' I said. ' You look worried. Mice been at the cheese ? '

" ' In a manner of speaking,' he answered. ' Only they're damned large mice. I'm floored, Bill, and that's straight : and it's a pretty serious business.'

" ' What's up,' I said. ' Can I help ? '

" He shook his head doubtfully.

" ' I'll tell you what it is, but I don't want it to go any further. You know I'm in charge of ' A ' dump, don't you ? Well about two months ago a bunch of indents were presented in the ordinary way for stuff. I think there were about half-a-million cigarettes, and some boots and two or three hundredweights of ham. Everything was perfectly in order—I've examined the vouchers myself—and so the stuff was loaded on to the lorry that had come for it, and the lorry was driven away.

" ' Naturally I thought no more about it, until the next morning produced another batch of similar indents from the same people. The storekeeper brought it to me—by mere luck it happened to be the same man who had handled the vouchers the previous day—and asked me what he was to do. Well, there was only one thing to be done. I got on the telephone to the people who wanted the stuff, and asked 'em what under the sun they wanted with two such big demands on consecutive days.

" ' The guy at the other end of the wire began to splutter and asked me what the devil I was talking about. He hadn't sent in two indents : he'd only sent in one. A lorry had left that morning for the stuff, driven by a man named Wilson. And sure enough Wilson was there right enough cursing good and strong at the delay. So there was nothing for it but to load up the lorry and let him go. Whatever mistake had occurred was nothing to do with him.

" ' Back I went to the office and hauled out yesterday's indents. Not a flaw to be found in 'em : they were, on the face of things, absolutely genuine. So then I got on the telephone all the way round. I rang up everyone I could think of, and asked them the same question. Had a lorry—and I gave 'em the type of bus it was—turned up for them with the following stores on board—and I gave 'em a detailed list of the stores. No—it hadn't : same answer everywhere. But in case it did arrive they'd ring me up.

" ' Well—I never got deafened with that telephone bell. Not only the stores but the whole blamed lorry were never heard of again. About seventy-five thousand dollars' worth of stuff completely vanished.

" ' There was always the possibility of accident, of course, and so I promptly reported the matter to the police. But as the days went by and no news came in, I had to come to the conclusion that we'd been had all right, and that a bare-faced robbery had been committed right under our noses.'

" ' Just a moment, John' I put in. ' Did no one recognize the driver ? '

" ' I thought of that,' he answered, ' but it's a blank. The driver and his mate had on goggles, and the other fellow who helped to load was just an ordinary sort of bloke—quite inconspicuous. My storeman says he might remember him, but he wouldn't swear to it. Don't forget Dick, we get 'em in by the score daily, and if a bunch are out on a game like that they're not going to employ a man with a wooden leg and a strawberry mark on his face.

" ' Now that was the beginning of it. Four days later, Anston who runs ' C ' store loaded up two thousand pairs of boots, two thousand cardigans, and two thousand suits of underclothes on another lorry. And, damn it, that disappeared into the blue also. Over I went as soon as I heard of it to see Anston, and we compared those indents. Not a trace of resemblance in the writing—not a clue. His, to all appearances, were just as genuine as mine, and there we were stung again good and hard. It was obvious what had happened : it was obvious that the stolen stuff had been sold to the French, or was being kept in some secret place for disposal to them in due course. It was also obvious that we were up against a thoroughly daring gang, of whom at anyrate some must be our own people.

" ' So that very morning we called a general meeting of all the fellows who were running stores to discuss what was to be done. They'd done it twice now with success, and we felt pretty sure they wouldn't be able to resist the temptation of trying it again. The point was how to catch 'em. They weren't fools, and they must know that the loss had been discovered. Recognition was well-nigh impossible. We had six big depots lying some distance apart, and granted that they only tried one robbery at each they'd be fairly safe in using the same men each time. But since it was more than likely that there was a biggish gang of them, there was nothing to prevent 'em changing round. So at last we decided that the only thing to do, in the event of a big indent coming in, was to ring up the formation making the demand and get it confirmed before issue.

" ' By Jove ! Dick. We got some pretty blasphemous confirmation down the telephone. What the hell, etc., etc. ? Wasn't the indent there staring us in the face ? Were we trying to be funny ? You see we weren't over communicative as to why we were doing it ? No one likes to admit he's been soaked properly.

" ' For a fortnight nothing happened. Then in comes Payton one morning to see me, gibbering at the mouth with rage.

" ' They've stung me, Bill. Three days ago. Jam, ham, tinned beef—every darned thing you can think of. Best part of fifty thousand dollars' worth. My telephone was out of action that morning, and I was infernally busy. The indent was signed by Jack Cooper : I'd swear to his signature in a thousand. If I've seen it once, I've seen it a hundred times. It was a forgery.'

" ' He lit a cigarette, and ramped up and down the office.'

" ' I took it out to him, and damn it! it even deceived him. It wasn't until we found there was no carbon duplicate in his office that he was quite sure he hadn't signed it himself and forgotten about it.

" ' Well that made three of us who had taken it in the neck and we were getting sorer than Hell. Cart-wright of " D " store, and the other two, Mason and Digby, who hadn't been caught were kind of tolerant about it—the implication being that we'd better come along to them and learn our job. At least that was the idea until Cartwright loaded up a lorry with a hundred thousand dollars' worth of stuff which was wanted urgently. He verified everything : had the driver brought into his office to have his photograph taken from about forty different angles, and generally read the riot act all round. That lorry broke down thirty miles out of Paris. The men had stopped at an inn to have their lunch, and no power on earth would start the engine after. I'm no motorist but I gather something had gone in the magneto.

" ' Well luckily another lorry—an empty one—passed shortly after going the same way. So they changed the stuff over, and that was that. Cartwright swelled our numbers to four, though he swears it wasn't his fault. Anyway none of the stuff was ever seen again.

" ' And that left Mason and Digby. Mason started the ball rolling in fine style. It seems one morning that he got suspicious of a driver who turned up, and there being no flies on Jake Mason he was hit with a brilliant idea. So he got himself nailed up in a packing case reputed to contain tinned meat, and was loaded up with the rest of the stuff. As far as I can make out he was put in upside down and had a sixty mile drive, so he must have had a real fine morning. Still he didn't care so long as he could run them to ground. He'd got two guns with him, and he wasn't going to hesitate about using them.

" ' Of course, as I said to him, it might have been a darned good show if the lorry hadn't been a perfectly genuine one. But when they unpacked Jake, the scene was a trying one. They first of all thought he was trying to be funny : then they insisted he was mad. And when poor old Jake tried to explain it wasn't a success. They had indented for tinned meat, and Jake as a substitute left them cold. However, he pacified them after a while, and went back to Paris by train, to find the line in his office darned near fused with the blasphemy coming over it from another quarter. What had happened to the lorry that had started off that morning for Beauvais ?

" ' At the time Jake had been packed up in his box, so he sent for his quarter-master. Yes—perfectly true. A lorry had started right enough, and the quarter-master had not only rung up to find out that it was all right, but in addition he knew the driver personally. They came from the same town in the States.

" ' And here, Bill, the matter becomes even more

C

serious than before. Up-to-date there had been no violence : this time there was. The driver was found more dead than alive in a ditch : his mate is still in hospital unconscious, and the lorry has never been seen again.'

" John Thripley lit a cigarette, and intimated that he was thirsty.

" ' That's a very strange story, John,' I remarked. ' For five lorries to disappear like that beats cock-fighting.'

" ' Five lorries worth a quarter of a million dollars at a conservative estimate,' he grunted. ' But it's not the money I mind so much—it's not mine. What gets my goat is being stung like that. And the point is, Bill, there is still the sixth lorry to go. Your criminal, and mark you this is no ordinary man, is a darned conceited fellow. And I'm open to a bet that he won't be happy till he's done in Digby. There's another thing too : he's getting to the end of his tether or he wouldn't have taken to violence. Highway robbery in broad daylight on a main road is a pretty dangerous operation.'

" ' They probably stopped the lorry and asked for a lift,' I said. ' And then laid out the driver and his mate at a suitable opportunity. Have you got no suspicions at all ? '

" ' Not the faintest vestige,' he answered. ' And the police seem as floored as we are. They take up the line, and I hardly blame 'em for it, that the criminals are our own people, and that we ought to be able to look after our own affairs. Of course they don't actually say that—but they imply it.'

" The door swung open at that moment, and an officer came in. I didn't know him but John Thripley did, and I heard him whistle under his breath.

" ' It's Digby,' he said. 'And something has happened.'

" Just then the newcomer saw John, and came over to our table.

" ' By God ! Thripley,' he said grimly, ' I don't rest until I've caught those swine. Have you heard what happened last night ? It's murder—cold-blooded murder this time.'

" ' The devil it is,' said John. ' You can speak out : I've just been telling my friend here all about it.'

" ' I was sitting in my office the night before last about five o'clock,' said Digby, ' when one of my sergeants came in.'

" ' Look here, Captain,' he said to me, ' I reckon I've got a line on those crooks.'

" ' Good man,' I cried. ' Who are they ? '

" ' I'd sooner not say, sir,' he said, ' for I may be wrong.'

" ' How did you get the line,' I asked him.

" ' Well,' he said with a bit of a grin, ' there's a little cabaret called the *Petit Souris* where I go sometimes to have a drink and a dance. And there's a girl there—Marie is her name, who seems to like dancing with me. I was sitting at a table with her last night, and I found I'd run out of cigarettes. So she pulls out a paper packet of Fatimas and offers it to me.

" ' Hullo ! Marie,' I said, ' Where did you get these
from ?   You're becoming a proper little American.'

" ' She laughed and told me that all the girls had
them now as they were so easy to get.

" ' Is that so,' I answered. ' I didn't know you
found it any easier to get 'em now than before.   Do
the boys give 'em to you ? '

" ' She shook her head, and then suddenly she sat
up in her chair and laid her hand on my arm.

" ' Do you see that man who has just come in ? '

" ' I looked over at the door, and saw an American
soldier standing there with a girl on each arm.   He'd
got the face of a Chicago tough, but in about ten
seconds you couldn't see him for girls.   They were
round him like bees round honey.

" ' He seems popular,' I said.

" ' Because he gives away so many presents,' said
Marie.   ' Cigarettes, and jam, and meat, and a pair of
boots to Lisette's father, and . . . '

" ' But I guess I wasn't listening, Captain : I was
just staring at her and then at him.

" ' Where does he get them from, Marie ? ' I said.

" ' She shrugged her shoulders : she wasn't interested
in that.

" ' But I don't like him,' she went on. ' He is a
cochon.'

" Digby chewed savagely at his cigar.

" ' There's no good my repeating the whole conversation,' he went on.   ' All that matters is that my

sergeant was pretty well convinced in his own mind that this fellow knew a good deal more than was healthy about these robberies. I don't know whether he gave himself away or not—he must have : but the fact remains that I've just been to the mortuary to identify his dead body. He'd been plugged through the heart at close range. You could see the mark of the scorch on his coat.'

" ' When did it happen ? ' I asked.

" ' Some time last night,' he answered. ' And I don't quit Paris till I've caught the guy who did it.'

" Which was a very fine sentiment, but easier to say than to carry out. The sergeant had not mentione l the man's name : in fact Digby couldn't say if he even knew it. All that we had to go on was that he looked like a Chicago tough, and had been in this cabaret place two nights previously. Also—and in this, so it seemed to me, lay our trump card—that he was well-known and popular with the little ladies of the quarter.

" Quite obviously the *Petit Souris* was our jumping-off ground, but at once there cropped up a difficulty. If this man was the man or one of the men we wanted, he was pretty well certain to know both Digby and Thripley by sight. And the instant he saw them in such an unexpected haunt he'd be bound to smell a rat. Now we hadn't an atom of proof to go on, and the one essential thing was not to scare our bird if we were to have a hope of bringing it home to him.

" ' There's only one thing to do,' I said. ' Let me go to this place alone. I've got plain clothes here, and he won't know me. I'll get in touch with this girl Marie if I can, and if I see this fellow I'll remember his face and that will put us a step forward anyway. Once he's known, it oughtn't to be difficult to get enough proof to convict him.'

" So that evening I went off to the *Petit Souris*. I got there about nine, and found it the usual sort of place. There were some twenty girls there, a few Frenchmen and two or three Britishers. But there was no sign of any American soldier.

" ' Tell me,' I said to the waiter who brought my drink, ' is there any girl here of the name of Marie ? '

" ' Mon Dieu, m'sieur,' he cried, ' half-a-dozen at least.'

" ' I guessed that,' I answered. ' But throw your memory back, my lad, three nights ago. Do you remember an American *sous officier* who was in here sitting at a table with one of those six Maries ? '

" He gave me a quick look of suspicion, and I knew I'd started one hare. His face assumed a look of bovine imbecility and he shook his head. So many people came in that he had completely forgotten the incident. He regretted it deeply, but he couldn't assist me.

" ' You may keep the change,' I remarked, showing him a twenty franc note, ' if your memory improves. But it must be the right Marie.'

" He hesitated : cupidity struggling with fear.

Then suddenly he leant forward on the pretence of drying the table with a napkin.

" ' This is not a good place for Americans, sir,' he whispered. ' I would go if I was you.'

" ' Well you're not me,' I said. ' And I'm not going. Now then—has your memory come back ? '

" He shrugged his shoulders.

" ' As M'sieur wishes. The girl you want is the one in green sitting by herself three tables away.'

" ' Good for you,' I said. ' There's the note.'

" He bustled away, and after a moment or two I glanced casually at the girl. She was a pretty little thing, and I noticed she kept looking at the door as if she was expecting someone. And very soon I noticed another thing, too. All the other girls—at least all those who hadn't got men with them—were looking at her surreptitiously and whispering amongst themselves. Evidently there was some secret which concerned her, and of which, so it struck me, she was in ignorance.

" Further it seemed to me that I was the object of a considerable amount of interest. At first I thought it was simply because I was a stranger, but after a while I began to realize that it was something more than that. It's hard to explain exactly what I mean, but it struck me that in some way my presence was being connected with this girl Marie. It wasn't the waiter because I'd noticed it before I spoke to him. It couldn't be me personally for I'd never been to the place before, and no one there knew me. So it boiled down to the fact that it must be because I was an American.

"Well there was no good wasting time. I was there to see Marie, and get what I could out of her. So when I'd finished my drink I got up and strolled over to her table, conscious that every girl in the room was watching me.

" 'Will you give me the pleasure of a dance, mam'selle,' I asked.

"She stared at me for a while without speaking.

" 'I am not dancing to-night,' she said quietly.

" 'Too bad,' I answered, sitting down beside her. ' I've been watching you, and it seems to me you're waiting for somebody. I wonder if I can guess who it is.'

" 'Are you an American officer ? ' she asked.

" 'I am,' I said. ' Why do you ask ? '

" 'Then, M'sieur—go away. This place is not safe for you. It is not safe for any American. Mon Dieu ! if I only knew what had happened . . . '

"She broke off, and sat there twisting her handkerchief between her fingers.

" 'Happened to whom,' I asked her.

" 'M'sieur—do you know a Sergeant Franklin ? '

"Now that was the name of Digby's murdered sergeant : I'd asked him.

" 'What do you know of Sergeant Franklin,' I said cautiously.

" 'Listen, m'sieur—he was my friend. He promised that he would be here last night—but he never came. And I must see him. I must warn him.'

" I took the bull by both horns.

" ' Marie,' I said : ' Sergeant Franklin was murdered last night.'

" For a moment I thought she was going to faint. Her face turned the colour of the tablecloth, and her breath came in little gasps.

" ' Take a pull at yourself, my dear,' I went on. ' It's because of that that I'm sitting here talking to you. Do you know who it was who killed him ? '

" But she hardly seemed to hear the question.

" ' So that's what all the mystery is,' she whispered savagely. ' They knew—these pigs.'

" She sat up suddenly and stared at the door.

" ' Mon Dieu ! he is early to-night. M'sieur, don't look round. For God's sake don't look round. Do you want me to help you to find the man who murdered Sergeant Franklin ? '

" ' Sure thing, Marie,' I said. ' But will you be all right. I don't want to get you into trouble.'

" She laughed a little harshly.

" ' What does it matter about me,' she cried impatiently. ' Don't you understand that I loved him. And that brute—that devil killed him. Because of what I said. Do you suppose I mind—now—if they kill me. As they will.'

" She added those last three words under her breath.

" ' Will you promise to do exactly what I say ? '

" ' I promise.' I saw there was no time for argument.

c*

" ' First—give me your address.'

" I told her the name of my hotel.

" ' Good. To-morrow morning I will ring you up there. Then come to the address I shall give you, and bring with you some friends. But now to-night there is not much time. In a few seconds a man will come up to this table. He will insult you : I, too, shall seem to agree with him. Say nothing : answer nothing—just go.'

" She sat back in her chair laughing, and snapped her fingers in my face. It was done so suddenly : her change of expression was so abrupt that for a moment I was nonplussed. Then as a coarse voice spoke from behind my shoulder, I understood.

" ' And who under the sun may you be ? '

I turned round to find an American private regarding me offensively, and for a moment my temper almost got the better of me. I'd forgotten that I was in plain clothes and that he couldn't know I was an officer. He was a villainous looking swine—one of the type it's better to avoid unless you're asking for trouble—and I guessed at once that this was the Chicago tough of whom Sergeant Franklin had spoken to Digby.

" ' Get out,' he snarled. ' Beat it while the going's good, or you may find yourself leaving feet first.'

" The girl laughed as I rose to my feet, and got rid of a choice bit of Parisian *argot* at my expense. And then for an instant the man turned away to shout to the waiter and her eyes rested on his back. By Jove ! I've never seen such a depth of concentrated hatred on anyone's face before or since. It was diabolical—devilish. But when I got to the door he was sitting beside her with his arm round her waist, and she was pointing a derisive finger at me. Evidently the game had commenced. The point that worried the others was whether it was genuine—or not.

" They were all round in my hotel early the next morning, to say nothing of the Provost Marshal, and we discussed it while we waited. Personally I felt sure that the girl was on our side, but they weren't so certain. They hadn't seen that look in her eyes, and were sceptical about the whole thing.

" ' On her own showing,' as Digby said, ' this fellow has been giving things away lavishly. Granted that it's the same man, didn't she tell that poor devil Franklin so? So is she likely to split on him ? '

" And at that very moment the telephone bell rang. I picked up the receiver and from the other end came her voice.

" ' Come at once to 15, Rue de St. Gare ! '

" It was tense, that voice of hers—tense and quivering with excitement, and her mood communicated itself to me.

" ' Come on, you fellows,' I cried. ' The Kid has done what she said.'

" We tumbled into a couple of taxis, each of us with a gun in his pocket. There was always the possibility of a trap, and we were taking no chances. And in ten minutes we arrived at her house. She came down to meet us at the door, and her face was white with dark rings under her eyes.

" ' Good morning, Marie,' I said, holding out my hand. ' What has happened ? '

" ' Come and see,' she answered briefly, and led the way upstairs.

" We crowded into the room after her to find a strange sight confronting us. Lashed hand and foot to a chair was the man I had met the night before, and he was unconscious.

" ' You want the truth,' she said quietly. ' All right : you're going to have it. Go in there.'

" ' Look here, Marie,' I said nervously. ' What are you going to do ? '

" With a girl of that type you never can tell, and I had visions of vitriol and other choice devices.

" ' Don't be afraid,' she said contemptuously. ' I'll leave the brute for you just as he is.'

" It was her bedroom we went into, and it was behind the chair where the man sat bound so that he couldn't see us though we could see him.

" ' Don't make a sound,' she said to us. ' I'm going to wake him.'

" She picked up a jug of cold water and flung it in his face, and after a moment or two he gave a spluttering cough and his head moved.

" ' What the hell has happened,' he muttered stupidly.

" Then he stared at the girl who was facing him across the table.

" ' I'll kill you for this,' he snarled, and she laughed and picked up that india-rubber strap.

" ' What are you going to do with that,' he shouted and there was terror in his voice.

" ' Get the truth, you devil,' she answered.

" You could see the man's great muscles heaving and straining at the ropes that held him, but she'd lashed him in too well, had Marie.

" ' What's the good of the truth,' he screamed. ' I'll deny it after, and there will be no proof.'

" ' I'll chance that,' she said quietly, and started in on him with the strap.

" Up one leg—down the other ; up one arm—down the other ; again and again and again, while we watched, fascinated. At the beginning of the third circuit he gave an awful groan and she paused.

" ' Who killed Sergeant Franklin,' she asked.

" A flood of abuse was the only answer.

" At the beginning of the fifth she repeated the question, and by this time the sweat had come clean through his clothes, and he was dripping like a sponge. But he still stuck it.

" At the beginning of the seventh he gave in.

" ' I did,' he croaked.

" ' Why did you kill him,' she demanded.

" ' Because he knew too much,' he muttered.

" ' About you stealing the lorries,' she went on.

" ' Of course,' he cried. ' What else ? Let me get up, you devil ; let me get up.'

" ' Not yet. I want the names of the men who have been helping you.'

" He gave 'em—half-a-dozen in all, and six men in the back-room jotted down those names as he said them.

" ' Now let me up, you she-cat,' he snarled. ' And may God help you when I get my hands on you.'

" But Marie had slipped suddenly to the floor, and when we got to her we found she'd fainted."

The American paused, fingering the rubber strap thoughtfully.

" What was the end ? " I asked.

" The chair in America for him," he answered grimly. " Our methods of examination are a little more drastic than yours, and we got the truth pretty effectively out of his confederates. They were deserters —the lot of 'em, and O'Brien, the leader, was an expert forger to boot. Moreover he was wanted for murder on our side as well : so, as there was a prejudice against killing an American in France they did the good deed in America."

" And Marie ? " I asked.

" They got her all right, though I don't know how. Someone gave her away I suppose. Personally I never saw her again. But once—just before I left Paris I was walking through the cemetery where Franklin was buried. And there was a little bunch of cheap flowers on his grave. They were old and faded, and I turned to an attendant near by :

" ' Who put these here ? ' I asked.

" He shrugged his shoulders.

" ' A girl, m'sieur,' he answered.   ' And I have let them remain.   They are dead—but then so is she.'

" ' What's that ? ' I cried.   ' Marie dead.'

" ' M'sieur knew her,' he said indifferently.   ' But yes—she is dead.   She was stabbed in the heart not a hundred yards from the cemetery gates the same evening that she put those flowers on the grave.   Who by ?   M'sieur, who knows ?   *C'est la guerre, n'est-ce-pas*—or very nearly.' "

IT is not advisable, when you speculate, to put your
money into a tin mine that contains no tin.   Further,
it is not advisable, when you speculate, to put *all* your
money into anything.   But if you combine the two,
and put all your money into a tin mine that contains
no tin, you are asking for the trouble that Major Jack
Delmont asked for—and got.   And with him in the
getting were his wife and his daughter, Molly.

She was twenty-one when it happened, was Molly,
and a combination of the astounding good looks of
both her parents.   And since it was a catastrophe
impossible to conceal, she was present at the council of
war which was held in the Delmont household.

Her father—utterly penitent—invited them both to
walk on his face and roast him over a slow fire ;   her
mother, after one " Oh ! Jack, *dear*, how could you ? "
went to her man and kissed him.   Molly went for a
walk.

She returned with her mind made up, and the next
morning, having bought a third return to London, she
departed for the day.

" I am," she announced on her return, " going to do
something terribly original.   I am going to be a
governess."

" Ye gods ! " said her father.

" Darling child," said her mother.

" Angels both," said Molly.   " If Daddy will make
a fool of himself, it's up to me to show that there are
still some brains in the family.   So I have taken a
post to-day."

" You don't mean you've done it already ? " cried
her father.

" Who with, dear ? " asked her mother.

" Mrs. Oliver Samuelson," said the girl.   " Who
says that's nothing ? "

" Who the deuce is Mrs. Oliver Samuelson ? "
demanded her father.

" The world's worst horror," laughed Molly.   " Told
me she didn't allow followers in the house.   Joking
apart, she's pretty grim, Daddy.   Rolls in boodle.
The woman in the office, who seemed quite a human
sort of soul, told me about her.   They've rented
Ladbroke Towers."

" Ladbroke Towers ! " cried her father.   " Why, I
used to shoot there with the old man.   He died about
a year ago.   It's a wonderful house, Kiddie."

" So I gathered from Mrs. Oliver Samuelson," said
the girl gravely.   " She expatiated at length on its
charms, and her great friendship with the present
Earl, and the social life that she led, and so on and so
forth.   Naturally, I was suitably impressed."

" I hate it, my dear," said her father gloomily.
" What a blithering idiot I was ! "

" Dry up, my pet," laughed Molly.   " It's no good
going into all that again."

" What's the family, Molly ? " put in her mother.

" I gather my principal charge is one Oswald, aged nine. A child who requires careful handling. Also, I am to help Mrs. Oliver Samuelson in her correspondence."

" I hate it," repeated her father, and Molly promptly kissed him on the top of his head.

" It won't be as bad as it sounds," she said, with a show of confidence she was far from feeling. " And if it is, I can always chuck it."

Which was not a good prophecy. For, six months later, she found that it was immeasurably worse than it had sounded, and she hadn't chucked it. Times out of number she had been on the point of doing so, and then the knowledge that the two people she loved most in the world could just get on on the pension, if she wasn't there, restrained her.

The Oliver Samuelsons were an altogether beastly family. And, let it be clearly understood, beastly is the *mot juste*. The family consisted of five members : father, mother, daughter and two sons, and it is a doubtful point as to which of the five was the most unpleasant. In fact, the generally accepted theory was that it was whichever you happened to be with last.

But they rolled in money—positively wallowed in it. Detach the Oliver, and the reason is clear. Who has not heard of Samuelson's Certain Cure for Chilblains, of Samuelson's Excellent Eradicator of Eczema, of Samuelson's Perfect Paralyser of Pimples ? Well— these were the people.

Now far be it from me to suggest that there is any

reason why the vendor of patent medicines should not be quite as charming a person as anyone else. There is nothing inherently debasing about paralysing pimples. There is, further, no earthly reason, as far as I can see, why a man should not reap a large reward for performing such a meritorious act. The cause of their beastliness was not that : it was simply them. If Mr. Samuelson had been the Archbishop of Canterbury, or a stockbroker, or even an author, he would still have been beastly. And the same applies to the rest of them.

It was the successful manipulation of a hundred thousand pounds during the rubber boom that caused the trouble. Before that they had been content to be beastly in comparative obscurity, but when Mrs. Samuelson had at last grasped the fact that they were millionaires, her social aspirations, always there, though hitherto suppressed, soared to dizzy heights. Such things have happened before : such things will happen again. It matters not whether one likes it or doesn't like it—the thing is inevitable. And, after all—why not ?

The man who makes a million pounds may be, and very often is, a nicer fellow than the heir to several thousand acres and a castle badly in need of repair. And had that been so in the case of the Oliver Samuelsons, these words would never have been written. At the risk of repeating myself, I wish that to be clear. What I am about to relate happened not because they were *nouveaux riches*, or patent medicine vendors, but simply because they were beastly. Had Mr. Oliver Samuelson been an author, as I said before, it would still have happened. I can't make it clearer than that.

Why their social aspirations should have been settled on a country place I do not profess to say. They none of them rode, shot or fished : they were all of them profoundly bored anywhere except in London. But since the motives inspiring the Oliver Samuelsons are, I am glad to say, a sealed book to me, I can only record the fact that they decided to obtain a country house—I beg your pardon, seat.

Now it so happened that, some three months previous to their momentous decision, the Earl of Ladbroke had consumed his last glass of port and been gathered to his forbears, leaving Ladbroke Towers sadly encumbered. His wife was dead : his only son was prospecting somewhere in the back of beyond. And the family lawyer was deteriorating badly at golf through worry over death duties. If only ne could let the house, all might yet be well ; but would the new Earl agree ? And if he did, could he find a tenant ?

To him, then, there came one day, like a direct answer to prayer, Mr. Oliver Samuelson. It was true that, dire though the necessity was, there were moments when the lawyer wondered if the price was not too great—moments when the full horror of his visitor sank into his soul. But, being a man of stern determination and a vigilant custodian of the Ladbroke interests, he banished these vacillating thoughts. He explained politely that to sell was out of the question, but that he had his lordship's authorization to let for five years. And he then mentioned a figure the size of which staggered even him.

Mr. Oliver Samuelson didn't turn a hair. He ejected from his mouth a considerable portion of chewed cigar; ground it into the carpet with his foot, and announced that a few odd thousand this way or that made no difference to him. And a month later the family was in residence

Now, as all the world knows, Ladbroke Towers is situated in the centre of the most cliquish county in England. And, as the months went by, the fact gradually penetrated into the brain of Mrs. Oliver Samuelson that, though money will obtain a country seat, money will not fill it. Not, at least, with the people whom she was desirous of knowing. Business friends of her husband were delighted to come and stay : acquaintances of her son and daughter were only too ready to drink her champagne and play poker till three in the morning. But the county families remained icily aloof.

A few called—once, and there the matter ended. Invitations to shoot and to dine were declined ; the large ball given at Christmas was exclusively attended by people from London. And there, but for one or two things, the matter would have ended.

The first concerned the matter of the head keeper, a man whose father and grandfather had been head keepers there before him. Annoyed by the smallness

of the bags, and refusing to realize that it was entirely
due to the badness of the shooting, Mr. Oliver Samuelson sacked him on the spot. The fact that his wife
was going to have a baby and that there was no
other cottage for him to go to, was nothing to do with
Mr. Samuelson.

"Get out, and get out quick. You're useless."

The second concerned a girl in the village and the
heir to the Samuelson fortune. An unpleasant case
without a redeeming feature.

There were other things, too—things which revealed
them in their true colours ; things which caused a
letter to be penned by a gentleman who signed himself
Bimbo. It breathed a certain despair, that letter ;
the writer realized that nothing could be done, since he
was fully aware that the state of the recipient's finances
was even more hopeless than usual. And the recipient,
a vast young man with a large mouth and a jink in his
nose, mopped his forehead in the stifling heat and
grinned gently to himself. Then he sat down and
answered Bimbo's letter. And the envelope of the
answer was addressed to His Grace the Duke of
Ledmonton. Moreover, its contents made that worthy
nobleman sit up with a gasp and hurriedly seek his wife.

"Impossible," she said. "Out of the question.
Tiny has got 'em again."

It was some two months later that an extremely
pretty girl, leading a singularly unpleasant-looking little
boy by the hand, walked through one of the many
copses which surround Ladbroke Towers. On her

face was an expression of utter weariness ; in her free hand she carried a book.

Molly Delmont was very near breaking-point. If only that beast of a man would leave her alone she could go on sticking it, but she knew his character far too well by now not to realize the futility of any such hope. Mr. Oliver Samuelson, junior—her present charge's brother—was of the brand that regards a pretty governess as fair game. It was his mother she was afraid of. Only too well did she know that once that lady got an inkling of what was going on she'd be kicked out of the house within an hour. And what on earth was she to do then ?

She sat down in a leafy glade, and opening the book at random she began to read mechanically. And it wasn't until she'd finished that a little twisted smile crossed her lips as she realized what she had been reading.

" There are no Prince Charmings to-day, dear. It's only a fairy story."

" What an exceedingly reprehensible statement to make to the young ! "

With a little gasp of surprise she swung round—only to gasp again at what she saw. Standing on his head in a clearing in the bushes was one of the largest young men she had ever seen in her life.

" Most reprehensible," he repeated. " I'm surprised at you."

" What's that man doing that for ? " demanded Oswald.

" I really don't know, dear," said the girl, sternly repressing a strong desire to laugh. " Do you know you are trespassing ? "

" That's why I'm standing on my head."

" But what on earth has that got to do with it ? " she cried helplessly.

" Absolutely nothing," he agreed. " Do go on reading."

" But I can't go on reading with you standing on your head. It's ridiculous."

" There I must beg to disagree," he remarked. " I take up no more room this way than any other ; I don't spoil the acoustics of the wood ; in fact, my position here doesn't affect the situation in the slightest."

" For goodness' sake," cried the girl, beginning to laugh helplessly, " do get the right way up."

" As you will," said the large young man, resignedly.

In his normal position, he seemed even vaster than before. He was wearing an old shooting coat and a pair of grey flannel trousers of great antiquity, and as he rose to his feet he picked up a large ash-plant stick. He was without a hat, and the sun striking through the trees glinted on fair, crisp hair. His mouth was big ; his nose had a jink in it—but all the girl could notice were his eyes. Big, brown eyes they were, steady and clear, and just at the moment bubbling over with laughter.

" Who on earth are you ? " she said at length.

" Prince Charming," he retorted gravely, to see her flush a little and bite her lip.

" That," she said quietly, " is rather impertinent. As I said before, you're trespassing ; so do you mind going ? "

" Strongly," he answered, sitting down on the grass. " In the first place, I should hate you to think that I meant to be impertinent ; in the second, I want to talk to you."

" But I don't know you," she cried.

" I rather anticipated you might say that," he agreed. " Hence my method of introducing myself. The ordinary common dictates of humanity require that you should satisfy yourself that I'm not insane. And that will take you a long time. May I smoke ? "

He held out his case to her, but she shook her head.

" Oswald," she called out. " Don't go too far away."

" His name is Oswald, is it ? " said the large young man, lighting a cigarette. " May I be pardoned for stating that he seems to me a singularly unpleasant child ? "

" He's the most abominable little beast I've ever met," answered the girl, and he saw that her eyes had suddenly filled with tears. " He's—— "

She broke off abruptly and rose.

" You must really go away," she said. " You don't understand."

" That's why I'm not going away," he answered. " I want to understand."

" He'll sneak to his mother about this—sneak in a beastly sort of way."

" Are you his—— "

" I'm his governess," she broke in defiantly. " And if it wasn't that I've got to, I'd sooner beg in the streets than have anything to do with these horrors."

" I like the way you said ' horrors,' " he said, with a smile. " I must make their acquaintance. The Oliver Samuelsons, aren't they ? "

" Yes. You know this part of the country, do you ? "

" Slightly," he answered gravely. " This is Lord Ladbroke's place, isn't it ? "

" Yes. He's abroad. And he let Ladbroke Towers to them for five years. They've been here a year now."

" I gather from your tone that you think that a year too long."

She shrugged her shoulders.

" It's nothing to do with me. They'd be equally horrible wherever they were. But it makes me wild to think of a wonderful old place like this being let to such people."

" Miss Delmont, may I ask for an explanation ? "

They both turned round to find a short, stout woman regarding them through lorgnettes.

" Where is Oswald ? And who is this person ? "

" He was here a moment ago, Mrs. Samuelson," said the girl, flushing, and wondering if her last remark had been heard. " He can't be far away."

" How often have I told you, Miss Delmont, about his getting lost ? "

" Not much danger of that," said the large young

man gravely. "Anyone finding him would return him at once."

For one moment the lorgnettes quivered. Was it conceivable that this unknown and badly-dressed young man intended anything by that remark? But no ; she dismissed the idea.

"What are you doing here ? " she demanded.

"At the moment, just standing on my feet," he answered. "But I can quite easily stand on my head, if you like. In fact, I prefer it."

"You must be mad," she gasped, as the large young man promptly proceeded to do so.

"Far from it," he answered happily. "Why don't you try it yourself ? "

A choking sound came from Molly Delmont, instantly suppressed as the voice she dreaded most in the world came from behind her shoulder.

"Hullo! What's all this? What's that fool doing there ? "

The large young man resumed his normal position, and stared at the newcomer. That sudden stiffening of the girl had not escaped his notice, and the reason thereof did not seem hard to find. With eyes in which there was no longer laughter, he took in every detail of the man confronting him—the coarse neck, the hairy hands, the sensual mouth—and what he saw was not good.

"Thought that would bring you to your senses," sneered the other. "You don't mind frightening women, but when a man comes along——" He shrugged his shoulders contemptuously. " Get off this land, or I'll have you run off."

The large young man smiled.

" I'm going. And you're quite right—it was entirely your appearance that brought me this way up. I could see your legs far too well before."

" What the devil do you mean ? " snarled the other thickly.

" Your tailor ought to know better," said the large young man placidly. " To send you out in plus fours is an outrage on public decency, and a probable cause of civil riot."

The next moment he was gone.

" Doubtless somewhat rude," he murmured to himself as he strolled along towards the road. " But how pleasant. Great Heavens ! the half of these people hath not been told me."

And then, somehow or other, the Oliver Samuelsons faded from his mind, and the picture of a girl with blue-grey eyes that were filled with tears replaced them.

" So there are no Prince Charmings to-day, aren't there ? " He apostrophized a squirrel that was regarding him from a tree. And then he thought of the face he contemplated every morning when shaving. " True, O Queen ! I suppose you're right."

He stepped out on to the road, and stood a moment thinking. There remained to be seen the father and daughter, and the large young man was cogitating on the best method of bolting that particular badger when he saw a car come out of the lodge gates some four hundred yards away.

It came rapidly towards him, raising a cloud of dust behind it, and his keen eyes saw at once that a man was sitting beside the driver. It might be or it might not, he reflected, and since from earliest infancy he had always believed in taking a chance, he stepped without further ado into the centre of the road and stood there waving his hands. There came a harsh scraping of brakes and the car pulled up. Whereupon the large young man leant upon the bonnet and realized that the chance had come off. Seated beside the chauffeur was the head of the family of Oliver Samuelsons.

" You were exceeding the speed limit," said the large young man accusingly.

Mr. Oliver Samuelson turned a deep magenta.

" What the—— ? Who the—— ? " he spluttered. " Are you in the police ? "

" No," conceded the other. " I am not in the police. But, as a law-abiding citizen, I felt impelled to reason with you. Once start on the downward path of sin, and you'd be setting fire to churches next. It's a fearful thing to set fire to a church, you know."

" Do you mean to say," howled the infuriated owner of the car, " that you had the confounded impertinence to stand in the middle of the road and wave your arms merely to tell me that I was exceeding the speed limit ? "

" Far from **it**," said the large young man. " But this is my only suiting, and you were making such an infernal dust. Besides, I wanted to meet you."

" You wanted to meet me ? " spluttered the other.

" And now that I have, I don't ever want to do so again."

The large young man came round and stood by the door of the car, and his face was very close to that of Mr. Oliver Samuelson.

" You miserable medicine-monger," he said grimly, " how dared you sack Rodgers ? You, who couldn't hit a sitting cat at five yards."

Then he stepped back.

" Don't let me detain you any more. If you're catching a train, I hope you've missed it."

He watched the car drive off, and after a while he strolled on slowly in the same direction.

" I have now seen eighty per cent. of the family," he murmured thoughtfully. " I will take the daughter on trust."

" Well, Tiny—was I right ? "

The large young man finished his whisky and soda and placed the empty glass on the table beside him with some deliberation.

" My dear old Bimbo," he remarked, " unless with mine own eyes I had seen them, I would not have believed them possible. But—and this is the point —if it was only that, I wouldn't feel justified in taking any further steps. After all, they cannot help their

D

appearance, and old Samuelson had a perfect right to refuse to cancel the lease and quit."

" You've heard from your lawyer definitely on that point ? "

" I was in London when the answer arrived," said the other. " Bimbo—they must go. Alexa, you tell me, was rude enough to say that I'd got 'em again when you read her my letter. Well—it's cut and dried : I heard two days ago. There's gold where I've been, and workable tin—and it's mine. Even if I'm not a millionaire, I've got ample to keep the place going. And, as I said before—the Oliver Samuelsons must go."

The Duke of Ledmonton thoughtfully lit a cigarette.

" How do you propose to do it ? "

" That, old boy, shall be revealed in due course. But there's one thing I can tell you now. Alexa and you will have to assist."

The large young man turned round as he got to the door.

" Have you seen the perfectly glorious girl with blue-grey eyes, whose job in life is to look after Oswald ? "

" Who on earth is Oswald ? " spluttered the other.

But he spoke to an empty room : the large young man had already departed on his more or less lawful occasions. Not that it mattered much to him whether they were lawful or not : all that he cared about was that they should be secret. And so it was with a distinct appearance of stealth that, as dusk was falling, he approached a certain building hidden in the woods some quarter of a mile from Ladbroke Towers. It was an old chapel, which, owing to lack of money, had been allowed to fall into disrepair.

It was a gloomy spot, and as he opened the door the air inside struck dank on his face. But the large young man never hesitated ; closing the door carefully behind him, he disappeared into the gloom beside the altar. And then there came a sudden click, and the chapel was empty.

Half an hour later another click might have been heard, as the large young man, with a faint smile on his face, stepped back into the chapel. And then with startling abruptness the smile faded and was replaced by something very different.

" You brute ; you brute—let me go ! "

" Not much, my dear," came in a coarse, triumphant voice. " You're altogether too pretty. I'm going to have a kiss."

Which, unfortunately for the heir of the Oliver Samuelsons, was where he was wrong. What he did have was a vague sort of feeling that a thing like a steam-hammer had met his face ; a further vague sort of feeling that the back of his head was being used as a pile-driver on a stone floor—and then oblivion.

"Good Heavens ! You haven't killed him, have you ?"

Molly Delmont gazed at the motionless figure on the floor, and then looked up, a little shyly, at the man who stood beside her.

" I fear not," said her companion gravely. " I think his jaw is broken, but that's all."

" Where did you come from ? " cried the girl.

" I told you this morning that fairy tales were not extinct," said the large young man with a smile. " I just appeared because you wanted me."

For a moment or two he stared straight into her eyes—stared until hers, misty and shining in the dim light, fell before his.

" I don't understand," she said, a little nervously. " What are you doing here ? "

" What are you ? " he countered.

" I often come here," she answered. " And this evening that brute followed me. What are we going to do about him ? "

" Leave him where he is to cool," he said calmly. He took her by the arm and gently forced her towards the door. " I don't particularly want him to recognize me when he comes to—so let's go."

" But who are you ? " she insisted.

" Well, you didn't like Prince Charming," he answered gravely. " So shall we cite another fairy story—Beauty and the Beast ? "

" Don't be ridiculous," she said, and the large young man saw the colour rise in her cheeks. " I do wish you'd tell me what you were doing in there."

" I will, if you promise not to pass it on."

" Of course I promise," she said, eagerly.

" I was seeking a method of ridding the locality of the Oliver Samuelsons."

" In that chapel ? " she said incredulously, and the large young man nodded.

" In that chapel," he repeated.

" Well, you'll never do it," answered the girl. " They got a letter only the other day from some lawyer in London asking them if they would cancel the lease, and they were furious. The old man is as stubborn as a mule. And, anyway "—she added curiously—" what on earth has it got to do with you ? "

" What do you bet I don't do it ? " he said, ignoring her last question.

" Anything you like."

" I shall hold you to that," he said quickly. " And now I'm going. But don't forget one thing. If that swine in there gives you any more trouble, or if you want me at any time, drop me a line to—to—— "

He hesitated for a moment or two.

" To Ely View Cottage," he concluded. " It's on the Duke of Ledmonton's place. Address it care of Mr. Rodgers."

" Is that the man Mr. Samuelson sacked ? " she said.

" It is. The Duke let him have a spare cottage on his place."

" You know Mr. Rodgers ? "

" Very well indeed," said the large young man.

" And that's why you're doing this. To pay out the Samuelsons." With a sudden little nervous movement she put her hand on his arm. " Do be

careful. I'd like to see them paid out ; they deserve
it. But they're vindictive—and if they find out—
Oh ! you see they've got money, and you haven't—
And it's money that counts."

" Not in fairy stories," he interrupted gravely.
" Then—it's only love."

And before she could think of anything further to
say, he was gone.

Exactly how the fact that the Duke and Duchess of
Ledmonton would accept an invitation to dinner,
should one be received from the Samuelson family,
became known to Mrs. Samuelson is one of life's little
mysteries. Perhaps it was due to a conversation
between the large young man and little Mrs. Carlton,
which caused that charming lady to laugh
immoderately and then go and call at Ladbroke Towers.
Certain it is that some three weeks after the use of
Mr. Samuelson junior's head as a pile-driver, invitations had gone forth far and wide requesting the
county to dine, and, to Molly Delmont's stunned
surprise, they had all been accepted.

" It's amazing," she said to the large young man,
whom she had happened to meet—not, strangely
enough, for the first time—in the ruined chapel.
" The whole bunch are coming to-night."

" It should be an amusing evening," he remarked
gravely. " How is our friend's jaw ? "

" He's been in London ever since you hit him," she
said happily. " But I have no doubt he'll be back

this afternoon. And, incidentally, what about your bet now ? This dinner will be the culminating moment of their lives. They have arrived. The only way to get rid of them after this will be to burn down the house."

" You have got the most angelic dimple," said the large young man earnestly. " But apart from that, I shall be there."

" You'll be there ? What do you mean ? "

" Fairy story again," he answered. " The invisible man."

And certainly there was no sign of him that evening when the guests had assembled in the hall, which was hardly surprising in view of the fact that Molly had written out the invitations herself. But he was such an amazing individual that she half expected suddenly to see him standing on his head at the top of the stairs, or popping up through the table at dinner.

He intrigued her so vastly, did that large young man, Rodgers' nephew, so the worthy gamekeeper had told her, but still——. Of all the perfect dears she had ever met—— !

What made her feel so nervous was the fear that he would do something rash. He was just the type who wouldn't care, and she'd hate it if anything happened to him. And it was as she reached that stage in her reflections that a loud, raucous laugh came from somewhere up in the ceiling. A sudden silence settled on the table, and everyone peered up into the dimness of the lofty dining-room.

" Good evening, Duchess," came in a harsh, metallic voice. " How are the corns to-night ? Samuelson's Certain Cure works wonders. Soak the feet in hot water, at the same time consuming one of Samuelson's Perfect Pink Powders."

Molly stole an aghast look at the Duchess, to find to her amazement that she was apparently shaking with uncontrollable laughter.

" I would like to take this opportunity," continued the voice, " of bringing to the notice of this august company all my wonderful medicines. As a family we admit frankly that our habits are awful and our appearance vile. That, however, does not alter the fact that we can eradicate eczema, intimidate itch, and paralyse pimples. In proof of this, ladies and gentlemen, a small box of my omnipotent ointment will be presented free, gratis, and for nothing, to each of you on your departure to-night. I thank you for your kind attention."

" Good evening, Duchess. How are the corns ? "

" Good God ! " howled Mr. Samuelson. " It's starting again."

The next day every servant was sacked : that evening at dinner, when only the family were present, the most lurid revelations descended upon their heads from the ceiling.

The following day an army of workmen appeared, with orders to discover the accursed thing or perish in the attempt. Hardly were their ladders in position when the family lawyer, whose golf still maintained its erstwhile brilliance, was announced.

" You will bear in mind, Mr. Samuelson," he said suavely, " that I cannot allow any tearing down of walls. I should regard that as a structural alteration, which would automatically cancel your lease."

The day after, the workmen having departed, Mr. Oliver Samuelson locked the dining-room door, and ordained that they should feed elsewhere. That afternoon, from far and near, came callers in ones and twos, in threes and fours, demanding with oaths and curses, with prayers and blandishments, to be allowed to hear the ghost. And even as they paused outside the door came the voice, muffled, it is true, but quite distinct : " Have you tried my purple pills ? "

Then the papers got hold of it, and reporters descended in hordes. A prominent member of the Society for Psychical Research gave it as his considered opinion that it was Mr. Samuelson's ectoplasm giving tongue from the roof—or words to that effect.

And finally, Mrs. Samuelson's nerve broke. She flatly refused to remain one day longer in the house. And her progeny backed her. It was the end. Beaten all along the line, the Oliver Samuelsons returned to their pristine obscurity, and with their departure silence came to the dining-room. No more could one hear the merits of the omnipotent ointment extolled : no longer were the habits of the Samuelson family pointedly discussed.

The prominent member of the Society for Psychical

D*

Research claimed that it proved his point : the reporters denounced the whole thing as an advertising stunt that had misfired : the county breathed freely again : and the vast young man emerged one morning from the ruined chapel bearing in his arms a gramophone and several records.

" There used," he explained to Molly Delmont, who was waiting for him outside, " to be a musicians' gallery in the dining-room, from which a secret passage ran to the chapel. The gallery has been removed, but the passage still remains. And that's that."

" But how did you know ? " she asked.

" I was sort of brought up on the place, you see," he said gravely. " But don't let's worry about that. All that matters is that I've won my bet. And, you remember, don't you, what the wager was for ? "

" No, I don't," she said, looking away.

" Anything I liked," he answered softly.

And suddenly she found both her hands in his.

" Molly, you know what I want."

" But, my dear," she cried, " it's madness. I haven't got a penny. What should we live on ? "

" Don't be basely utilitarian," he laughed. " I love you. That's all that matters in a fairy story. Except one thing. You've got to love me."

" Idiot," she whispered.

" Do you, darling, do you ? "

" Of course, we're both qualifying for an asylum," she said helplessly. " But I do : I can't help it. I take back what I said about there being no Prince Charmings."

And still he looked at her gravely, but with a wonderful light in his eyes.

" You darling," he said. " You darling. Molly— haven't you guessed ? I'm not Rodgers' nephew. And it wasn't for his sake that I drove those people into outer darkness, but for yours and mine. We must have somewhere to live. And I thought the old place would do."

" So you're Lord Ladbroke," she said, slowly.

" Terrible thing to have to admit," he answered. " But I am. Moreover, we have a custom in our family. Every Ladbroke carries his bride through the front door when she first arrives—and kisses her. I've just invented a new one. In future, every Lad- broke will carry the girl he is going to marry through the chapel door—and kiss her. The custom starts now."

" But, my dear," she whispered. " I don't even know your name."

" Just Beauty and the Beast, darling. Though most people call me Tiny."

Half an hour later the new custom was still being rehearsed.

THE HORROR AT STAVELEY GRANGE

I

" A FACT pointing in a certain direction is just a fact :
two pointing in the same direction become a
coincidence : three—and you begin to get into the
regions of certainty.   But you must be very sure of
your facts."

Thus ran Ronald Standish's favourite dictum : and
it was the astonishing skill with which he seemed to
be able to sort out the facts that mattered from the
mass of irrelevant detail, and having sorted them out,
to interpret them correctly, that had earned him his
reputation as a detective of quite unusual ability.

There is no doubt that had he been under the
necessity of earning his own livelihood, he would have
risen to a very high position at Scotland Yard; or, if
he had chosen to set up on his own, that his career
would have been assured. But not being under any
such necessity, his gifts were known only to a small
circle of friends and acquaintances. Moreover, he
was apt to treat the matter as rather a joke—as an
interesting recreation more than a serious business.
He regarded it in much the same light as solving a
chess problem or an acrostic.

In appearance he was about as unlike the con-
ventional detective as it is possible to be.   Of medium

height, he was inclined to be thick-set. His face was ruddy, with a short, closely-clipped moustache—and in his eyes there shone a perpetual twinkle. In fact most people on first meeting him took him for an Army officer. He was a first-class man to hounds, and an excellent shot ; a cricketer who might easily have become first class had he devoted enough time to it, and a scratch golfer. And last, but not least, he was a man of very great personal strength without a nerve in his body.

This, then, was the man who sat opposite to me in a first-class carriage of a Great Western express on the way to Devonshire. On the spur of the moment that morning, I had rung him up at his club in London— on the spur of the moment he had thrown over a week's cricket, and arranged to come with me to Exeter. And now that we were actually in the train, I began to wonder if I had brought him on a wild-goose chase. I took the letter out of my pocket—the letter that had been the cause of our journey, and read it through once again.

" Dear Tony," it ran, " I am perfectly distracted with worry and anxiety. I don't know whether you saw it in the papers, and it's such ages since we met, but I'm engaged to Billy Mansford. And we're in the most awful trouble. Haven't you got a friend or someone you once told me about who solves mysteries and things ? Do, for pity's sake, get hold of him and bring him down here to stay I'm nearly off my head with it all —Your distracted Molly."

I laid the letter on my knee and stared out of the window. Somehow or other I couldn't picture pretty little Molly Tremayne, the gayest and most feckless girl in the world, as being off her head over anything. And having only recently returned from Brazil I had not heard of her engagement—nor did I know anything about the man she was engaged to. But as I say, I rang up Standish on the spur of the moment, and a little to my surprise he had at once accepted.

He leant over at that moment, and took the letter off my knee.

" The Old Hall," he remarked thoughtfully. Then he took a big-scale ordnance map from his pocket and began to study it.

" Three miles approximately from Staveley Grange."

" Staveley Grange," I said, staring at him. " What has Staveley Grange got to do with the matter ? "

" I should imagine—everything," he answered. " You've been out of the country, Tom, and so you're a bit behindhand. But you may take it from me that it was not the fact that your Molly was distracted that made me give up an excellent I.Z. tour. It was the fact that she is engaged to Mr. William Mansford."

" Never heard of him," I said. " Who and what is he ? "

" He is the younger and only surviving son of the late Mr. Robert Mansford," he answered thoughtfully. " Six months ago the father was alive—also Tom, the elder son. Five months ago the father died : two months ago Tom died. And the circumstances of their deaths were, to put it mildly, peculiar."

" Good heavens ! " I cried, " this is all news to me."

" Probably," he answered. " The matter attracted

very little attention. But you know my hobby, and it was the coincidence of the two things that attracted my attention. I only know, of course, what appeared in the papers—and that wasn't very much. Mansford senior and both his sons had apparently spent most of their lives in Australia. The two boys came over with the Anzacs, and a couple of years or so after the war they all decided to come back to England. And so he bought Staveley Grange. He had gone a poor man of distinctly humble origin : he returned as a wealthy Australian magnate. Nine months after he stepped into the house he was found dead in his bed in the morning by the butler. He was raised up on his pillows and he was staring fixedly at a top corner of the room by one of the windows. And in his hand he held the speaking tube which communicated with the butler's room. A post-mortem revealed nothing, and the verdict was that he had died of heart failure. In view of the fact that most people do die of heart failure, the verdict was fairly safe."

Ronald Standish lit a cigarette.

" That was five months ago. Two months ago, one of the footmen coming in in the morning was horrified to find Tom sprawling across the rail at the foot of the bed—stone dead. He had taken over his father's room, and had retired the previous night in the best of health and spirits. Again there was a post-mortem—again nothing was revealed, And again the same verdict was given—heart failure. Of course, the coincidence was commented on in the press, but there the matter rested, at any rate as far as the newspapers were concerned. And therefore that is as much as I know. This letter looks as if further developments were taking place."

" What an extraordinary affair," I remarked, as he finished. " What sort of men physically were the father and Tom ? "

" According to the papers," answered Standish, " they were two singularly fine specimens. Especially Tom."

Already we were slowing down for Exeter, and we began gathering our suitcases and coats preparatory to alighting. I leant out of the window as we ran into the station, having wired Molly our time of arrival, and there she was sure enough, with a big, clean-cut man standing beside her, who, I guessed, must be her fiancé. So, in fact, it proved, and a moment or two later we all walked out of the station together towards the waiting motor car. And it was as I passed the ticket collector that I got the first premonition of trouble. Two men standing on the platform, who looked like well-to-do farmers, whispered together a little significantly as Mansford passed them, and stared after him with scarcely veiled hostility in their eyes.

On the way to the Old Hall, I studied him under cover of some desultory conversation with Molly. He was a typical Australian of the best type : one of those open-air, clear-eyed men who came over in their thousands to Gallipoli and France. But it seemed to me that his conversation with Ronald was a little forced : underlying it was a vague uneasiness—a haunting fear of something or other. And I thought he was studying my friend with a kind of desperate hope tinged with disappointment, as if he had been building on Ronald's personality and now was unsatisfied.

That some such idea was in Molly's mind I learned as we got out of the car. For a moment or two we were alone, and she turned to me with a kind of desperate eagerness.

" Is he very clever, Tom—your friend ? Somehow I didn't expect him to look quite like that ! "

" You may take it from me, Molly," I said reassuringly, " that there are very few people in Europe who can see further into a brick wall than Ronald. But he knows nothing, of course, as to what the trouble is—any more than I do. And you mustn't expect him to work miracles."

" Of course not," she answered. " But oh ! Tom—it's—it's—damnable."

We went into the house and joined Standish and Mansford, who were in the hall.

" You'd like to go up to your rooms," began Molly, but Ronald cut her short with a grave smile.

" I think, Miss Tremayne," he said quietly, " that it will do you both good to get this little matter off your chests as soon as possible. Bottling things up is no good, and there's some time yet before dinner."

The girl gave him a quick smile of gratitude and led the way across the hall.

" Let's go into the billiard room," she said. " Daddy is pottering round the garden, and you can meet him later. Now, Billy," she continued, when we were comfortably settled, " tell Mr. Standish all about it."

" Right from the very beginning, please," said Ronald, stuffing an empty pipe in his mouth. " The reasons that caused your father to take Staveley Grange and everything."

Bill Mansford gave a slight start.

" You know something about us already then."

" Something," answered Ronald briefly. " I want to know all."

" Well," began the Australian, " I'll tell you all I know. But there are many gaps I can't fill in. When we came back from Australia two years ago, we naturally gravitated to Devonshire. My father came from these parts, and he wanted to come back after his thirty years' absence. Of course he found everything changed, but he insisted on remaining here and we set about looking for a house. My father was a wealthy man—very wealthy, and his mind was set on getting something good. A little pardonable vanity perhaps—but having left England practically penniless to return almost a millionaire—he was determined to get what he wanted regardless of cost. And it was after we had been here about six months that Staveley Grange came quite suddenly on to the market. It happened in rather a peculiar way. Some people of the name of Bretherton had it, and had

been living there for about three years. They had
bought it, and spent large sums of money on it :
introduced a large number of modern improvements,
and at the same time preserved all the old appearance.
Then as I say, quite suddenly, they left the house and
threw it on the market.

" Well, it was just what we wanted. We all went
over it, and found it even more perfect than we had
anticipated. The man who had been butler to the
Brethertons was in charge, and when we went over,
he and his wife were living there alone. We tried to
pump them as to why the Brethertons had gone, but
they appeared to know no more than we did. The
butler—Templeton—was a charming old bird with side-
whiskers ; his wife, who had been doing cook, was a
rather timorous-looking little woman—but a damned
good cook.

" Anyway, the long and short of it was, we bought
the place. The figure was stiff, but my father could
afford it. And it was not until we bought it, that we
heard in a roundabout way the reason of the Brethertons' departure. It appeared that old Mrs. Bretherton
woke up one night in screaming hysterics, and alleged
that a dreadful thing was in the room with her. What
it was she wouldn't say, except to babble foolishly
about a shining, skinny hand that had touched her.
Her husband and various maids came rushing in, and
of course the room was empty. There was nothing
there at all. The fact of it was that the old lady had
had lobster for dinner—and a nightmare afterwards.

At least," added Mansford slowly, " that's what we thought at the time."

He paused to light a cigarette.

" Well—we gathered that nothing had been any good.   Templeton proved a little more communicative once we were in, and from him we found out, that in spite of every argument and expostulation on the part of old Bretherton, the old lady flatly refused to live in the house for another minute. She packed up her boxes and went off the next day with her maid to some hotel in Exeter, and nothing would induce her to set foot inside the house again.   Old Bretherton was livid."

Mansford smiled grimly.

" But—he went, and we took the house.   The room that old Mrs. Bretherton had had was quite the best bedroom in the house, and my father decided to use it as his own.   He came to that decision before we knew anything about this strange story, though even if we had, he'd still have used the room.   My father was not the man to be influenced by an elderly woman's indigestion and subsequent nightmare.   And when bit by bit we heard the yarn, he merely laughed, as did my brother and myself.

" And then one morning it happened.   It was Templeton who broke the news to us with an ashen face, and his voice shaking so that we could hardly make out what he said.   I was shaving at the time, I remember, and when I'd taken in what he was trying to say, I rushed along the passage to my father's room with the soap still lathered on my chin.   The poor old man was sitting up in bed propped against the pillows. His left arm was flung half across his face as if to ward off something that was coming : his right hand was grasping the speaking-tube beside the bed. And in his wide-open, staring eyes was a look of dreadful terror."

He paused as if waiting for some comment or question, but Ronald still sat motionless, with his empty pipe in his mouth. And after a while Mansford continued :

" There was a post-mortem, as perhaps you may have seen in the papers, and they found my father had died from heart failure. But my father's heart, Mr. Standish, was as sound as mine, and neither my brother nor I were satisfied. For weeks he and I sat up in that room, taking it in turns to go to sleep, to see if we could see anything—but nothing happened. And at last we began to think that the verdict was right, and that the poor old man had died of natural causes. I went back to my own room, and Tom—my brother—stayed on in my father's room. I tried to dissuade him, but he was an obstinate fellow, and he had an idea that if he slept there alone he might still perhaps get to the bottom of it. He had a revolver by his side, and Tom was a man who could hit the pip out of the ace of diamonds at ten yards. Well, for a week nothing happened. And then one night I stayed chatting with him for a few moments in his room before going to bed. That was the last time I saw him alive. One of the footmen came rushing in to me the next morning, with a face like a sheet—and before he spoke I knew what must have happened. It was perhaps a little foolish of me—but I dashed past him while he was still stammering at the door—and went to my brother's room "

" Why foolish ? " said Standish quietly.

" Some people at the inquest put a false construction on it," answered Mansford steadily. " They wanted to know why I made that assumption before the footman told me."

" I see," said Standish. " Go on."

" I went into the room, and there I found him. In one hand he held the revolver, and he was lying over the rail at the foot of the bed. The blood had gone to his head, and he wasn't a pretty sight. He was dead, of course—and once again the post-mortem revealed nothing. He also was stated to have died of heart failure. But he didn't, Mr. Standish." Mansford's voice shook a little. " As there's a God above, I swear Tom never died of heart failure. Something happened in that room—something terrible occurred there which killed my father and brother as surely as a bullet through the brain. And I've *got* to find out what it was : I've *got* to, you understand—because "— and here his voice faltered for a moment, and then grew steady again—" because there are quite a number of people who suspect me of having murdered them both."

" Naturally," said Standish, in his most matter-of-fact tone. " When a man comes into a lot of money

through the sudden death of two people, there are
certain to be lots of people who will draw a connection
between the two events."

He stood up and faced Mansford.

" Are the police still engaged on it ? "

" Not openly," answered the other. " But I know
they're working at it still. And I can't and won't
marry Molly with this cloud hanging over my head.
I've got to disprove it."

" Yes, but, my dear, it's no good to me if you
disprove it by being killed yourself," cried the girl.
Then she turned to Ronald. " That's where we
thought that perhaps you could help us, Mr. Standish.
If only you can clear Billy's name, why——"

She clasped her hands together beseechingly, and
Standish gave her a reassuring smile.

" I'll try, Miss Tremayne—I can't do more than
that. And now I think we'll get to business at once.
I want to examine that bedroom."

.   .   .   .

II

Ronald Standish remained sunk in thought during
the drive to Staveley Grange. Molly had not come
with us, and neither Mansford nor I felt much inclined
to conversation. He, poor devil, kept searching
Ronald's face with a sort of pathetic eagerness, almost
as if he expected the mystery to be already solved.

And then, just as we were turning into the drive, Ronald spoke for the first time.

" Have you slept in that room since your brother's death, Mansford ? "

" No," answered the other, a little shamefacedly. " To tell the truth, Molly extracted a promise from me that I wouldn't."

" Wise of her," said Standish tersely, and relapsed into silence again.

" But you don't think——" began Mansford.

" I think nothing," snapped Standish, and at that moment the car drew up at the door.

It was opened by an elderly man with side whiskers, whom I placed as the butler—Templeton. He was a typical, old-fashioned manservant of the country-house type, and he bowed respectfully when Mansford told him what we had come for.

" I am thankful to think there is any chance, sir, of clearing up this terrible mystery," he said earnestly. " But I fear, if I may say so, that the matter is beyond earthly hands." His voice dropped, to prevent the two footmen overhearing. " We have prayed, sir, my wife and I, but there are more things in heaven and earth than we can account for. You wish to go to the room, sir ? It is unlocked."

He led the way up the stairs and opened the door.

" Everything, sir, is as it was on the morning when Mr. Tom—er—died. Only the bedclothes have been removed."

He bowed again and left the room, closing the door.
" Poor old Templeton," said Mansford. " He's
convinced that we are dealing with a ghost. Well,
here's the room, Standish—just as it was. As you see,
there's nothing very peculiar about it."

Ronald made no reply. He was standing in the
centre of the room taking in the first general impression
of his surroundings. He was completely absorbed,
and I made a warning sign to Mansford not to speak.
The twinkle had left his eyes : his expression was one
of keen concentration. And, after a time, knowing
the futility of speech, I began to study the place on
my own account.

It was a big, square room, with a large double bed
of the old-fashioned type. Over the bed was a canopy,
made fast to the two bedposts at the head, and supported
at the foot by two wires attached to the two corners of
the canopy and two staples let into the wall above the
windows. The bed itself faced the windows, of which
there were two, placed symmetrically in the wall
opposite, with a writing table in between them. The
room was on the first floor in the centre of the house,
and there was thus only one outside wall—that facing
the bed. A big open fireplace and a lavatory basin
with water laid on occupied most of one wall ; two
long built-in cupboards filled up the other. Beside
the bed, on the fireplace side, stood a small table, with
a special clip attached to the edge for the speaking-
tube. In addition there stood on this table a thing not
often met with in a private house in England. It was

a small, portable electric fan, such as one finds on board ship or in the tropics.

There were two or three easy chairs standing on the heavy pile carpet, and the room was lit by electric light. In fact the whole tone was solid comfort, not to say luxury; it looked the last place in the world with which one would have associated anything ghostly or mysterious.

Suddenly Ronald Standish spoke.

" Just show me, will you, Mansford, as nearly as you can, exactly the position in which you found your father."

With a slight look of repugnance, the Australian got on to the bed.

" There were bedclothes, of course, and pillows which are not here now, but allowing for them, the poor old man was hunched up somehow like this. His knees were drawn up: the speaking-tube was in his hand, and he was staring towards that window."

" I see," said Standish. " The window on the right as we look at it. And your brother now. When he was found he was lying over the rail at the foot of the bed. Was he on the right side or the left ? "

" On the right," said Mansford, " almost touching the upright."

Once again Standish relapsed into silence and stared thoughtfully round the room. The setting sun was pouring in through the windows, and suddenly he gave a quick exclamation. We both glanced at him and he was staring up at the ceiling with a keen, intent look

to be made up, while Ronald had shrugged his shoulders and shaken his head.

" Understandable, Mansford," he remarked, " but unwise. My advice to you is to have that room shut up."

And the old butler, shutting the door of the car, had fully agreed.

" Obstinate, sir," he whispered, " like his father. Persuade him to have it shut up, sir—if you can. I'm afraid of that room—afraid of it."

" You think something will happen to-night, Ronald," I said as we turned into the Old Hall.

" I don't know, Tom," he said slowly. " I'm utterly in the dark—utterly. And if the sun hadn't been shining to-day while we were in that room, I shouldn't have even the faint glimmer of light I've got now. But when you've got one bit of a jig-saw, it saves trouble to let the designer supply you with a few more."

And more than that he refused to say. Throughout dinner he talked cricket with old Tremayne : after dinner he played him at billiards. And it was not until eleven o'clock that he made a slight sign to me, and we both said good-night.

" No good anyone knowing, Tom," he said as we went upstairs. " It's an easy drop from my window to the ground. We'll walk to Staveley Grange."

The church clock in the little village close by was striking midnight as we crept through the undergrowth towards the house. It was a dark night—the moon was not due to rise for another three hours—and we finally came to a halt behind a big bush on the edge of the lawn from which we could see the house clearly. A light was still shining from the windows of the fatal room, and once or twice we saw Mansford's shadow as he undressed. Then the light went out, and the house was in darkness : the vigil had begun.

For twenty minutes or so we waited, and Standish began to fidget uneasily.

" Pray heavens ! he hasn't forgotten and gone to sleep," he whispered to me, and even as he spoke he gave a little sigh of relief. A dark figure was lowering itself out of the window, and a moment or two later we saw Mansford skirting the lawn. A faint hiss from Standish and he'd joined us under cover of the bush.

" Everything seemed perfectly normal," he whispered. " I got into bed as you said—and there's another thing I did too. I've tied a thread across the door, so that if the ghost goes in that way we'll know."

" Good," said Standish. " And now we can compose ourselves to wait. Unfortunately we mustn't smoke."

Slowly the hours dragged on, while we took it in turns to watch the windows through a pair of night glasses. And nothing happened—absolutely nothing. Once it seemed to me as if a very faint light—it was more like a lessening of the darkness than an actual light —came from the room, but I decided it must be my imagination. And not till nearly five o'clock did Standish decide to go into the room and explore. His face was expressionless : I couldn't tell whether he

E

was disappointed or not. But Mansford made no effort to conceal his feelings : frankly he regarded the whole experiment as a waste of time.

And when the three of us had clambered in by the window he said as much.

" Absolutely as I left it," he said. " Nothing happened at all."

" Then, for heaven's sake, say so in a whisper," snapped Standish irritably, as he clambered on to the bed. Once again his objective was the right hand wire stay of the canopy, and as he touched it he gave a quick exclamation. But Mansford was paying no attention : he was staring with puzzled eyes at the electric fan by the bed.

" Now who the devil turned that on," he muttered. " I haven't seen it working since the morning Tom died." He walked round to the door. " Say, Standish —that's queer. The thread isn't broken—and that fan wasn't going when I left the room."

Ronald Standish looked more cheerful.

" Very queer," he said. " And now I think, if I was you, I'd get into that bed and go to sleep—first removing the thread from the door. You're quite safe now."

" Quite safe," murmured Mansford. " I don't understand."

" Nor do I—as yet," returned Standish. " But this I will tell you. Neither your father nor your brother died of heart failure, through seeing some dreadful sight. They were foully murdered, as, in all probability you would have been last night had you slept in this room."

"But who murdered them, and how and why?" said Mansford dazedly.

"That is just what I'm going to find out," answered Standish grimly.

. . . .

As we came out of the breakfast-room at the Old Hall three hours later, Standish turned away from us. "I'm going into the garden to think," he said, "I have a sort of feeling that I'm not being very clever. For the life of me at the moment I cannot see the connection between the canopy wire that failed to shine in the sunlight, and the electric fan that was turned on so mysteriously. I am going to sit under that tree over there. Possibly the link may come."

He strolled away, and Molly joined me. She was looking worried and *distraite*, as she slipped her hand through my arm.

"Has he found out anything, Tom?" she asked eagerly. "He seemed so silent and preoccupied at breakfast."

"He's found out something, Molly," I answered guardedly, "but I'm afraid he hasn't found out much. In fact, as far as my brain goes it seems to me to be nothing at all. But he's an extraordinary fellow," I added, reassuringly.

She gave a little shudder and turned away.

" It's too late, Tom," she said miserably.

" Oh ! if only I'd sent for you earlier. But it never dawned on me that it would come to this. I never dreamed that Bill would be suspected. He's just telephoned through to me : that horrible man McIver —the Inspector from Scotland Yard—is up there now. I feel that it's only a question of time before they arrest him. And though he'll get off—he must get off if there's such a thing as justice—the suspicion will stick to him all his life. There will be brutes who will say that failure to prove that Bill did it, is a very different matter to proving that he didn't. But I'm going to marry him all the same, Tom—whatever he says. Of course, I suppose you know that he didn't get on too well with his father."

" I didn't," I answered. " I know nothing about him except just what I've seen."

" And the other damnable thing is that he was in some stupid money difficulty. He'd backed a bill or something for a pal and was let down, which made his father furious. Of course there was nothing in it, but the police got hold of it—and twisted it to suit themselves."

" Well, Molly, you may take it from me," I said reassuringly, " that Bob Standish is certain he had nothing to do with it."

" That's not much good, Tom," she answered with a twisted smile. " So am I certain, but I can't *prove* it."

With a little shrug of her shoulders she turned and

went indoors, leaving me to my own thoughts. I could see Standish in the distance, with his head enveloped in a cloud of smoke, and after a moment's indecision I started to stroll down the drive towards the lodge. It struck me that I would do some thinking on my own account, and see if by any chance I could hit on some solution which would fit the facts. And the more I thought the more impossible did it appear : the facts at one's disposal were so terribly meagre.

What horror had old Mansford seen coming at him out of the darkness, which he had tried to ward off even as he died ? And was it the same thing that had come to his elder son, who had sprung forward revolver in hand, and died as he sprang ? And again, who had turned on the electric fan ? How did that fit in with the deaths of the other two ? No one had come in by the door on the preceding night : no one had got in by the window. And then suddenly I paused, struck by a sudden idea. Staveley Grange was an old house - early sixteenth century ; just the type of house to have secret passages and concealed entrances . . . There must be one into the fatal room : it was obvious.

Through that door there had crept some dreadful thing—some man, perhaps, and if so the murderer himself—disguised and dressed up to look awe-inspiring. Phosphorus doubtless had been used—and phosphorus skilfully applied to a man's face and clothes will make him sufficiently terrifying at night to strike terror into the stoutest heart. Especially someone just awakened from sleep. That faint luminosity which we thought we had seen the preceding night was accounted for, and I almost laughed at dear old Ronald's stupidity in not having looked for a secret entrance. I was one up on him this time.

Mrs. Bretherton's story came back to me—her so-called nightmare—in which she affirmed she had been touched by a shining skinny hand. Shining— here lay the clue—the missing link. The arm of the murderer only was daubed with phosphorus ; the rest of his body was in darkness. And the terrified victim waking suddenly would be confronted with a ghastly shining arm stretched out to clutch his throat.

A maniac probably—the murderer : a maniac who knew the secret entrance to Staveley Grange : a homicidal maniac—who had been frightened in his foul work by Mrs. Bretherton's shrieks, and had fled before she had shared the same fate as the Mansfords. Then and there I determined to put my theory in front of Ronald. I felt that I'd stolen a march on him this time at any rate.

I found him still puffing furiously at his pipe, and he listened in silence while I outlined my solution with a little pardonable elation.

" Dear old Tom," he said as I finished. " I congratu- late you. The only slight drawback to your idea is that there is no secret door into the room."

" How do you know that ? " I cried. " You hardly looked."

" On the contrary, I looked very closely. I may say that for a short while I inclined to some such theory as the one you've just put forward. But as soon as I saw that the room had been papered I dismissed it at once. As far as the built-in cupboard was concerned, it was erected by a local carpenter quite recently, and any secret entrance would have been either blocked over or known to him. Besides McIver has been in charge of this case—Inspector McIver from Scotland Yard. Now he and I have worked together before, and I have the very highest opinion of his ability. His powers of observation are extraordinary, and if his powers of deduction were as high he would be in the very first flight. Unfortunately he lacks imagination. But what I was leading up to was this. If McIver failed to find a secret entrance, it would be so much waste of time looking for one oneself. And if he had found one, he wouldn't have been able to keep it dark. We should have heard about it sharp enough."

"Well, have you got any better idea," I said a little peevishly. "If there isn't any secret door, how the deuce was that fan turned on ? "

"There is such a thing as a two-way switch," murmured Ronald mildly. "That fan was not turned on from inside the room : it was turned on from somewhere else. And the person who turned it on was the murderer of old Mansford and his son."

I stared at him in amazement.

"Then all you've got to do," I cried excitedly, " is to find out where the other terminal of the two-way switch is ? If it's in someone's room you've got him."

"Precisely, old man. But if it's in a passage, we

haven't. And here, surely, is McIver himself. I wonder how he knew I was here ? "

I turned to see a short thick-set man approaching us over the lawn.

" He was up at Staveley Grange this morning," I said. " Mansford telephoned through to Molly."

" That accounts for it then," remarked Standish waving his hand at the detective. " Good-morning, Mac."

" Morning, Mr. Standish," cried the other. " I've just heard that you're on the track, so I came over to see you."

" Splendid," said Standish. " This is Mr. Belton— a great friend of mine—who is responsible for my giving up a good week's cricket and coming down here. He's a friend of Miss Tremayne's."

McIver looked at me shrewdly.

" And therefore of Mr. Mansford's, I see."

" On the contrary," I remarked, " I never met Mr. Mansford before yesterday.

" I was up at Staveley Grange this morning," said McIver, " and Mr. Mansford told me you'd all spent the night on the lawn."

I saw Standish give a quick frown, which he instantly suppressed.

" I trust he told you that in private, McIver."

" He did. But why ? "

" Because I want it to be thought that he slept in that room," answered Standish. " We're moving in deep waters, and a single slip at the present moment may cause a very unfortunate state of affairs."

" In what way ? " grunted McIver.

" It might frighten the murderer," replied Standish. " And if he is frightened, I have my doubts if we shall ever bring the crime home to him. And if we don't bring the crime home to him, there will always be people who will say that Mansford had a lot to gain by the deaths of his father and brother."

" So you think it was murder ? " said McIver slowly, looking at Standish from under his bushy eyebrows.

Ronald grinned. " Yes, I quite agree with you on that point."

" I haven't said what I think ! " said the detective.

" True, McIver—perfectly true. You have been the soul of discretion. But I can hardly think that Scotland Yard would allow themselves to be deprived of your valuable services for two months while you enjoyed a rest cure in the country. Neither a ghost nor two natural deaths would keep you in Devonshire."

McIver laughed shortly.

" Quite right, Mr. Standish. I'm convinced it's murder : it must be. But frankly speaking, I've never been so absolutely floored in all my life. Did you find out anything last night ? "

Standish lit a cigarette.

" Two very interesting points—two extremely interesting points, I may say, which I present to you free, gratis and for nothing. One of the objects of oil is to reduce friction, and one of the objects of an electric

E*

fan is to produce a draught. And both these profound facts have a very direct bearing on . . . " He paused and stared across the lawn. " Hullo ! here is our friend Mansford in his car. Come to pay an early call, I suppose."

The Australian was standing by the door talking to his fiancée, and after a glance in their direction, McIver turned back to Ronald.

" Well, Mr. Standish, go on. Both those facts have a direct bearing on—what ? "

But Ronald Standish made no reply. He was staring fixedly at Mansford, who was slowly coming towards us talking to Molly Tremayne. And as he came closer, it struck me that there was something peculiar about his face. There was a dark stain all round his mouth, and every now and then he pressed the back of his hand against it as if it hurt.

" Well, Standish," he said with a laugh, as he came up, " here's a fresh development for your ingenuity. Of course," he added, " it can't really have anything to do with it, but it's damned painful. Look at my mouth."

" I've been looking at it," answered Ronald. " How did it happen ? "

" I don't know. All I can tell you is that about an hour ago it began to sting like blazes and turn dark red."

And now that he had come closer, I could see that there was a regular ring all round his mouth, stretching up almost to his nostrils and down to the cleft in his chin. It was dark and angry-looking, and was evidently paining him considerably.

" I feel as if I'd been stung by a family of hornets," he remarked. " You didn't leave any infernal chemical in the telephone, did you, Inspector McIver ? "

" I did not," answered the detective stiffly, to pause in amazement as Standish uttered a shout of triumph.

" I've got it ! " he cried. " The third point—the third elusive point. Did you go to sleep this morning as I suggested, Mansford ? "

" No, I didn't," said the Australian, looking thoroughly mystified. " I sat up on the bed puzzling over that darned fan for about an hour, and then I decided to shave. Well, the water in the tap wasn't hot, so——"

" You blew down the speaking-tube to tell someone to bring you some," interrupted Standish quietly.

" I did," answered Mansford. " But how the devil did you know ? "

" Because one of the objects of a speaking-tube, my dear fellow, is to speak through. Extraordinary how that simple point escaped me. It only shows, McIver, what I have invariably said : the most obvious points are the ones which most easily elude us. Keep your most private papers loose on your writing-table, and your most valuable possessions in an unlocked drawer, and you'll never trouble the burglary branch of your insurance company."

" Most interesting," said McIver with ponderous

sarcasm. " Are we to understand, Mr. Standish, that you have solved the problem ? "

" Why, certainly," answered Ronald, and Mansford gave a sharp cry of amazement. " Oil reduces friction, an electric fan produces a draught, and a speaking-tube is a tube to speak through secondarily ; primarily, it is just—a tube. For your further thought, McIver, I would suggest to you that Mrs. Bretherton's digestion was much better than is popularly supposed, and that a brief perusal of some chemical work, bearing in mind Mr. Mansford's remarks that he felt as if he'd been stung by a family of hornets, would clear the air."

" Suppose you cease jesting, Standish," said Mansford a little brusquely. " What exactly do you mean by all this ? "

" I mean that we are up against a particularly clever and ingenious murderer," answered Standish gravely. " Who he is—I don't know ; why he's done it—I don't know ; but one thing I do know—he is a very dangerous criminal. And we want to catch him in the act. Therefore, I shall go away to-day ; McIver will go away to-day ; and you, Mansford, will sleep in that room again to-night. And this time, instead of you joining us on the lawn—we shall all join you in the room. Do you follow me ? "

" I follow you," said Mansford excitedly. " And we'll catch him in the act."

" Perhaps," said Standish quietly. " And perhaps we may have to wait a week or so. But we'll catch him, provided no one says a word of this conversation."

"But look here, Mr. Standish," said McIver peevishly, " I'm not going away to-day. I don't understand all this rigmarole of yours, and. . . . "

" My very good Mac," laughed Standish, " you trot away and buy a ticket to London. Then get out at the first stop and return here after dark. And I'll give you another point to chew the cud over. Mrs. Bretherton was an elderly and timorous lady, and elderly and timorous ladies, I am told, put their heads under the bed-clothes if they are frightened. Mr. Mansford's father and brother were strong virile men, who do not hide their heads under such circumstances. They died, and Mrs. Bretherton lived. Think it over— and bring a gun to-night."

For the rest of the day we saw no sign of Ronald Standish. He had driven off in the Tremayne's car to the station, and had taken McIver with him. And there we understood from the chauffeur they had both taken tickets to London and left the place. Following Ronald's instructions, Mansford had gone back to Staveley Grange, and announced the fact of their departure, at the same time stating his unalterable intention to continue occupying the fatal room until he had solved the mystery. Then he returned to the Old Hall, where Molly, he and I spent the day, racking our brains in futile endeavours to get to the bottom of it.

" What beats me," said Mansford, after we had discussed every conceivable and inconceivable possibility, " is that Standish can't know any more than we do. We've both seen exactly what he's seen ; we both know the facts just as well as he does. We're neither of us fools, and yet he can see the solution—and we can't."

" It's just there that he is so wonderful," I answered thoughtfully. " He uses his imagination to connect what are apparently completely disconnected facts. And you may take it from me, Mansford, that he's very rarely wrong."

The Australian pulled at his pipe in silence.

" I think we'll find everything out to-night," he said at length. " Somehow or other I've got great faith in that pal of yours. But what is rousing my curiosity almost more than how my father and poor old Tom were murdered is who did it ? Everything points to it being someone in the house—but in heaven's name, who ? I'd stake my life on the two footmen—one of them came over with us from Australia. Then there's that poor old boob Templeton, who wouldn't hurt a fly—and his wife, and the other women servants, who, incidentally, are all new since Tom died. It beats me—beats me utterly."

For hours we continued the unending discussion, while the afternoon dragged slowly on. At six o'clock Mansford rose to go : his orders were to dine at home. He smiled reassuringly at Molly, who clung to him nervously ; then with a cheerful wave of his hand he vanished down the drive. My orders were equally concise : to dine at the Old Hall—wait there until it

was dark, and then make my way to the place where
Standish and I had hidden the previous night.

It was not till ten that I deemed it safe to go ;
then slipping a small revolver into my pocket, I left
the house by a side door and started on my three-
mile walk.

As before, there was no moon, and in the shadow of
the undergrowth I almost trod on Ronald before I
saw him.

" That you, Tom ? " came his whisper, and I lay
down at his side. I could dimly see McIver a few
feet away, and then once again began the vigil. It
must have been about half-past eleven that the lights
were switched on in the room, and Mansford started
to go to bed. Once he came to the window and leaned
out, seeming to stare in our direction; then he went
back to the room, and we could see his shadow as he
moved about. And I wondered if he was feeling
nervous.

At last the light went out, and almost at once
Standish rose.

" There's no time to lose," he muttered. " Follow
me—and not a sound."

Swiftly we crossed the lawn and clambered up the
old buttressed wall to the room above. I heard
Ronald's whispered greeting to Mansford, who was
standing by the window in his pyjamas, and then
McIver joined us, blowing slightly. Climbing walls
was not a common form of exercise as far as he was
concerned.

" Don't forget," whispered Standish again, " not a sound, not a whisper. Sit down and wait."

He crossed to the table by the bed—the table on which stood the motionless electric fan. Then he switched on a small electric torch, and we watched him eagerly as he took up the speaking-tube. From his pocket he extracted what appeared to be a hollow tube some three inches long, with a piece of material attached to one end. This material he tied carefully round the end of the speaking-tube, thereby forming a connection between the speaking-tube and the short hollow one he had removed from his pocket. And finally he placed a cork very lightly in position at the other end of the metal cylinder. Then he switched off his torch and sat down on the bed. Evidently his preparations were complete ; there was nothing to do now but wait.

The ticking of the clock on the mantelpiece sounded incredibly loud in the utter silence of the house. One o'clock struck—then half-past—when suddenly there came a faint pop from near the bed which made me jump violently. I heard Ronald drawing his breath sharply and craned forward to see what was happening. There came a gentle rasping noise, as Standish lit his petrol cigarette lighter. It gave little more light than a flickering glimmer, but it was just enough for me to see what he was doing. He was holding the flame to the end of the hollow tube, in which there was no longer a cork. The little pop had been caused by the cork blowing out. And then to my amazement a blue flame sprang from the end of the tube, and burnt steadily. It burnt with a slight hiss, like a bunsen burner in a laboratory—and it gave about the same amount of light. One could just see Ronald's face looking white and ghostly ; then he pulled the bed curtain round the table, and the room was in darkness once again.

McIver was sitting next to me and I could hear his hurried breathing over the faint hiss of the hidden flame. And so we sat for perhaps ten minutes, when a board creaked in the room above us.

" It's coming now," came in a quick whisper from Ronald. " Whatever I do—don't speak, don't make a sound."

I make no bones about it, but my heart was going in great sickening thumps. I've been in many tight corners in the course of my life, but this silent room had got my nerves stretched to the limit. And I don't believe McIver was any better. I know I bore the marks of his fingers on my arm for a week after.

" My God ! look," I heard him breathe, and at that moment I saw it. Up above the window on the right a faint luminous light had appeared, in the centre of which was a hand. It wasn't an ordinary hand— it was a skinny, claw-like talon, which glowed and shone in the darkness. And even as we watched it, it began to float downwards towards the bed. Steadily and quietly it seemed to drift through the room—but always towards the bed. At length it stopped, hanging directly over the foot of the bed and about three feet above it.

The sweat was pouring off my face in streams, and I could see young Mansford's face in the faint glow of that ghastly hand, rigid and motionless with horror. Now for the first time he knew how his father and brother had died—or he would know soon. What was this dismembered talon going to do next ? Would it float forward to grip him by the throat—or would it disappear as mysteriously as it had come ?

I tried to picture the dreadful terror of waking up suddenly and seeing this thing in front of one in the darkened room ; and then I saw that Ronald was about to do something. He was kneeling on the bed examining the apparition in the most matter of fact way, and suddenly he put a finger to his lips and looked at us warningly. Then quite deliberately he hit at it with his fist, gave a hoarse cry, and rolled off the bed with a heavy thud.

He was on his feet in an instant, again signing to us imperatively to be silent, and we watched the thing swinging backwards and forwards as if it was on a string. And now it was receding—back towards the window and upwards just as it had come, while the oscillations grew less and less, until, at last it had vanished completely, and the room once more was in darkness save for the faint blue flame which still burnt steadily at the end of the tube.

" My God ! " muttered McIver next to me, as he mopped his brow with a handkerchief, only to be again imperatively silenced by a gesture from Standish. The board creaked in the room above us, and I fancied that I heard a door close very gently : then all was still once more.

Suddenly with disconcerting abruptness the blue flame went out, almost as if it had been a gas jet turned off. And simultaneously a faint whirring noise and a slight draught on my face showed that the electric fan had been switched on. Then we heard Ronald's voice giving orders in a low tone. He had switched on his torch, and his eyes were shining with excitement.

" With luck we'll get the last act soon," he muttered. " Mansford, lie on the floor, as if you'd fallen off the bed. Sprawl : sham dead, and don't move. We three will be behind the curtain in the window. Have you got handcuffs, Mac," he whispered as we went to our hiding place. " Get 'em on as soon as possible, because I'm inclined to think that our bird will be dangerous."

McIver grunted, and once again we started to wait for the unknown. The electric fan still whirred, and looking through the window I saw the first faint streaks of dawn. And then suddenly Standish gripped my arm ; the handle of the door was being turned. Slowly it opened, and someone came in shutting it cautiously behind him. He came round the bed, and paused as he got to the foot. He was crouching— bent almost double—and for a long while he stood there motionless. And then he began to laugh, and the laugh was horrible to hear. It was low and exulting—but it had a note in it which told its own story. The man who crouched at the foot of the bed was a maniac.

" On him," snapped Ronald, and we sprang forward simultaneously. The man snarled and fought like a tiger—but madman though he was he was no match for the four of us. Mansford had sprung to his feet the instant the fight started, and in a few seconds we heard the click of McIver's handcuffs. It was Standish who went to the door and switched on the light, so that we could see who it was. And the face of the handcuffed man, distorted and maniacal in its fury, was the face of the butler Templeton.

" Pass the handcuffs round the foot of the bed, McIver," ordered Standish, " and we'll leave him here. We've got to explore upstairs now."

McIver slipped off one wristlet, passed it round the upright of the bed and snapped it to again. Then the four of us dashed upstairs.

" We want the room to which the speaking-tube communicates," cried Standish, and Mansford led the way. He flung open a door, and then with a cry of horror stopped dead in the doorway.

Confronting us was a wild-eyed woman, clad only in her nightdress. She was standing beside a huge glass retort, which bubbled and hissed on a stand in the centre of the room. And even as we stood there she snatched up the retort with a harsh cry, and held it above her head.

" Back," roared Standish, " back for your lives."

But it was not to be. Somehow or other the retort dropped from her hands and smashed to pieces on her own head. And a scream of such mortal agony rang out as I have never heard and hope never to hear again. Nothing could be done for her ; she died in five minutes, and of the manner of the poor demented thing's death it were better not to write. For a large amount of the contents of the retort was hot sulphuric acid

.   .   .   .

" Well, Mansford," said Standish a few hours later, " your ghost is laid, your mystery is solved, and I think I'll be able to play in the last match of that tour after all."

We were seated in the Old Hall dining-room after an early breakfast and Mansford turned to him eagerly.

" I'm still in the dark," he said. " Can't you explain ? "

Standish smiled. " Don't see it yet ? Well—it's very simple. As you know, the first thing that struck my eye was that right-hand canopy wire. It didn't shine in the sun like the other one, and when I got up to examine it, I found it was coated with dried oil. Not one little bit of it—but the whole wire. Now that was very strange—very strange indeed. Why should that wire have been coated with oil—and not the other ? I may say at once that I had dismissed any idea of psychic phenomena being responsible for your father's and brother's death. That such things exist we know—but they don't *kill* two strong men.

"However, I was still in the dark; in fact, there was only one ray of light. The coating of that wire with oil was *so* strange, that of itself it established with practical certainty the fact that a human agency was at work. And before I left the room that first afternoon I was certain that that wire was used to introduce something into the room from outside. The proof came the next morning. Overnight the wire had been dry; the following morning there was wet oil on it. The door was intact; no one had gone in by the window, and, further, the fan was going. Fact number two. Still, I couldn't get the connection. I admit that the fact that the fan was going suggested some form of gas—introduced by the murderer, and then removed by him automatically. And then you came along with your mouth blistered. You spoke of feeling as if you'd been stung by a hornet, and I'd got my third fact. To get it pre-supposed a certain knowledge of chemistry. Formic acid—which is what a wasp's sting consists of—can be used amongst other things for the manufacture of carbon monoxide. And with that the whole diabolical plot was clear. The speaking-tube was the missing link, through which carbon monoxide was poured into the room, bringing with it traces of the original ingredients which condensed on the mouthpiece. Now, as you may know, carbon monoxide is lighter than air, and is a deadly poison to breathe. Moreover, it leaves no trace—certainly no obvious trace. So before we went

into the room last night, I had decided in my own
mind how the murders had taken place. First from
right under the sleeper's nose a stream of carbon
monoxide was discharged, which I rendered harmless
by igniting it. The canopy helped to keep it more or
less confined, but since it was lighter than air, something was necessary to make the sleeper awake and
sit up. That is precisely what your father and brother
did when they saw the phosphorescent hand—and they
died at once. Mrs. Bretherton hid her face and lived.
Then the fan was turned on—the carbon monoxide
was gradually expelled from the room, and in the
morning no trace remained. If it failed one night it
could be tried again the next until it succeeded.
Sooner or later that infernal hand travelling on a little
pulley wheel on the wire and controlled from above
by a long string, would wake the sleeper—and then
the end—or the story of a ghost."

He paused and pressed out his cigarette.

" From the very first also I had suspected Templeton.
When you know as much of crime as I do—you're
never surprised at anything. I admit he seemed the
last man in the world who would do such a thing—
but there are more cases of Jekyll and Hyde than we
even dream of. And he and his wife were the only
connecting links in the household staff between you
and the Brethertons. That Mrs. Templeton also was
mad had not occurred to me, and how much she was
his assistant or his dupe we shall never know. She
has paid a dreadful price, poor soul, for her share of

it ; the mixture that broke over her was hot concentrated sulphuric acid mixed with formic acid.
Incidentally from inquiries made yesterday, I
discovered that Staveley Grange belonged to a man
named Templeton some forty years ago. This man
had an illegitimate son, whom he did not provide for—
and it may be that Templeton the butler is that son—
gone mad. Obsessed with the idea that Staveley
Grange should be his perhaps—who knows ?   No man
can read a madman's mind."

He lit another cigarette and rose.

" So I can't tell you why.   How you know and
who : why must remain a mystery for ever.   And
now I think I can just catch my train."

" Yes, but wait a moment," cried Mansford.
" There are scores of other points I'm not clear on."

" Think 'em out for yourself, my dear fellow,"
laughed Ronald.   " I want to make a few runs
to-morrow."

CYNTHIA DELMORTON'S MISTAKE

CYNTHIA DELMORTON was a singularly beautiful girl, and for all I know is so still. Her figure was perfect : her face almost flawless. There were critics who said that her nose was a trifle too long : there were others, on the contrary, who denied the fact with oaths and curses. But seeing that she had been painted by three of London's leading artists who one and all declared that she was the most perfect thing they had ever seen, the nose question cannot have been very serious.

Her origin was a little obscure. She lived in a charming house in South Audley Street with an elderly lady who rejoiced in the name of Aunt Hester. Moreover she undoubtedly had money—lots of it. There was a rumour that the late Mr. Delmorton had really been Smithson and Co. Ltd.—one of those charitable firms whose aim in life is to ease other people's financial troubles by lending them money on note of hand alone. And if such a base rumour over the lovely Cynthia could possibly be true, she had certainly possessed the most notorious blood-sucker in London as her father—a man without a tinge of mercy or a thought of compassion.

The fact however remained, that she was extremely wealthy. Which was a far more important matter than the method by which the money had been obtained. And the result had been that divers men of all ages and positions had laid their hands and hearts at her disposal. Some of them had been genuinely infatuated by her beauty : others by her bank balance But one and all of them when their offer was turned down, thanked almighty Heaven for their escape. Except one poor boob, who blew out his brains . . . For the beautiful Cynthia had one very unpleasant trait, which never manifested itself until the last moment. She would lead a man on until he was well-nigh crazy—and then laugh in his face.

Of course when the man she did decide to marry appeared, there would be no laughter. At least if there was it would be carefully concealed. But so far that lucky being had not arrived. And when he did he would have to be something pretty special. Cynthia Delmorton was essentially not one of those who—to paraphrase the well-known line—had danced with Princes and kept the common touch. Nothing under an Earl would be good enough for her final choice—and not a modern creation at that. But until that blissful day arrived, she saw no reason why good-looking men should not go wild about her, and throng her charming drawing-room.

And then one spring that complete disrespecter of persons—influenza, descended upon the house. Within an hour so did Sir William Harbottle, London's most fashionable and futile doctor. He consumed a glass of port and ate a biscuit, and with deadly accuracy diagnosed the disease. He continued to descend at ten guineas a time, more port and more biscuits, and finally pronounced his lovely patient convalescent.

" But, my dear young lady," he announced as he stroked her arm, " we require setting up. We are a little run down."

The " we," needless to state, was a pleasing conceit of Sir William's : no one regarding his ample presence need have panicked unduly.

" We will take a sea voyage."

" Dear Sir William," she murmured. " A sea voyage ? "

" Where the bracing ozone will set us up again. Restore our wasted tissues : remove our lassitude. And then we shall return fresh and invigorated for the ardours of June in London."

And the more she thought of the idea the more she liked it. Up to date her sea voyages had consisted of occupying a cabin whilst crossing the Channel : this was going to be something quite different. Some new frocks : a flirtation or two—there was bound to be some man on board who would fill the bill : and a real rest cure.

Aunt Hester proved the first obstacle. For that usually malleable woman having heard of Cynthia's decision, stuck in her toes and jibbed definitely. Nothing would induce her to go on the sea. She loathed it and detested it : she was always seasick— and in short, rather than do so she would resign her position as Cynthia's companion.

" If you must have someone with you, my dear,"

she said, " why not ask Marjorie. She's a nice girl :
she won't get in your way and you'll be doing her a
real kindness as well."

Cynthia cogitated. Yes : Marjorie Blackton would
do. Better perhaps than Aunt Hester. Her idea of
a companion was what most people would describe as
an unpaid maid, and if her Aunt was continually seasick she would be more nuisance than she was
worth.

" Write and ask her," she said thoughtfully. " Tell
her that as far as clothes are concerned, she can send
any reasonable bill in to me."

Marjorie Blackton was an old school friend of hers.
At least she was the only girl at the very expensive
place at which Cynthia had been " finished " whom
she did not actually dislike. For even at that age
she neither loved nor was loved by her own sex. But
for some strange reason Marjorie bestowed on her one
of those peculiar adorations which arise and flourish
in girls' schools.

Strange, because it would have been impossible to
find two more totally dissimilar characters. Marjorie
was everything that her idol was not. Unselfish,
utterly lovable, frank and open, she was the exact
antithesis of Cynthia. And the latter, though slightly
flattered for a time, soon took advantage of the state
of affairs. She practically made the younger girl her
fag. It was " Marjorie, do this " and " Marjorie, fetch
that," from the beginning of term till the end. And
the same relationship had continued after they felt

school, though necessarily not to the same extent.

Then quite suddenly Mr. Blackton lost most of his
money, and for a while Cynthia had debated whether
to ask Marjorie to come as her companion. As far
as she was capable of affection for anybody she was
fond of her, but having given the matter due consideration she had come to the conclusion that an older
woman would be more suitable from every point of
view. And so she dismissed Marjorie from her scheme
of things, as was her custom when a person was no
longer of use to her. Now she proposed to bring her
back temporarily into that scheme : a proposal which
met with the other girl's delighted approval as soon
as she heard of it.

And so, some three weeks later the two of them
stepped into the boat train at Waterloo bound for
Southampton. The most luxurious cabin in the *S.S.
Ortolan*, 12,000 tons, of the Union Steamship Line had
been engaged : a number of immaculately-clothed
young men, who had pleaded in vain to be allowed to
accompany them as far as the ship, clustered round
the carriage door.

" Now you must all promise to be good while I am
away," said Cynthia impartially. " And when I come
back in June. . . ."

It was at that moment that the train began to move,
but she managed that every member of the group
should think that her unfinished sentence was addressed
to him personally.

" Thank God that's over, my dear " she said

languidly. " What a bore they are. Do give me my rug, will you ? "

She looked up with a sudden frown : a man was standing in the door leading into the corridor. Moreover he seemed to be on the point of depositing a weather-beaten suit-case on one of the spare seats.

" This carriage is engaged," she remarked haughtily.

The man turned round with a smile.

" Am I to understand," he said, " that you are the proud possessor of six tickets ? I'm really very sorry but this is the only compartment in the train that isn't full."

" I gave orders that I required a carriage to myself," she said with her most freezing look.

" Dear me," he answered politely. " If it wasn't for the fact that you can't give orders for anything of the sort, I should say that someone had blundered. However, what would you like me to do ? Stand in the corridor, or go into the guard's van ? "

" If you persist in intruding," she said icily, " I would prefer that you do so in silence."

" Why—sure," he remarked genially. " Doubtless we shall have lots of time for conversation before we get to the Cape."

He buried himself behind a newspaper, leaving Cynthia gasping. The Cape ? Was this odious mortal going to the Cape with her ? True he was young, and of pleasing appearance, but he must clearly be put in his place and punished. And she was an adept at doing both.

It was at that moment that she got her second shock. Marjorie was undoubtedly smiling at the man behind her magazine ; the man was grinning at Marjorie behind his paper. She knew it : she had done it so often herself with other men.

But what she could do was one thing : what Marjorie could do was quite another. For her companion and a strange man to indulge in mutual smiles at her expense was a state of affairs not to be tolerated for an instant. And the small fact that she was completely wrong—that all that had happened was, that Marjorie suddenly seeing him grinning at her had involuntarily smiled back just because it was good to be alive—cut no ice. She wouldn't have believed it anyhow ; but then Cynthia Delmorton's joy in living lay, not in just life but merely in what she could get out of it.

They were running through Eastleigh when the man spoke again. Five times during the journey had Marjorie got up to do something for Cynthia—and three out of the five times she could far more easily have done it for herself. And five times during the journey had an amused and faintly contemptuous glint come into the man's eyes. But he remained buried behind his paper until the train began to slacken, when he folded it up.

" Would you care to sit at my table," he asked gravely. " I'm the second officer, and I generally manage to collect a cheery bunch."

For a moment Cynthia stared at him speechlessly ; the second officer. . . .

" Surprised at my not being on board, I suppose," he went on cheerfully. " Pretty exceptional, I agree. But the old man is a sportsman, and my business was sudden and urgent. However, would you like me to fix it up about the table ? "

" I think it would be very nice," said Cynthia quietly, and Marjorie glanced at her in some trepidation. She knew that tone of old—knew what it portended. She knew that before the end of the voyage this poor young man was going to wish he had never been born. And it was a shame. . . .

But she couldn't warn him, and he rushed into the trap.

" Splendid. I'll arrange it. But I warn you from what I hear we're going to have it a bit choppy as far as Madeira."

They did : and Marjorie for the first time began to see Cynthia in her true light. She was loyal clean through : she tried to make excuses—but the plain fact emerged that for selfishness her employer was in a class by herself. True, she was ill—slightly, for a couple of days ; but until they anchored off Funchal Cynthia treated her and the stewardess like a couple of slaves. Then she was graciously pleased to emerge from her cabin, and show herself for the first time to the admiring gaze of her fellow passengers.

" Well, well, how are you ? "

A cheerful voice hailed the lovely invalid, and she

looked up from her deck chair to see their travelling companion. He looked different in uniform ; in fact honesty compelled her to admit that he looked extremely nice in uniform. So she gave him one of her most bewitching smiles, and confessed that she felt a little better.

" Good," he cried. " We shall be dancing to-night, and you must play a bit of deck tennis. Miss Blackton is a nailer at it."

He moved off and she watched him cursing four Portuguese lace vendors for blocking the gangway— watched him through narrowed eyes. How that young man was going to suffer before she'd finished with him ! And what a lucky thing it was that he was really quite presentable ; it made things so much pleasanter for her.

" My dear ! that is Cynthia Delmorton. You must have seen her pictures in the *Tatler* and *Sketch*."

The words carried to her during a sudden lull in the raucous babel around her, and a sense of pleasant well-being stole over her. Yes ; she was Cynthia Delmorton . . . And the sun was shining, and the water was blue, and the brown-skinned boys diving off the deck for threepenny bits thrown into the water amused her. Also there was an extremely bumptious and conceited young man to punish. She smiled slightly to herself . . . Fancy wasting her time on an officer in the Merchant Service. Still, she would do it quickly, and then turn to worthier game.

" Mr. Fraser," she called gently as he passed—

Marjorie had found out his name—" won't you come and cheer me up ? Besides I want to apologize. I'm afraid I was rather rude to you in the train."

" Rude ! " he laughed. " Not a bit. You were just natural. Sorry I can't stop now, but I've got to see a man about a dog in the smoking room. You shall apologize at lunch . . . You're sitting next to me."

And with that he was gone leaving Cynthia Delmorton utterly speechless. Never in the course of her life had any man spoken to her like that before. " See a man about a dog in the smoking room." When she had invited him to sit by her . . . " Not rude : only natural." Was the man mad ?

He certainly showed no signs of insanity at lunch. He included her breezily in the conversation ; chaffed Marjorie Blackton, who had been ashore and done the time-honoured toboggan trip over the cobbles from Terreiro da Lucta, and finally challenged her to a game of deck quoits later on.

" When you're a little stronger," he remarked, " you must play tennis."

And there was a twinkle in his eyes as he spoke, the sort of twinkle a parent might have when dealing with a fractious child.

And so it went on. The trouble about the man was that he seemed impervious to snubs. He had a hide like a rhinoceros ; delicate satire flew off him like water off a duck's back. Of course he missed the point of it all—that was the reason. Completely lacking in breeding, he was unable to understand her subtle irony

And Marjorie, who understood it only too well, felt her heart grow sick within her. At last her final delusions about Cynthia were gone. Coming out to Madeira they had began to totter ; by the time they were crossing the line the crash was complete. Thank Heavens ! Jim Fraser didn't appreciate the position of affairs : that was her only compensation.

And then one evening something occurred which brought her up with a start. She was sitting out by herself on the boat deck, in the shadow of one of the funnels, when two people passed her. They didn't see her, but she recognized them at once . . . They paused between two of the boats, not three yards away from her, and she heard Cynthia's voice.

" You really are the most attractive man, Jim."

Marjorie could have screamed. It was too cruel. Surely, surely she needn't carry her vindictiveness to such a point as that. The poor devil had done her no harm : she cared not the snap of a finger about him. But just to gratify her petty spite, she was going to lead him on—and then shake with laughter in his face. Marjorie half rose ; then with a little gasp that was half a sob she crouched back again. For Cynthia was in his arms.

With a sick numbness she watched him kiss her : heard Cynthia's low triumphant laugh : heard her whispered " Darling."

Then she was gone, leaving him standing by the boats. For a second she paused by the top of the companion, and her words floated back—" There is always to-morrow."

For a little while he stood there ; then suddenly with a little start he saw Marjorie. He came over to her slowly, and sat down beside her.

" You saw," he said quietly. " I'm sorry."

" So am I," she answered gravely. " Very sorry. Oh ! Mr. Fraser," she went on impulsively, " don't think me impertinent and foolish. But I—oh ! it's so difficult to say."

He was staring at her steadily, and she went stumbling on bravely.

" You see—I know Cynthia. And I don't want to be disloyal to her—after all, she's paying everything for me. But please, please be careful. She's—she's different to most girls. She's been spoilt, I suppose— and she doesn't mean to be cruel."

" No," he agreed quietly. " It's just natural."

But she hardly heard.

" She just plays with men . . . And then she turns them down without a thought. Can't you see—oh ! can't you see ? I don't want to hurt your feelings, but you must realize that she has the world at her feet, and . . . and. . . ."

" And therefore is hardly likely to pay serious attention to the second officer of the good ship *Ortolan*," he said, lighting a cigarette.

She looked at him surprised : he seemed singularly calm about it.

" That's why I am so sorry you saw," he concluded.

"But I don't want you to be hurt," she cried. "And you will be."

"Why don't you want me to be hurt," he said gently.

"Oh! because . . . Of course, I don't. I hate to see anybody hurt."

"You dear! You dear girl." And now she was staring at him in genuine amazement, and dimly realizing that both her hands were in his. "I'm only sorry you saw it, Marjorie, because I can't now do what I would like to. At least not at this moment."

And then he too was gone, and after a while Marjorie got up a little stiffly and went below. What on earth had he meant?

"My dear," said Cynthia, "too humorous! Our worthy pachyderm has kissed me. Up on the boat deck."

"I saw you," she answered dully. "Oh! Cynthia— can't you leave him alone?"

"What on earth do you mean?" cried the other. And then she suddenly burst into a peal of laughter. "Why I believe you're in love with him yourself."

"I am," said Marjorie gravely, and started to undress.

Of course this was too much of a scream altogether: it really added relish to the jest. That Marjorie— demure little Marjorie—should have fallen in love with the second officer was too exquisite.

"My dear," she cried, "but this is Romance with a capital R. Does he reciprocate your feelings?"

" Of course he doesn't," answered the other flushing. " And Cynthia—you won't say anything, will you ? "

" My dear—trust me. Perish the thought that I should spoil love's young dream. But I must insist on being allowed to deal with the dear man just once. I'll let him down mildly, I promise you, but he has been exceedingly rude to me—and he's got to take his gruel like a good boy."

" But I'm sure he didn't mean it, Cynthia," said Marjorie miserably.

" Then he's got to learn. And anyway, my dear," she went on with a smile, " you have the remedy in your own hands. Get him to take *you* up on the boat deck to-morrow night."

" You know I don't stand a chance if you're about," said Marjorie simply. " Anyway I'm nothing to him. But I don't think you're playing the game. He's— he's not the type of man . . . It's not fair to a man like him, Cynthia : it's not fair."

" Then he had better not go and see people about dogs, my dear, when I've asked him to come and talk to me," said the other softly. " I don't like men who do that. Besides he must be trained—if you're going to marry him."

She got into her bunk and opened a book, and with a little shiver, though the night was tropical, Marjorie followed her example. And when at last she did fall asleep, she got no rest. For she dreamed without cessation—dreams in which she saw Cynthia, gloating and devilish, and a white-faced sobbing man—a man she tried to comfort, but who always turned away from her.

It was the day after that a piece of information arrived in the Wireless Bulletin, which for nearly six hours annoyed Cynthia thoroughly. Marjorie saw it first, just as she was going in to breakfast, and thought no more about it. The news that the Earl of Axminster had been killed in a motor accident, interested her but little more than the fact that the French exchange was 129.47. It was otherwise with Cynthia. Not that the death of that well-known and sporting nobleman at the early age of fifty-six distressed her in the slightest, but merely because it made her wish that she had acted otherwise. And it is annoying when one cannot rectify a mistake. She might now have been the Countess of Axminster. And she wasn't. Which was a distressing thought—most distressing. Had not Hedderton—his eldest son—sat in her pocket for a complete season ? In fact she had almost—but not quite—become Viscountess Hedderton. And if she had, Hedderton would not have gone his fool journey to Central Africa, picked up some horrible tropical disease and died. Undoubtedly most annoying.

She recalled that last evening perfectly. She had known he was coming for her answer, and during the the afternoon she had finally made up her mind— balancing the points for and against. And the result had been against. Hedderton's father, she had decided, was more than likely to live another thirty years, and that was too long to wait even for one of the oldest

F*

titles in England. The fact that he was utterly
infatuated with her was his misfortune and not her
fault. And so without the smallest tinge of compunc-
tion she turned him down. She could see him now—
white-faced and stammering . . . He couldn't quite
understand : he'd been so sure . . . He had kissed
her so often . . . And she had laughed softly.

" My dear man," she had said, " if I married all the
men who have kissed me, I'd want an hotel to stow
them in."

And he had failed to see the cheapness of the remark
because, poor devil, he was still infatuated. Instead
he had gone off to Africa and died. Not four months
previously . . . Most annoying . . . In fact when she
went in to lunch she was feeling thoroughly
irritable.

Jim Fraser was already there, and he bowed to her
gravely. He was looking strained about the eyes, she
noticed : all through lunch he hardly spoke. Hooked
already : hardly worth powder and shot. Still in her
present mood she felt like making someone suffer, so
she gave him her sweetest and most alluring smile.

" I'm feeling terribly depressed," she murmured.
" Poor Lord Axminster is dead. Such a charming
man."

A woman opposite looked at her with interest.

" Of course you knew him well, Miss Delmorton."

" Naturally," remarked Cynthia languidly. " You
see, Hedderton and I were very great friends."

Marjorie squirmed, and when Jim Fraser leaned

forward with a puzzled frown she could have screamed. She guessed what was coming.

" Hedderton," he said. " I don't quite follow."

" Viscount Hedderton," she explained politely. " Axminster's son. They have different names, you know."

" I see," he answered. " I suppose that is done to make it harder."

She smiled, and glanced round the table.

" What funny ideas you have, Mr. Fraser. Yes— Hedderton died in Africa."

" And who is the heir ? " asked someone.

" I really don't know," she answered. " He had no brothers. There was a cousin of sorts, I believe."

She relapsed suddenly into silence ; what was it Hedderton had said on that point ? It was a cousin— a very charming fellow, but a rolling stone. Un- married. Of course he might be impossible, but it was worth while bearing in mind against her return to London. She would write Aunt Hester a letter from Cape Town telling her to make enquiries . . . It would be funny if, after all, she did pull it off. The thought of it put her in quite a good temper again.

" Don't forget you promised to show me the Southern Cross to-night, Mr. Fraser," she said as he rose from his seat.

" Am I likely to," he answered fervently.

And across the table her eyes met Marjorie's mock- ingly. Really life wasn't so bad after all : it had its humorous side.

But it was a side that was taxed to the uttermost that evening. The pachyderm was so terribly intense and gauche. And he would persist in harking back to Lord Axminster's death.

" It must be wonderful," he said humbly, " to know all those people who are just names to us, as intimately as you do."

He was holding her hand at the time, and gazing at her adoringly.

" I very nearly married Hedderton," she said softly. " But I'm glad I didn't—now."

" And if you had," he puzzled it out, " you would be the—the Earless of Axminster."

She gave a delighted gurgle of laughter.

" Countess," she corrected him. " But then, you see—the poor fellow is dead."

" But I'm sure he wouldn't have gone to Africa if you had married him," he said gravely.

" Well, if he hadn't and was alive, and I had married him—then I should be the Earless of Axminster. You delicious person."

" And instead of that," he cried eagerly, " you're going to be . . . "

Really, she'd die of suppressed laughter in a second. The pachyderm was on the verge of proposing : she looked round to see if by any chance Marjorie was about. This was going to be a thing too good to be missed.

" What am I going to be ? " she whispered.

" Cynthia—wouldn't you rather be my wife than the Countess of Axminster ? "

That finished it : self-control could stand it no longer. She burst into a peal of laughter : then she pulled herself together. The thing had become a bore ; so she'd punish the pachyderm now and finish with it.

" This," she said as soon as she had recovered herself sufficiently to speak, " is the funniest thing that has ever occurred to me. My poor dear young man, are you mad ? Do you really imagine, even for one second, that I should marry you ? " Laughter again overcame her.

" But you deserved a little lesson, you know. As a matter of fact I intended to give you a longer one, but I couldn't help laughing. You were so supremely ridiculous."

Once more she began to shake.

" No, Mr. Fraser, I am afraid that I must decline the riotous future you offer me. I feel it would be too much for my nerves. But as a reward for having made me laugh, I'll tell you a secret. Put the excellent alternative you gave me before Marjorie . . . Not that the poor dear is ever likely to be Countess of anything, but still. . . . "

She rose with a smile—a smile which suddenly faded from her face. For this uncouth boor was lying back in his deck chair, literally holding his sides.

" Rich," he almost sobbed. " Not to say ripe and fruity. You're quite right, my dear woman ; we've hurried matters. This jest would have stood another three days."

" What on earth do you mean ? " she said.

And then he, too, rose to his feet, and stood facing her.

" Listen to me, Cynthia Delmorton," he said quietly. " In the course of my wanderings round the globe I've met some pretty rotten women. You're just about the rottenest."

" How dare you ? "

In her stunned rage she could hardly get the words out.

" You're going to hear one or two home truths now," he went on calmly. " You're a calculating, mercenary snob—and you killed Hedderton as surely as if you'd shot him yourself. Only no jury, unfortunately, could convict you. I happened to see him the night before he left for Africa, poor devil."

" Will you kindly take me straight to the captain," she said icily. " I can only conclude that you're drunk, and I wish to make a complaint."

" Certainly," he answered. " What are you going to tell him ? That I was drunk last night, too—when I kissed you ? "

For a moment or two she stared at him white and rigid with rage. He had got her, and she knew it : this common man had beaten her at her own game. Why he had done it was beyond her : her brain was still too dazed at the sudden turning of the tables to think clearly.

" You set out to teach me a lesson." He was speaking again. " I fully intended that you should. Your only miscalculation was that I had already determined to teach you one—one that you richly deserved. But I admit that I never even dreamed that the lesson would prove quite so subtly successful until this morning. And I'm profoundly sorry it has. I was very fond of my uncle."

" Your uncle," she stammered. " What do you mean ? "

" There was a cousin of sorts, I believe," he said gravely. " There was, and—is. And he happens to be the second officer of the *Ortolan*."

" You mean," she almost screamed, " that you're Lord Axminster ? "

" Precisely," he answered. " And since you have mercifully refused my invitation to become my Earless, I think we might conclude the interview. You see I want to follow your advice, and put the alternative I gave you in front of Marjorie . . . Er—good-night. Oh ! and the captain's cabin is the fourth from this end . . . It's the big one . . . And incidentally— one other small point. Had I not been perfectly certain that you didn't know who I was, I should never have risked proposing. The danger of your acceptance would have been too great. Still it was kind of you to explain about us having different names."

A moment later he was alone : Cynthia Delmorton still retained sufficient thinking capacity to realize that, if she was going to have hysterics, her cabin was the most suitable place. For a while he stood looking after her : then half consciously he turned and stared over the water towards Africa.

" Yes, old man," he muttered, " she killed you. And I loved you. Life's a funny thing."

Then with a faint smile on his lips, he strolled down to the main deck. They were dancing, and he stood in the smoking-room door watching. Life, indeed, was a funny thing. And then he saw her, coming towards him with a startled look on her face.

" What on earth has happened to Cynthia ? " she cried. " She's in the most extraordinary condition."

" Biting the bed clothes," he said lazily. " Splendid. I asked her a question, you see, and she got the answer wrong. I asked her if she would sooner be my wife or Countess of Axminster."

" Jim—you proposed. But I don't understand. Did she refuse you ? "

" My dear," he cried, " you don't suppose I'd be as pleased as I am if she'd accepted me. And now I want to ask you the same question. . . . "

And then suddenly he grew serious.

" Marjorie—Marjorie darling, come up on the boat deck. I don't make a hobby of this, my dear—and there's a lot you don't understand. But I haven't got time to explain it to you now—not until you've answered that question. Will you marry me ? "

" Jim—you're mad," she whispered. " And you can't propose in the smoking-room."

" Can't I ? I've just done it. But come up above and I'll do it again."

And she went. And she stayed. And an hour later he still hadn't explained ; explanations are tedious things. In fact it wasn't until the following morning that she thought about the explanation, and then for a while she couldn't grasp it.

For Jim wasn't at breakfast, and a note lay on her plate. She tore open the envelope, and read the contents.

" Second Officer Jim Fraser presents his compliments to the future Countess of Axminster, and trusts that the beautiful Miss Delmorton is not still biting the bedclothes. He further solicits her company at the eleven o'clock issue of beef tea.

" P.S. You're an adorable darling. Jim."

THE ELEVENTH HOUR

" DANGEROUS things—Primo Packs," remarked the nondescript man to me with a faint smile.

I was focussing my camera for that oft-taken photograph of the Castle of Chillon with the Dents du Midi in the background, and I stared at him in mild surprise.

" What on earth do you mean ? " I said. " Why— dangerous ? "

" Take your photo," he answered. " The light is just right. And then, if you have the time and would care to listen I'll tell you how the use of a Primo Pack very nearly cost an innocent man his life."

It sounded good to me, and I told him so. A casual hotel acquaintance, he had strolled with me along the shore of the Lake of Geneva that morning. Quite a nice fellow, though a little dull, was the impression he had given me ; and I remember I wondered as I lit my pipe whether he belonged to that portion of humanity that can tell a story, or the other.

" They were a comparatively new innovation at the time when it happened," he began. " The ordinary rolls, of course, were well known, and the plate—so cumbrous and heavy for the average amateur—was the only alternative for most people. I mention that fact, because to-day, there would be but little possibility of a similar tragedy occurring. The mechanism of the film pack is common property.

"With which preamble I'll get down to it. The first character I will introduce to you is Sir John Brayling—fifteenth baronet. In many ways he was quite a decent fellow, and yet he was never popular. Partially, perhaps, because, though he lived in the centre of a sporting county, he didn't care about sport. An occasional day with a gun was his limit: the rest of his time he devoted to photography. In addition he was apt to be a bit morose; if he gave a dinner party at Brayling House it was even money that he would sit in almost unbroken silence all through the meal. Which cannot be said to make for the gaiety of nations.

"I have mentioned photography as being his obsession: he had another—his wife. And small blame to him. Hester Brayling was the most gloriously attractive woman. She was considerably younger than he was—fifteen years to be exact, and she possessed every quality that he lacked. She rode magnificently, and played tennis and golf better than most. Also she was brimming over with *joie de vivre*.

"In her way she was undoubtedly very fond of her husband, but her affection was not comparable with his. He simply idolised the ground she walked on, and the great grief of his life was that there were no children. And as they had been married seven years it rather looked as if there never would be.

" It was when she was twenty-nine that Ronald Vane came on the scene. He was a man in the early thirties —good-looking, wealthy and a bachelor. He had taken a neighbouring house, and every mother of daughters for miles around sat up and took notice. Quite legitimately, too : Ronald Vane was one of the most delightful men I have ever met."

The nondescript man smiled as he lit a cigarette.

" Quite right," he said. " They did. I was down there a good deal at the time, and I watched the affair developing under my nose. Vane sat in her pocket out hunting : used to motor her over to play golf : danced with her just as often as the dictates of society would allow. But—and I want to make this clear—that was all. Vane was as straight a man as ever lived : so was she—if I may be pardoned the Irishism.

" Now it happened that I was a fairly privileged person. I'd known Hester since she was a child, and one day I seized a suitable opportunity to talk to her. Foolish perhaps, but I was afraid of what was going to be the result. So I tackled her point blank on the subject.

" She looked at me quite steadily and shrugged her shoulders.

" ' What am I to do, Bill ? ' she said. ' I'm in love with Ronald : he's in love with me. One can't help a thing like that : it just happens. But there's nothing more to it than that I can assure you.'

" ' That's all right, my dear,' I answered, ' but how long is that state of affairs going to continue ? I don't want to appear an interfering busybody, but, situated as you two are, only a miracle from Heaven can prevent John finding out sooner or later. Don't forget that every mother around here has already visualised Ronald as a prospective son-in-law. And it isn't going to be long before one of them finds it her duty to acquaint John.'

" She stared out of the window in silence for a while. Then—' What do you advise ? '

" I laughed.

" ' My dear,' I said, ' I may be a fool, but I'm not a damned fool. I'd sooner keep my breath. But as a plain statement of fact from a partially sane onlooker I would offer you two suggestions. Either cut the painter and go away with him, or else suggest to him that he should give up the remainder of his lease and go big game shooting for a couple of years or so. I admit that the novelty of my remarks almost staggers me, but at this stage of the world's history it is hardly likely that anyone will discover a new way out of your present situation. It is not exactly the first time it has happened.'

" ' I wonder what John would say,' she said thoughtfully. ' I should hate to hurt him.'

" ' You'll hurt him even more,' I answered, ' if he finds out by roundabout means. And, Hester, this I do say with certainty : he's bound to do so. If you were in London it might be different—but down here it's hopeless. You and Ronald are both far too well known.'

" ' I'll think it over, Bill,' she said. ' I suppose Ronald and I, like most people in similar circumstances, have imagined that no one guessed. We've let things drift. But if you've spotted it—so have other people. I'll think it over.'

" At that I left it, and two days later I went back to London. She had taken my remarks exactly as I expected she would : she wasn't the type to be offended or annoyed. But I confess that during the next few weeks I continually found myself wondering as to whether they were going to bear any fruit."

The nondescript man paused and stared at a passing steamer.

" It's funny when one looks back on things," he continued after a while, " and tries to trace cause and effect. Would the tragedy have happened but for what I had said to her ? Heaven knows. All I do know is that some two months after that conversation, in the middle of the month of July, I returned to my rooms for lunch to find a telegram awaiting me. It was short and to the point and ran as follows : ' Come at once. Hester.' So I threw some things into a suit-case and caught the afternoon train.

" I was met at the station by a man whose face was vaguely familiar, and who was in a state of considerable agitation.

" ' You probably don't remember me,' he said. ' I'm John's brother.'

" I placed him then : I'd met him once some years before staying at Brayling House. His name was Richard, and in character, appearance and everything he was the exact opposite of John. Save for a slight family likeness it was almost impossible to believe they were brothers. Richard was fair where John was dark : Richard was one of those men who can go on talking by the hour in quite an amusing way, and he was fond of sport. In fact—John's antithesis.

" ' What's the trouble ? ' I said as we shook hands.

" ' John has been murdered,' he answered. ' And Ronald Vane has been arrested for doing it.'

" I don't know how long I stood there staring at him foolishly : the thing was so completely unexpected.

" ' Hester wants to see you as soon as possible,' he went on. ' I've got the car.'

" All the way up to the house I bombarded him with questions, but it will make it clearer for you if I go on a few hours and tell you the story as I pieced it together after having heard everyone.

" It appeared then, that after my departure some two months previously, Ronald Vane himself had gone away for six weeks. And during that six weeks Hester had somewhat naturally let things drift. On Vane's return he and she had had things out, with the result that they decided that the only fair and straight thing to do was to tell her husband.

" Accordingly, one morning Vane came over to Brayling House with the definite intention of tackling Sir John. That was the day before the tragedy took place. It was not a pleasant undertaking as you can imagine, but Vane was not the man to shirk it.

"Well, to put it tersely, the interview was not a success. At first Sir John had been so flabbergasted that he could hardly take it in. But as soon as he had grasped that this unbelievable thing had happened : that here standing in his house was a man who was calmly informing him that he proposed in the near future to run away with his wife, his rage became ungovernable. No one will deny that there was a good deal of excuse for him : but he seemed totally unable to grasp the fact that Vane was really doing the straight thing in telling him the state of affairs, instead of leaving him to discover it as a *fait accompli*.

"To cut it short, however, he went for Vane with a hunting-crop, and Vane, who was considerably the more powerful man, had some difficulty in wresting it away without hurting him. Which was the last thing he wanted to do : he felt so desperately sorry for him.

"In the middle of what was practically a hand to hand fight a table was knocked over, and the noise brought in the butler. He stood in the doorway aghast at what he saw, and a moment later Vane having got possession of the crop managed to half-push, half-throw Sir John away from him.

"' Show this blackguard to the door,' Sir John panted to the servant. 'And never let him inside this house again or I'll sack you.'

"Well—Vane went. He got back to his house and

rang up Hester, asking her to come to him at once. But now a further complication had arisen. Sir John, whose mood of ungovernable fury had been succeeded by one of sullen rage, flatly refused to even consider the question of divorce.

" ' I can't lock you up,' he said to his wife. ' I can't prevent you going to him. But I can prevent you marrying him, and I will.'

" That, then, was the situation on the following morning—the morning of the tragedy : a situation which, as you can well imagine, was common property in the servants' hall. Moreover it was a situation which in view of what was to come was just about as damning as it could well be.

" At nine o'clock Sir John went out armed with his camera. There was one particular bit of wood some half-mile from the house that he apparently wanted to get. At a quarter past nine one of the gardeners saw him focussing his camera : at half-past ten he was discovered by another gardener with his head battered in lying on the ground in front of his camera. Not much you say up to date to incriminate Vane. Wait. At half-past nine two children, belonging to one of the keepers, passed close to the glade. They were on their way to the village to do some shopping for their mother, and when they came back they told her what they'd seen.

" First they had heard two men shouting at one another. They'd crept up behind some bushes to see Sir John and Ronald Vane having a furious quarrel. Mark you, there was no doubt about the identification : they knew Vane—everybody did, and, of course, they knew Sir John. They watched for a little and then, getting frightened they ran away.

" Pretty black now you'll admit—but worse was to come. Vane himself admitted that he had met Sir John that morning, and had had a terrible row with him. He stated that he was on his way to Brayling House. It was a short cut that he frequently used. Quite unexpectedly he saw Sir John in front of him, and since it was he whom he was going to see he stopped and spoke to him. He refused to say what the quarrel was about : all he would say was that he had been unsuccessful in his request and after, he thought, about ten minutes, he left Sir John and returned to his own house, which he reached at ten-fifteen. Moreover, he utterly and flatly denied that he had killed Sir John.

" But now even worse was to come. Vane had in his possession a very heavy stick—almost a club. What strange freak of fate had induced him to take it out with him that morning he couldn't say. He admitted that he had done so : he further admitted that he lost his temper so completely with Sir John that he flung the thing at his head. It missed him, and fell in some bushes where Vane left it. It was found in the bushes right enough, but with its top covered with blood. In short, it was obviously the weapon with which Sir John had been murdered.

" I suppose," went on my companion with a short

laugh, " that if you deliberately went out of your way
in a work of fiction to surround your hero with every
damning circumstance you could think of, it would be
impossible to weave a tighter web than that which
hemmed in Ronald Vane. Motive, weapon, opportunity, witnesses—everything combined to make his
case hopeless from the start. In fact, on two or three
occasions when I went to see him he admitted as much
to me.

" ' That I didn't do it I know,' he said. ' But were
I in the position of the jury I should find myself
guilty.'

" A further trouble was his inevitable unpopularity.
To the man in the street who believed in his guilt he
was merely a scoundrel who not only had fallen in
love with another man's wife, but had murdered her
husband.

" I won't bore you with an account of the trial.
From the start the result was a foregone conclusion.
Ronald Vane could bring no witnesses, but he insisted
on giving evidence himself. It was useless. The
jury only retired for a quarter of an hour.

" And then came the end, and the episode that
lingers most in my mind. Asked by the Judge if he
had anything to say, I can still see Ronald Vane, his
arms folded, his face grave and a little stern.

" ' Nothing, my Lord,' he said, and his voice was
quite steady. ' You have awarded me a perfectly
fair trial. It is not your fault—nor is it mine that you
have come to the conclusion that you have. It is the

fault of a set of utterly unprecedented circumstances. I cannot but believe that in time some fact will come to light which will prove my innocence. And if it is too late '—for the fraction of a second his voice shook— ' do not reproach yourselves too bitterly. On the evidence as it is I quite understand that your verdict is the only one possible.'

"And I don't believe there was a person in court whose conviction of his guilt was not a little shaken. He was a big man, Vane—big in every way—and there was something about him as he stood there that was great. No recrimination : no bitterness : almost, if I may be allowed the analogy, was it a repetition of two thousand years ago.

"'Father forgive them for they know not what they do.'

"And then he disappeared from sight, and I led a white-faced woman back to her hotel.

"I suppose you're wondering," he went on after a while, "as to when I'm going to justify my original remark about Primo Packs. I'm coming to it now. Hester had gone back to Brayling House : her brother-in-law had insisted on that. And the days ticked on : days during which I wandered aimlessly about, racking my brains for some clue, some possibility that might have been overlooked. Nothing : it was a blank wall. Sometimes I even began to wonder if he hadn't done it : gone mad for a moment and killed Sir John without being aware of the fact.

" And then one morning I was in a chemist's shop getting some aspirin. There was only one attendant and he was explaining to a customer the working of a Primo Pack. I listened idly—I'm not interested in photography—until a sudden sentence caught my ear

" ' As each film is taken one of these pieces of black paper is pulled out and torn off. That has the effect of moving the taken film to the back of the pack leaving the next one in front.'

" Even then the possibility did not strike me : I just bought my aspirin and walked out. And it was only as I sat down to lunch at my club that a thought —a wild possibility—dawned on me. Wild though it was—well-nigh crazy—it was sufficient to send me dashing and lunchless to Scotland Yard.

" ' Where,' I demanded of the first official I saw, are the various exhibits in the Ronald Vane case ? '

" He stared at me as if I was mad, and I realized I must take a pull at myself. Anyway, I finally convinced him that I was a respectable person, and he became quite helpful. You see Sir John had been using a Primo Pack of which one film had been taken. Ronald Vane, in the course of his evidence, had stated that he had waited while Sir John had taken it : waited for him to enter up the details in his pocket book. That film had been taken at 9.15, and the wild idea had occurred to me that possibly another film had been taken too—one of which we knew nothing, because it was still in the front of the pack."

" Great Scott ! " I cried. " I get you. Only

one piece of black paper had been torn off."

"Two to be exact," he replied. "The covering and the one marked 1. Both those pieces had been found. So that number 2 film was in position for exposure. Had any photograph been taken on it ?

"Jove ! I don't think I'll ever forget that afternoon. I chased round various departments trying not to be buoyed up by such a wildly fantastic hope. A dozen times I solemnly adjured myself not to be a fool: a dozen times I forced myself to remember that even if a photograph had been taken the chances were a hundred to one against it being of any use to us.

"However, at last we ran the man to ground who had developed number 1, and to him I explained my idea. At first he was politely sceptical, but after a time he began to share my enthusiasm.

"'We'll go and try,' he said. 'The pack is in my dark-room.'

"I don't think I'd got a dry thing on me by the time he started. He was one of those maddeningly deliberate individuals, and in the state I then was I felt I could have drowned him in a bath of his own developer. He insisted on lecturing me on chemicals till I forgot my manners and cursed him foolishly. And then he showed himself human and apologised.

"The agony of the moment when he put the film in the dish ! Subconsciously I realized that it was the last chance : that if nothing happened Ronald would die in two days. I closed my eyes : I couldn't bear to look.

G

" ' My God ! ' I heard his tense whisper. ' There's something coming out.'

" Wiping the sweat from my eyes I peered over his shoulder. And now he was as keen as I was : almost without breathing we watched a picture form and materialize on the yellow film.

" ' Now we'll fix it,' he cried, ' and then we'll know.'

" His hand was shaking as he put the negative into a bath of hypo, and then we both sat there and waited. It was an eternity, so it seemed to me, before he took it out and opened the door. He held it up to the light, and then he turned and looked at me gravely.

" ' If anything was wanting,' he said, ' to prove Ronald Vane's guilt, this film supplies the deficiency. If you will wait a moment I'll give you a print of it.'

" He disappeared, and I think I cried. I had only vaguely glanced at the negative ; I had no idea as to what had caused his words. All I could feel was the sickening reaction after hope that had risen to a dizzy height.

" And then I began to think. If what he said was right, Ronald Vane *had* done it. And he hadn't : I felt he hadn't : I knew he hadn't.

" ' An astounding photograph : quite astounding.'

" His voice cut into my thoughts, and I got up and bent over the dish he had placed on the table. He was right : it was an astounding photograph. Occupying half of it was Sir John's face. He was staring towards the camera and above it, and in his

eyes was a look of dreadful terror. He was looking
at someone who stood behind the camera—someone
whose shadow fell on the ground, someone with arm
upraised to strike. He was looking at his murderer.

" ' Evidently adjusting his stop,' said the chemist.
' He looked up suddenly : saw Vane coming for him
and unconsciously pressed the bulb.

" ' Why should you assume it was Vane ? ' I said
dully.

" He shrugged his shoulders, and turned away.

" ' I apologize,' he said. ' But I fear, sir, that this
photograph is not going to help you to clear your
friend.'

" ' I suppose it won't,' I muttered. ' May I take
it with me ? '

" I spoke without thought : the thing was no good
to me.

" ' Certainly,' he answered courteously. ' And if
you like I'll give you a copy of the other one—the
print of number 1 film.'

" I thanked him mechanically, and a few minutes
after I left. So it was no use : I began to wish I'd
never overheard that chemist in the morning. To
have hoped so much and then suffer such a disappointment was the refinement of cruelty.

" For hours that evening I sat staring at the two
photos. The first was just a clear-cut print of the glade
with light and shade exquisitely defined : it was the
second that fascinated me. That monstrous distorted
shadow of the murderer : that ashen face of terror :

the rest of it the glade as in the first. Astounding as he had said : unique. No such photograph had ever been taken before. And I found myself cursing childishly because it couldn't speak when I shouted at it—' Whose is that shadow ? ' Almost I tore it up, and then—suddenly . . . "

The nondescript man paused and lit another cigarette.

" Confound you, sir," I cried, laughing. " I understand your feelings towards the chemist."

" Are you a mathematician ? " he went on irrelevantly. " I am. And if you are you will appreciate the feeling of almost frozen calm that comes to the brain when the step of some intricate problem that has eluded you for hours, reveals itself. Such became my condition suddenly—in the twinkling of an eye. I have said that the second photograph showed one half of the glade, and that had been the part of it at which I'd scarcely glanced. Now with every sense alert I riveted my attention on it. Then realizing I'd missed the last train I rung up and ordered a motor car.

" It was dawn when I reached Brayling House, and I ordered the car to wait for me in the road. It would be four hours at least before I could prove my theory, but I was too excited to think of food. The one essential thing—a cloudless sky—was present, and going to the glade I sat down and waited.

" It was two months later in the year, and so I knew that times would be different. That didn't matter. The actual directions of the shadows would be different. And that didn't matter. The essential thing would be the same.

" And it was. I dashed from the wood into the car, and drove to Brayling House.

" ' Hester,' I howled from the hall. ' It's all right. We'll save him.'

" I had a dim vision of a woman's white face with hope too marvellous for words dawning on it : then I was back in the car driving full speed for London. Only the Home Secretary would do for me, and I caught him as he was dressing for dinner.

" ' What on earth,' he began, as I burst past the butler into his room.

" ' Sorry,' I gasped, ' I'm not an anarchist. Look at these two photos. Ronald Vane case.'

" ' Two,' he cried, ' I've only seen one.'

" I handed them to him in silence, and for a while he stared at them.

" ' Well,' he said. ' What of it ? I don't know how this second one was obtained, but it doesn't seem to me to alter matters. That presumably is Ronald Vane's shadow.'

" ' It isn't,' I cried. ' It can't be. If Vane committed the murder, what time was it done ? It is a proven fact that he was back in his own house at 9.45. Therefore the latest at which it was done—if he did it—was 9.30. And if that is so those two photographs were taken within a quarter of an hour of one another. Which is impossible.'

" ' Why is it impossible ? ' he snapped

" ' Take number 1,' I cried. ' Do you see the end of the shadow of that pointed tree on the ground ? Now take number 2. Do you see where it is in that one ?

" ' Now, sir, the sun cannot lie. I went down there this morning and measured things, and do you know how long it takes for that shadow to move that distance ? One hour and five minutes. That second photograph was taken at twenty minutes past ten, when Ronald Vane can be proved to have been in his own house. The other shadow is the murderer all right, but it's not Ronald Vane.'

" ' Good God ! ' he said. ' Good God ! '

" A narrow shave I think you'll agree," went on the speaker after a moment. " And a shave which— given a roll of films—would never have been necessary. Someone with due time at his disposal would certainly have spotted it, had the two photos been developed simultaneously. But the result was all right : Ronald Vane did not go to the gallows, and in due course he married his Hester.

" But," I cried, " who did it ? Was that ever found out ? Whose was the shadow ? "

For a while he stared over the lake without speaking.

" No," he said at length, " it was never found out. The generally accepted theory is that it was some tramp who meant to stun him for his money, and then realizing what he'd done fled in a panic. Maybe that's right : maybe not."

" You have a theory of your own," I demanded.

He smiled.

"About time we got back for lunch, isn't it? Or do you want to take some more photographs? No. Then let's stroll. Only I've often wondered what Sir John did between 9.30 and 10.15. Obviously he took no photographs. Was he raging about the glade in a distracted way by himself, or was he talking to someone else? If so, whom would he be likely to talk to for such a long period? You remember I told you he was inclined to be morose. Was someone lying up, hidden in the bushes, who desired his death and seized such a golden opportunity for throwing suspicion on another man?

"His brother Richard," he continued irrelevantly, "suffered like so many younger sons from a champagne taste with a gin income. He has since inheriting the property demolished all that part of the wood. Both very natural things to do—but I wonder."

THREE OF A KIND

G*

HENRY PARTINGTON was a jovial-looking man of about fifty. His hair was turning distinctly grey, but his face had that cheerful ruddiness of colouring which made him appear several years younger. A permanent twinkle in his clear brown eyes, and a pleasant, infectious laugh completed the picture of a care-free, middle-aged man who found life good, and who wanted other people to find it good also.

Being clean-shaven, the first impression he generally gave was that he was a retired naval officer, and his intimate knowledge of various odd corners of the globe helped the illusion. Other people, on the contrary, were wont to put him down as one of that fine, but alas! diminishing band of landed gentry whose principal occupations are riding to hounds, shooting and fishing. And only one or two shrewd, hard-faced men put him down for what he really was—a rascal who lived by his wits.

But such a pleasant rascal! In fact it was his delightful charm of manner that had made him a rascal in the first place. If he had been a morose and forbidding individual, it is more than likely that he would have become a bank manager of unimpeachable morals and intense dullness. He had started life as a bank clerk, and it was the daily contemplation of incomes so immeasurably larger than his own ever could be, that had led him to formulate the simple rule that had been his through life. And the rule was that any large difference between his own worldly possessions and the other person's should be adjusted as far as lay in his power and as soon as possible. Simultaneously with arriving at this resolve he ceased to be a bank clerk, which was just as well for all concerned.

He was what would be described professionally as a first-class confidence man. He stole with the victim's full knowledge and approval. And he stole so charmingly that the victim never had an inkling that the operation was in progress. Frequently, in fact, the poor fish returned for more. Investments, real estate, transactions over jewellery, anything and everything came equally easily to Henry Partington, provided a large wad of the money that passed remained in his pocket. As a side line he counted on bridge for a thousand a year, and billiards kept him in cigars. Even golf, with a handicap of sixteen, paid for itself, and golf afforded the exercise necessary for his figure.

It was just before he had reached the age of thirty that in a moment of mental aberration he had taken unto himself a wife. Whether it was to try and make amends for having swindled the poor girl's father out of five thousand of the best, or whether he really loved her, was a point Henry Partington had frequently debated in his own mind since. But it was an academic debate since she died a year later when presenting him with Joan, his daughter. And

Joan, during the early part of her life, was a sad worry to her father. As a small girl, and later as a long-legged flapper, there was no evident niche for her in Henry Partington's scheme of things. True, she lent an air of respectability—allusions to my poor dear wife and motherless child always impressed the ladies —but in her early days she was undoubtedly more trouble than she was worth.

Until one day he woke with a slight start to the knowledge that his daughter was a singularly pretty girl. He was smoking his after luncheon cigar at a fashionable hotel on the South coast, and his glance rested casually on the tennis courts. And there he perceived his daughter holding a court. No less than seven young men were around her, and the crowd seemed to be increasing. For a moment or two his eyes narrowed : the train of thought that the spectacle had suggested to his astute brain was not very pleasant. No : a thousand times—no.

But though he banished the idea from his mind at the moment, it had returned. After all, she need never know : she could act in all innocence. The more innocent she was, in fact, the better she would act. And one day, a few months later, he finally threw his scruples overboard.

" There's a young fellow here, my darling," he murmured, " young Teffington, to be exact, whom I'd rather like you to be nice to. He's a good boy, and he's a bit worried over some of his investments. I thought I'd try and help him : a little private dinner in our sitting-room, don't you know ? If you give him one or two of your angelic smiles, it will make the lad more at his ease."

So Lord Teffington got his smiles, and they cost him, at a conservative estimate, a thousand pounds apiece.

It was rapid then : he didn't even try to fight against it. Joan became bait, and the game went merrily on. And if at times the remnant of a conscience pricked him for using his daughter in such a cause, he assuaged it by assuring himself that as she had no idea what she was doing, no blame could be attached to her. Which admirable piece of casuistry might have had something to be said for it : if it had not been built on a funda-mental error.

Exactly when Joan began to have her suspicions, it is difficult to say. They grew gradually in her mind, though she fought against them indignantly at first. But she was no fool, and by the time she was nineteen the polite myth of her father being something in the City was finally exploded. She knew that he wasn't anything of the sort, and though she was still far from realizing what a confounded old scamp he really was, she had a pretty shrewd idea that his method of liveli-hood would not stand a close scrutiny. In fiction, of course, she would have broken away from him in righteous horror at this point, and earned her own living as a governess ; in practice she did nothing of the sort. In the first place, she knew nothing about teaching ; in the second, no female parent would have employed her—she was far too pretty ; thirdly, and most important of all, such a proceeding would have bored her to death.

And so she did what many people have done before her—she drifted. She was genuinely fond of her father, and in spite of herself, his free and easy philosophy of life made her laugh. For, after a while, though the matter had never been definitely mentioned between them, that astute gentleman had sensed that she was not quite so ignorant as he thought. And imperceptibly the mask had dropped off when they were alone, until, at the age of twenty, Joan had but few illusions left with regard to her father's ideas on the subject of *meum* and *tuum*. Which was all very reprehensible, and might have ended Heaven knows how unless Bill Longworth had appeared on the scene.

Bill was something completely different to anybody she had ever met before. In her wanderings around hotels with her father the average man Joan had encountered had been cast in a mould. It was, doubtless, a good mould, but honesty compels the admission that it was a dull one. They were all very nice boys, who played tennis and golf quite well and danced quite passably : but sooner or later they all stammered and became hot in the hand as a preliminary to blurting out their undying passion. And there was another mould—not a good mould—of elderly men who also grew hot in the hand. They made her sick.

And then, one August, when she and her father were staying at the Grand Hotel at Westbourne, Bill Longworth arrived. It was tea-time, and from behind her table she watched him covertly as he got out of the bus. And as he disappeared into the hotel, he left her with a vivid impression of clear blue eyes set in a keen, tanned face ; of physical fitness and intense virility ; of well-fitting clothes on a perfect figure. A bag crammed with golf clubs followed him, together with several suit-cases plastered with the fancy labels of foreign hotels and steamship companies.

" An undoubted lamb," she reflected in the vernacular. " Him for little Joan."

" A soldier, I should imagine," remarked her father thoughtfully. " Probably penniless, but they sometimes think they can play poker."

" Can't you ever get away from it, Dad," she cried, irritably. " One of these days you'll strike a man who *can* play, and get bitten good and hard."

" Don't mock your poor old parent, my darling," he answered amiably. " I have often struck such scoundrels in the past, and I always develop a headache when I've lost a fiver."

She didn't see the stranger again till dinner, and then, as luck would have it, he had been placed at a table directly facing her. And it was over the fish that their eyes met and held for a second. Quite accidental, of course—but a second is a deuced long time—on certain occasions. Quite long enough to establish very pleasant hopes for the future—or to completely annihilate them.

He really was astoundingly pleasant to look at. And unconsciously Joan found herself building fancy pictures in her mind about him. A soldier probably, as her father had said : a clean-cut, straight-living man, with hard, cut and dried ideas on honour and the thing to do. And what would he think of her if he knew ? A wave of bitterness against her father passed over her : she felt a sudden intense envy for the red-cheeked dowdy girl at the next table eating her second large helping of apple-tart. She would break away: she would. Go and typewrite or something : at anyrate be honest.

Still silent and distraite she followed her father into the lounge. Out of the corner of her eye she saw the stranger's tall, spare figure standing by an open window, and then she resolutely tried to banish him from her thoughts. Which, if she'd stopped to think of it, was a very dangerous sign. . . .

She started talking to a dull and worthy woman next to her—one of her father's many smaller irons in the fire. And then the band struck up in the ball-room—the signal for an immediate rush of callow youths to her side. But as she went to dance with the first her heart gave a sudden little pound of excitement : her father was talking to the stranger in the window.

He didn't come up to her till near the end, and then her father introduced him. And there was a glint in Henry Partington's eyes which his daughter interpreted perfectly. It filled her with a sick hopelessness : it meant that something was doing. And Joan knew what that something was. She wouldn't help him over this : she'd tell him later that this stranger *must* be left alone. Because—oh ! because. . . .

" You dance divinely, Miss Partington."

The band had stopped ; the cool, grave voice in her ear pulled her together. She looked up at him to find his steady eyes fixed on hers with a strange, baffling expression in them.

" Are you staying long ? " she asked lightly, as they left the room.

" My plans are always a little vague," he answered. " Are you ? "

" About another month, I expect."

" That is my own present intention," he said, gravely. " I hope we shall have some more dances."

For about a quarter of an hour he stayed with her talking, and all the time she was conscious of that inscrutable look in his eyes. It defeated her : she couldn't interpret it. It seemed at times so utterly impersonal—almost as if she was a specimen under examination ; and then, quite suddenly, it would alter, and give her the intensely personal message which she had received so often from men before and never wanted till now.

For she made no bones about it to herself when she went to bed. She had only seen him for a few hours and spoken to him for a few minutes, but this man Bill Longworth could not be dismissed as all the others had been. He was going to mean something in her life, and the question was, how big a thing he was going to be. And her last coherent thought before

she fell asleep was that she would insist on her father
leaving him alone. On that point she was absolutely
determined. . . .

But it is one thing to be determined about a thing :
it is another to carry that determination into effect.
During the days that followed Bill Longworth seemed
to deliberately lay himself out to play straight into her
father's hands. He started off the very next morning
by announcing casually that he had a few thousands
lying idle and that he was wondering what to do with
them. And Joan all but heard her father's mental
snort of pure joy, like a thirsty war-horse scenting
water in the distance.

So that she wasn't in the least surprised when
Henry Partington casually suggested some three days
later that they should ask him to dinner in their
sitting-room.

" A little business talk, my pet," he remarked
casually. " A very nice fellow—young Longworth :
plays a rattling good game of golf. But the old
man with his strokes managed to beat him all
right."

" I wish you'd leave him alone, father," she said
quietly. " You know perfectly well why you want him
to dinner. And so do I."

" My darling," he cried, " you misunderstand me
this time, I assure you. It is true that in the past
certain schemes in which I have interested myself
have gone wrong, but I give you my word that on this
occasion I'm on a cast-iron certainty. Our

fortune, my pet, will be made. And I want that nice young fellow in on the ground floor with me."

She gave a short laugh and left the room. It wasn't the first time she had heard similar sentiments from her father, and she knew exactly what they were worth. And as she went to her room to change—she was playing golf with Longworth in a few minutes—she came to a sudden resolve. Without giving her father away—she was too loyal for that—she would try and persuade him not to part with his money. It would be difficult, but that couldn't be helped : it just had to be done.

They had played nine holes before she broached the subject, and the half-round had opened her eyes to another aspect of the case—an aspect which made her heart beat a little quicker, but which also made her resolve the more imperative. Bill Longworth was a class golfer ; anyone could see that with half an eye. And not in a hundred years would her father beat him, even with twice his allowance of strokes. Why, therefore, had Bill lost ? He *must* have done it deliberately. And if so—why ?

There could be only one answer. Joan was no fool : she knew she attracted him even as he attracted her. And he'd lost merely to ingratiate himself with her father. Which didn't matter much over a game of golf, but was a totally different thing when it came to business.

" Were you playing very badly against my father,

Mr. Longworth ? " she asked, as she watched him hit a screamer from the tenth tee.

" Couldn't get the putts down," he answered gravely, after she'd driven. " Good shot."

She shook her head.

" I don't believe you," she said quietly. " Do you mind if we sit down for a little. I want to talk to you."

" There is an excellent seat by the eleventh tee," he remarked. " Let us smoke a cigarette there, and look at the sea."

" Mr. Longworth," she said, when the caddies had been dismissed to a suitable distance. " Daddy has asked you to dinner to-night, hasn't he ? "

" An invitation greedily accepted," answered the man.

" Well, I want you to regard what I'm going to say in the strictest confidence," she went on quietly. " Daddy is a dear, but—but he's got one failing. He thinks he's a financial genius. He's always putting his money into the most wonderful schemes, which invariably go bust. And he's always persuading his friends to do likewise. He means it for the—for the best, but that's not much comfort when you lose your money. So I want you to promise me that whatever he says to you to-night you won't part with any of your money. I'm—I'm sure you'll only lose it."

She caught her breath a little quickly, and glanced at the man beside her. He was staring out to sea, and the knuckles of the hand which grasped the arm of the seat were gleaming white. And then he suddenly relaxed and looked at her, with the look that no woman can mistake.

" You darling," he said under his breath. " You darling."

For a moment or two she was so amazed that she could only stare at him blankly ; then the warm colour flooded her cheeks, and her eyes fell.

" What do you mean ? " she whispered faintly.

" Only that I adore you," he answered. " And what you've just said to me has made me the happiest man in the world."

" But why ? I don't understand." And she was staring at him blankly again.

" I don't expect you do," he said, with a little smile. " And maybe you never will. Anyway, it doesn't matter. Nothing matters except one thing. Can you guess what it is ? "

" No," she answered, very low.

" You angelic little liar," he laughed. " You care, Joan ? "

For a while she stared at the ground : then she raised her eyes to his.

" Like Hell, Bill. But oh !—it's impossible. Let's go on playing."

For the moment there was no one in sight, and she felt his arm like a steel bar round her waist. Gasping, half suffocated, she raised her lips to his ; then he let her go.

" Nothing is impossible, my beloved," he cried, triumphantly. " Absolutely nothing. Come along and finish the round. I have an irresistible longing to drive into the back of the gent in plus fours with the strawberry fair isle."

II

"My dear," remarked Henry Partington complacently, "I am glad to say that my brokers see their way to letting young Longworth have five thousand founder's shares in that new company I am interested in. The one I talked to him about at dinner that night."

It was three days later, and Joan and her father were sitting on the front listening to the band.

"He returns, I believe, this evening," he went on, "and to-morrow morning I will tell him the good news. Let us hope he won the cup ; he is undoubtedly a very good golfer."

With a little frown the girl contemplated her shoe : she felt out of her depth. For Bill Longworth had come to dinner as arranged, and instead of doing as she expected him to do—turn down her father firmly but politely—he had opened his mouth for the hook wider than ever. And here he was—caught.

True, when Henry Partington had left them alone for a few minutes while he went to look for a prospectus, Bill had taken her in his arms and kissed her till she was breathless and exhausted—but that was nothing to do with it. And the next day he had gone off to Portsdown to play for the Autumn Gold Cup.

What did it mean ; what could it mean, except that he didn't believe the warning she had given him ? And she couldn't let him be swindled by her father. Not Bill. She'd have to stop it even if it meant telling him the truth. And if she told him the truth, what would he think ? What would he think of her ?

" Dad, I beg of you—don't do it," she cried, suddenly. " I beseech of you, don't take Bill's money."

" My dear child," he answered, pompously, " as I've told you before, you're mistaken this time. This really is the goods : on my word of honour, I assure you. I'm putting him into a gold mine."

With a little sigh of utter weariness, she rose.

" I'm going back to the hotel," she said. " I've got a bit of a headache."

There was nothing for it : she'd have to tell him herself. And if it meant the end, well—it was only fair that she should pay. It was the price for being her father's daughter, and for acquiescing in his mode of life. But until now she had never realized how terribly big it was going to be.

She didn't see him until dinner-time, and then he came over to their table with the usual lazy smile on his lips, and a special private message in his eyes for Joan.

" Did you win," said Henry Partington.

" By two strokes," answered Bill Longworth.

" Everything went well : in fact a most successful trip. And how is Miss Joan ? "

" The same as before," she said, forcing a smile. " You must tell me about the game after dinner."

She would do it then ; she'd get him alone and tell him the truth. Tell him that she'd lied to him on the golf links when she'd implied what she had about her father ; tell him that they were just a pair of crooks and swindlers, and that this wonderful scheme was just another of the same old ramps. She could picture him now as he realized the truth ; see the light die out of those dear blue eyes of his ; the contempt and scorn on his face as he looked at her. But it had to be done ; yes—it had to be done. You can't kiss a man as she'd kissed Bill, and swindle him.

And so, with her mind made up, she left the dining-room to find that her father appeared to have made up his mind also. Henry Partington had not lived the life he had for thirty years for nothing, and that evening he remained glued to her side. Whether his astute mind suspected something of the truth or whether it was pure chance, she didn't know, but the fact remained that her father gave her no opportunity for even the shortest of private talks with Bill. And bed-time came without her having said a word.

She went up to her room leaving the two men together, and slowly undressed. She must get at him somehow : to-morrow morning might be too late. They were probably talking business now, and Bill was believing everything her father told him. People always did : he was so terribly plausible. And Bill would put down what she had told him on the links as just a girl's ignorance.

She was in bed before the idea struck her, and she realized the only thing to do. For a moment or two she hesitated as she glanced at her watch. After midnight. . . . Then, with sudden, quick decision, as if she was afraid of changing her mind, she got up and slipped on a wrap. She opened her door and looked out ; the passage was empty. And, without any further hesitation she walked along it in the direction of Bill's room.

She had seen the number in the visitors' book, and with her heart beating in great thumps she stopped outside the door of 213. For a moment she hesitated and almost fled back to her own room : then she knocked.

There was a short pause during which she heard what sounded like the rattle of golf clubs ; then the door was opened and Bill stood looking at her.

" Joan," he whispered. " What do you want ? Come in, my dear."

He closed the door behind her, but made no movement to touch her. He had evidently been polishing his clubs, for a mashie was lying across the chair and some sandpaper was on the floor. And having cleared his golf bag away from the easy chair, he stood watching her with that same baffling expression in his eyes that she had noticed the first time they met.

" Bill," she said steadily, " I've got something to

say to you. I wanted to say it after dinner to-night, but Daddy never gave me a chance. Are you going to put any money into this scheme of his ? "

" I think so," he answered. " It seems a very good opportunity."

She wouldn't meet his eye, and so she didn't see the tender look on his face.

" Bill you mustn't," she stammered. " Oh ! but it's difficult. Bill—I lied to you on the links, don't you understand ? I let you think that Daddy was just an ass who always lost his own money as well as other people's. I hoped that would be enough to put you off, but it evidently hasn't. Bill, we're—we're crooks."

Once again she failed to see the sudden smile that glinted on the man's face.

" That's how we live, Bill : by swindling people. You'll never see a penny of your money again if you give father that five thousand."

She stared miserably into the empty grate, only to give a sudden little gasp as his arms went round her and she felt his cheek against hers.

" And why, girl of mine," he whispered, " are you telling *me* all this ? You didn't tell the others."

She twisted in his grasp so that she faced him.

" Because I love you," she said simply. " And I didn't love the others."

" You darling," he breathed. " You darling. That's all I wanted to hear."

His lips met hers, her arms stole round his neck
And then she pushed him away.

"Bill, we're mad. Don't you see that what I'v
told you makes—everything—impossible."

He stood up, and his smile was twisted.

"That's for you to say, my sweetheart. For I'v
got something to tell you . . . My God! who's that?"

On the door had come a quick, imperative knock

"Quick, Joan," he whispered. "Through there
and into the bathroom. And not a sound, darling
not a sound. Lock the door."

Bill Longworth cast one rapid glance round the room
and straightened his tie. Then he strolled over to the
door and opened it. Two men were standing outside
with the assistant manager hovering nervously in the
background.

"Good evening, Bill," said the larger of the two
men. "I presume you know why we're here."

"You can presume anything you like," said
Longworth pleasantly. "But there's no need to do
it in the passage."

The large man smiled.

"Then we'll come inside. Now Bill, where are
they?"

"Where are what?" asked Longworth lighting a
cigarette.

"Lady Gallader's diamonds," said the large man
wearily. "We've got you this time, Bill, and as we
all want to go to bed it will save a lot of
trouble if you fork 'em out at once. Because if you

don't I warn you I'm going to find 'em if I have to rip
up every floor board in the room."

"Most interesting," drawled Bill. "At the moment,
however, the connection seems a little obscure. I
rather Lady Gallader has lost her diamonds; but
why this vicious animosity towards my harmless
apartment."

"Look here, Bill," said the large man patiently,
"in order that things may be quite clear to you I'll
tell you one or two small points that you don't know.
Last night at Portsdown Lady Gallader's house was
broken into, and her diamonds were stolen. Don't
look bored : I haven't come to the points you don't
know yet. This morning at four o'clock, Greystone—
you remember Inspector Greystone—was out for a
very early walk. A pure fluke I admit, Bill ; and bad
luck for you. And he happened to see a very old
friend having a morning walk also. This friend was
coming from the direction of Lady Gallader's house.
Been paying a call, Bill, had you ? So Greystone hid
behind a hayrick and wondered. Of course he knew
nothing about the burglary, but he did know a good
deal about the other early walker. So he followed him
back to his hotel, and from then till now, Bill, you've
never been out of our sight. As soon as Greystone
heard about the burglary, he 'phoned me. Then he
followed you in another car ; I got a warrant to search
you and here we are. Bill those stones are on you, or
they're in this room. We know you haven't got rid
of 'em to-day. And we're going to have 'em, if it

takes us a week. You've done us every time up-to
date, but we've got you at last."

"Most interesting," said Bill languidly. "But to
my uninitiated eye the evidence seems a trifle flimsy
Is our one and only Greystone the only man who i.
allowed to take an early morning walk?"

"What where you doing down there anyway,"
snapped the detective.

"Oh! ephemeral fame," sighed Bill. "Let me show
you the morning paper, MacAndrew. There—W
Longworth $72 + 73 = 145$. And Lord Gallader him
self presented me with a lovely medal. One over fours
my boy—for two rounds."

MacAndrew snorted.

"I'm not denying you can play golf. Maybe
you'll want a bit of practice after a few years' rest
though. Now then—where are they?"

"My dear Mac, I haven't got 'em. You've made a
boss shot this time, believe you me. As, I may say, you
always have on other occasions. In fact I regard myself
as a most hardly used individual. This atmosphere of
harsh suspicion in which I live is not conducive to good
putting."

"Cut it out," snarled MacAndrew. "If you won't
tell us, we've got to do it ourselves. But I can promise
you, Longworth, you'll regret it. Take that end of
the room, Johnson, and start with the bed."

It was three o'clock before they had finished, and
if Inspector MacAndrew had not actually fulfilled his
threat of ripping up the floor boards he had done

everything short of doing so. And he had drawn absolutely blank.

" Damn you, Longworth," he cried angrily. " I know you've got 'em."

He was standing in the centre of the room regarding Bill Longworth balefully. And Bill, who was carefully cleaning his niblick, looked up with a pleasant smile.

" Sorry for your disappointment, Mac," he murmured, " but I told you you'd made a howling error. And now, if you don't mind, I'd like to turn in. There's a big open competition at Le Touquet in three days, and late nights are the devil for one's golf."

And then suddenly his eyes narrowed : MacAndrew was looking at the bathroom door.

" What is through there, Bill ? " he asked.

" My bathroom," answered Longworth, getting up and strolling over to the door.

" Then I think we'll just search your bathroom, Bill," said MacAndrew quietly.

" And I think you won't," replied Longworth, equally quietly.

A gleam of triumph had come into the Inspector's eyes.

" Getting hot, are we," he remarked grimly. " Longworth, I order you to stand on one side."

" MacAndrew," said Longworth, and his face was set and strained, " I give you my most solemn word of honour that there is nothing in the bathroom that will interest you."

" That is a point I prefer to settle myself," answered

the detective. " Once again I order you to stand
aside."

And Bill Longworth's forehead was wet.

" Look here, MacAndrew," he cried desperately
" if I tell you . . . "

And at that moment the bathroom door opened
and Joan stepped into the room.

" My dear," cried Bill in agony. " Oh ! my dear."
But Joan took no notice of him.

" Search the bathroom," said Joan scornfully to
the Inspector. " And then go."

For a while there was absolute silence in the room
then the Inspector turned to Bill.

" You didn't want that door opened, Longworth—
quite naturally. To prevent it you were just going to
tell me—what. ' If I tell you '—you said."

" The great secret, MacAndrew. The thing I've
never told a soul. But I'd have told you to prevent
this happening." His hands were clenched : his
face was stern. " Keep your eye on the ball, and
your head still, and in a year or two you'll win one of
the monthly spoons."

A soft gurgle of laughter from Joan broke the
oppressive tension, and even the manager's face
twitched into a smile.

" MacAndrew," went on Bill quietly, " you've
made a mistake. It's true I was out early this morning,
I don't deny it. I couldn't sleep and I went for a
walk. But I don't even know where Lady Gallader's
house is."

" I've not made a mistake, Longworth," answered the other through his clenched teeth. " That was your work last night. But as usual, you've left no trace. Never mind, my friend : it's only a question of time before I prove it."

" Well, laddie," said Bill wearily, " it's a question of half-past three now. And as you said yourself, we all want to go to bed. Could we postpone the proof till to-morrow, or rather till later to-day."

" We cannot," snarled MacAndrew. " You were going to tell me where you'd hidden those stones, Longworth. And unless you do—now, this instant, I shall make it my business to see that this young lady's presence in your room—in that rig, is duly known to her father."

" You ineffable swine," said Bill tensely. " You supreme cur."

He was crouching a little, and his eyes, hard and merciless, were fixed on the Inspector's face. And then, just as he was going to spring, Joan's hand was laid on his arm.

" You will be a little late, Inspector," she said quietly. " I propose to tell my father to-morrow morning first thing that I came round to my fiancé's room to-night to talk a certain matter over with him, when you interrupted us."

She felt the muscles in Bill's arm relax, and not till then did her hand drop to her side.

" Would you now be good enough to search the bathroom, and then go ? "

H

But MacAndrew had had enough : and with a
stifled curse he swung on his heel and crossed to the
door.

" Sooner or later, Longworth : sooner or later I'll
catch you. And as for you, Miss, I wish you joy o
your choice. You've got the smartest jewel-thie
in Europe to-day."

But Bill Longworth was taking no notice : he was
staring at the girl by his side.

" Did you mean it, Joan ? " he said a little hoarsely
" When you said—' my fiancé.' "

The detectives had gone : the two of them were
alone.

" If you want me, Bill," she answered.

" If I want you," he almost shouted. " Why, I'm
mad for you."

And then his hands dropped to his sides.

" But, my dear—it's the truth : what MacAndrew
said."

" I guessed that," she said quietly. " And you
were going to tell him where the diamonds were,
rather than that he should open that door ? "

" Why yes, dear, I was," said Bill gravely. " Listen,
my darling. That was the thing I had to tell you.
I've done it for years. It's I who am the sinner—not
you. I spotted your father for what he was within
five minutes. And I wondered about you. Did you
know, or did you not ? On the golf links I was nearly
sure : to-night you told me."

Half unconsciously he had picked up one of

his brassies and was balancing it in his hand.

" Joan, I'm sick of it. MacAndrew is right : sooner or later he'll catch me. I want to marry and settle down. And you—oh ! my darling—it was first sight as far as I was concerned. But before I asked you I had to make sure. So I played into your father's hands, and found out what I wanted to know. And then when you came out of the bathroom and saved the situation—why, Joan dear, the world just stopped for a moment. Crooks, my darling, both of us : you such a tiny little one—me pretty black. But if we run straight, Joan . . . "

" Why, yes, Bill, we'll do that."

His arms were round her : his face close to hers.

" We'll run straight, boy : and we'll run together."

And then a sudden thought struck her and she smiled.

" Where are the diamonds ? "

" Where everything has always been," grinned Bill.

He took a screwdriver out of his pocket, and picked up a brassic.

" You pulled my leg once about the excessive number of my wooden clubs. But I don't play with them all."

The brass plate was off the bottom of the club, and Joan saw that the head was hollow. And in the cavity was something carefully wrapped in cotton wool.

" They're all there, and in three of the other clubs," he said.

" But, Bill," she cried, " this is Daddy's precious

pearl and diamond tie-pin that he values so much."

" I know, my angel," he admitted. " I was going to give it back to him to-morrow morning as a sort of solatium for not getting my five thousand and for losing his daughter."

THE IMPASSIVE FOOTMAN

1

JOHN MARWOOD stirred irritably in his chair, and pulled the shawl tighter round his shoulders. On his face was the peevish, complaining look which of late years had become chronic : his whole bearing suggested the man who has a grievance against everything and everybody : the man who has decided that life has not given him a square deal. It makes no difference to such a man that in the game it is often he who deals the cards : and that it is up to him to make the best of the bad hands when they come. Far from not meeting trouble half-way, the particular breed to which John Marwood belonged anticipate it before it starts. They seize it, they canter back with it, and they then exclaim triumphantly : " I told you so." In fact, the only thing which seems to annoy them, and make them really aggrieved, is when they can find nothing to complain about. It is a very rare occurrence, and mercifully for John Marwood things were not as bad as that. One of those wretched pin-pricks with which life delighted to buffet him had occurred : no one had come to give him his medicine. . . .

Out of the whole houseful of lazy, incompetent servants, not one of them could take the trouble to remember his sufferings. He fumed angrily and muttered under his breath. Three o'clock was the time for his tonic : it was now nearly five past. And, of course, Grace was out—she would be. Just when he wanted her. . . . And the fire wanted attention. . . . Moreover, that symptom of his which he had described to her last night, that sharp stabbing pain near the right shoulder blade was becoming increasingly acute. He felt convinced it was something serious, though his wife had not seemed very impressed when he had told her. But then, she never was : she seemed to have absolutely no conception of how he suffered.

Once again he moved irritably in his chair. Unless one of these fat brutes brought his medicine shortly he could have to get up and ring the bell. And any walking hurt his right leg abominably. But what did they care ? He might die at that moment, and not one of the great staff he employed would feel one single twinge of regret. They would afterwards, of course, when they were kicked out of a soft job into the world. Then they might begin to realize what he had done for them, and then it would be too late. He gloated over the thought for a moment or two : he almost felt as if it would be worth while dying just to score off them. But then, he wasn't likely to die : he never had any luck. . . .

Suddenly he heard footsteps approaching the door, and the need for rapid thought arose. When had he last endeavoured to show his callous household a little of the torture he endured ? Of course, it was acting

in a way—but a very necessary piece of acting. . . .
Only it didn't do to carry it out too often : otherwise
it lost its point. . . . It was as the knock came on
the door, and the handle turned, that he remembered
it was at least a week since he had done it last, and
that it was, therefore, quite time to do it again. . . .

With an agility remarkable considering the agony
in his right leg he rose and took a couple of steps
forward. Then he clutched the mantelpiece with one
hand, and his right side with the other. It was as
the door opened that he groaned. . . .

A man came in with a glass of medicine on a tray,
and for a moment he stood watching his master with
a contemptuous smile on his face. Then the mask of
the good servant replaced it, and, coming forward, he
placed the medicine on the table, and solicitously
helped the sufferer back to his chair, where he lay with
closed eyes.

" Your tonic, sir," murmured the servant, after a
decent interval.

After a long pause Marwood looked wearily up at
him. " How many of you are there below ? "

" Four, sir." The man's eyebrows went up slightly.

" Is it too much to hope that among four of you
there is one who can remember to bring me my
tonic in time ? "

" Very sorry, sir. The clock in the servants' hall
is slow."

" Then, is it too much to hope that among four of
you there is one who can remember to put it

H*

right ? " He put out a languid hand towards the glass. " If it is too much to hope for, I suppose I shall have to resign myself to the agony of getting up to ring the bell to remind you." With a profound sigh he looked at the pink liquid. " Is this a table-spoonful ? "

" Yes, sir."

With an expressionless face the man watched Marwood drain the glass : then, picking it up, he turned to go.

" Wait." Marwood's tired voice stopped him on his way to the door. " What sum of money do I pay you a year ? "

" Forty-eight pounds, sir."

" Forty-eight pounds." The speaker's eyes were closed : his weariness seemed to be increasing. " Then do you think it would be possible for you to tear your-self away from your arduous pleasures downstairs for a sufficiently long period to attend to one or two of the things that so very obviously want doing in this room ? I am fully aware that my comfort is a matter of supreme indifference to the entire house-hold ; but, in return for your forty-eight pounds a year, I hope I am not asking too much. For instance —the fire. It occurs to me that it might be saved from complete extinction if you could bring yourself to place a little coal on it."

As noiselessly as is humanly possible, the operation was performed, and the man stood up. He had only given his employer the opportunity for two agonized starts of nerve-wracked anguish, which was distinctly annoying to the invalid. Making up the fire was the invariable occasion of some of his very choicest flights of martyred cynicism. (And what made the servants' hall snarl with rage was the fact that for hours on end, when Marwood had given strict orders that he should not be disturbed, the fire was kept up and tended by the sufferer himself. Those were the occasions when he found the strength to totter alone to the door, and hang on the outside a red board, which informed the household that his nerves were in such a condition that he required complete solitude.)

At length the man in the chair opened his eyes, and gazed at the motionless servant. Long experience had taught him that the most potent weapon in the world, with what he was pleased to term " the lower orders," was a cold, malevolent sarcasm. Cursing anyone can stand—so John Marwood never cursed. He specialized in the icy sneer, and he was a fairly capable specialist. He enjoyed seeing a man writhe under his tongue : it afforded him an intense satisfaction, which can only be properly appreciated by the born bully. . . .

For a few moments the silence remained unbroken. There was no hurry, and undue precipitancy always spoilt these interviews. Each particular phase must be played to the end in order to get the full enjoyment, and the present phase was the silent interlude. It varied with the different servants, as to the length of time they could stand Marwood's eye without growing restless. And this man gave the best sport of all.

In fact, on two or three occasions he had actually beaten Marwood at his own game : forced him to speak before he had intended to, before he had really prepared his remark. He stood now calmly gazing out of the window, perfectly deferential, perfectly self-composed, until Marwood could have struck him in his rage. He felt that he would willingly have given all he possessed just to see this man squirming and writhing in front of him . . . like a small boy who impales an insect on a pin. . . .

"Is there anything more you wish, sir ? " Quite calmly the servant picked up the empty medicine glass.

"I suppose," said Marwood, striving to speak in his usual expressionless voice, "that you consider you have fulfilled all the obligations that can reasonably be expected of you in return for forty-eight pounds a year. Nevertheless, if it is not too much to ask, perhaps you would be kind enough to hand me that red volume from the bookshelf."

The man crossed the room and returned with the book.

"You would, of course," remarked Marwood, "give it to me upside down. And now—the evening paper . . . on that table . . ." He lay back completely exhausted. "At five o'clock—not five past or ten past—but at five, unless you are all too engrossed to think of the matter, perhaps one of you would again bring me my tonic. And until then I do not wish to be disturbed. Place the board on the door after you go out, and if it is within your power I entreat of you do not make a noise doing so."

"Very good, sir." With an inscrutable expression in his eyes the man stood watching Marwood to see if he had any further instructions. But the invalid apparently had not. He remarked " Forty-eight pounds a year. My God ! " twice, in a resigned whisper, and then complete prostration supervened.

It was as the door was closing behind the servant that Marwood once more found his voice.

" It was forty-eight pounds you said," he called feebly.

" Yes, sir." Very deliberately the man held the door open, and stared at his employer's back. " In addition, however, there is a shilling a month for insurance stamps, and the usual washing bills. I will prepare a complete statement for you."

Marwood's eyes opened in speechless fury, and he sat up with a jerk. But the door had shut, and the sound of the man's footsteps had died away before he could think of a suitable answer to such a piece of gratuitous insolence. . . .

After a while he calmed down, and opened the book on his knees. As might have been expected, it was a medical treatise—one of the popular type. Couched in comprehensible language, the symptoms of every disease from housemaid's knee to consumption were set forth in its pages, and there were very few of those diseases which, at some period or other during the last six years, Marwood had not suffered from according to himself. That he had been completely unable to find any doctor who would support his diagnosis was merely a proof that all doctors were fools. Far better results could be obtained, he had come to the conclusion, by looking after oneself : and since chemists—who were also a race of fools—had a rooted objection to making up prescriptions unless they were ordered by a doctor, he had been compelled by *force majeure* to fall back on patent medicines. Of these, he consumed annually an incredible amount : and only his naturally strong constitution had enabled him to stand the strain.

This afternoon he was desirous of finding out what that sharp pain in his right shoulder blade indicated. If he sent for one of those damned doctors, he would be told it was liver, and recommended to take exercise. . . . Exercise ! Exercise ! ! ! . . . With agonizing neuritis in his right leg.

It was no question of liver, that he knew. Heart, possibly—no, that was on the left side . . . or a tubercular growth. . . . There was a slight swelling as far as he had been able to make out the night before, by twisting round and moving a couple of looking glasses into more favourable positions. And then the light had been wrong, and Grace had come in and laughed at him. She would : there wasn't a soul who cared in the whole house—not one. But they'd think differently . . . they'd think differently —when . . .

Rigid, motionless, Marwood stared in front of him,

gripping the arms of his chair. Stab . . . stab . . .
stab . . . an excruciating pain had suddenly begun to
pierce him like a knife. It started from the region of
his right shoulder and spread to his chest. With
monotonous regularity it continued, while the flames
flickered in the grate, and fantastic shadows danced
round the darkening room. Stab . . . stab . . . every
four or five seconds : till his whole body seemed to be
burning with the agony.

Once he raised his voice in a feeble little whining
cry. " Liver ! They'll say it's liver." He threw out
his hands with an impotent wail, only to put them
back on the arms of the chair again, as the pain
jumped viciously with the movement.

And then slowly it died away ; the stabs became
fewer and fewer, and finally ceased altogether. Very
carefully he lay back in his chair, and after a while
put a shaking hand to his forehead. It was wet with
perspiration, and even at that moment he experienced
a grim satisfaction at this conclusive evidence of the
agony he had suffered. It was a pity Grace was not
there to see. Then she wouldn't have laughed.

He lay very silent, staring at the wall. He was
still shaking from the effects of the bout, though the
relief from the actual pain was exquisite. And it
was not for half an hour that the satisfaction he felt
at this proof of his sufferings was replaced by another
feeling which at first he found hard to analyse. He
shied away from the analysis like a frightened colt ;
he assured himself that it was only what he had known

all along, though none of these cursed doctors would believe him ; he proved conclusively that it only showed what he had always said—that he was a very sick man. But he proved it too conclusively ; he proved it so that at last he really did believe it himself. And the feeling which replaced the satisfaction was fear-sickening, gripping fear. He who had called Wolf so often when others were about, and had raged fretfully because they had taken no notice, realized suddenly that, in truth, the Wolf had come. And John Marwood knew the conclusion of that fable.

Once again he wiped the sweat from his forehead, and, reaching out a trembling hand, he raised a glass of water to his lips. His throat felt dry and parched ; the room seemed strangely hot. And then, with a sudden crash a coal fell into the grate and lay there smoking.

With a little whimper of fear he dropped the glass and soaked himself with water.

2

You may know Tearle's Tea Shop in a certain little street off Shaftesbury Avenue ; on the other hand, you may not. If you are supremely great and very beautiful, you probably patronize Rumpelmeyer's ; if you aspire solely to the consumption of a good, wholesome bun, an A.B.C. is not to be despised. In fact, London's teashops are legion, and between them every taste from Tooting to Mayfair, and thence down again to Whitechapel is catered for. But there is only one Tearle's.

It would be hard to define the *clientèle* of Tearle's. All that one can say is that once a Tearleite always a Tearleite. The tables are sufficiently secluded to allow people to eat the mustard and cress, which is Tearle's speciality, in decency ; they are not so completely hidden that it is unwise to take a step without a warning cough. In short, it is Tearle's, and, if you don't know it, go there and find out for yourself.

Grace Marwood had been sitting at her usual table in the corner for ten minutes before Bryan Daventry came in. He saw her as he reached the door, and, a little abruptly, he stopped and hung up his coat and hat. There were other pegs vacant nearer her table, but, not for the first time, Daventry wanted those few seconds' breathing space while he was still too far away for her to see the expression on his face. Because Daventry, being an ordinary decent man, to say nothing of being a brilliantly successful doctor, had decided some months ago that the intense, overpowering love he felt for Grace Marwood had got to stop. Which, incidentally, is the sort of foolish thing a man does decide.

He had never spoken about it to her. If you speak about love, and mean it, to another man's wife, you cannot change the conversation to easy prattle about the weather. Something will happen one way or the other ; either you will be taken at your word, or the lady will become peevish. And neither of these alternatives appealed to Daventry. If he had had to choose, it would have been the first without hesitation ; the thought of making Grace angry, of cutting out these occasional meetings, when he could sit near her, and watch the little dark tendrils of hair curling over her ears, could see the curve of her cheek and the soft light in her wonderful deep blue eyes—the thought of missing all that was inconceivable. And so he had compromised, as has been known to happen before. He continued to meet her, and discuss all those vague, intimate things which mean such a big side of life to a normal human being. But he never mentioned love, and, of course, she had no idea of his feelings on the matter. Which, incidentally, is the sort of foolish thing a man does think.

" You're late, *mon ami*," she said, holding out her hand as he came up.

" The ailments of the human race increase and multiply daily," he answered gravely, taking a cup of tea. " I investigated two completely fresh diseases to-day, and effectually cured both the proud proprietors."

" Bright man ! Have a bun."

" I looked out the Latin for cauliflower, and told 'em they were suffering from that. Pleased as Punch —both of 'em. Then, with the help of a little Eno's, suitably coloured—— " He shrugged his shoulders. " And what has Mrs. Marwood been doing to-day ? "

" Existing, Bryan ; just existing. John has discovered an entirely new pain."

For a moment their eyes met, and then Daventry looked away a little quickly.

" Where is the location this time ? " he asked, stirring his tea.

" Oh, somewhere in his back. I found him balanced on his chest of drawers last night, with his shaving glass in one hand, and an electric torch that wouldn't work in the other, trying to see if there was a swelling." She smiled—a fleeting, bitter smile. " Poor old John ! "

" Poor old John ! " echoed Daventry savagely. " My dear Grace, if poor old John took a two-mile run in the Park, wet or fine, every morning of his life for the next six months, there would be no new pains— as I told him myself."

The girl gurgled gently. " I remember the occasion perfectly. His remarks after you had gone, on your personal appearance, your ability, your utter lack of even the remotest claim to be considered fitted to qualify as an assistant to a dresser, are indelibly stamped on my brain."

Daventry laughed with her, and for a while neither of them spoke. There was never any necessity for speech between these two ; it came spontaneously when the spirit moved them ; at other times they were both very content to sit and watch the pictures that dance in the flames, or twist gently upwards in the hazy blue smoke of a cigarette. His dreams were always the same, impossible of fruition, and so, maybe the more wonderful. With her they were not so clear they were vaguer, more rambling, less personal. She knew his feelings for her, not, perhaps, in all their intensity, but she knew he cared. And as for herself —well, only once had she really faced it. She had realized then that if she was not in love with him, it was merely because it had never been crystallized into so many words. Poor old John stood in the way, and so what was the use ? For a time after that realization she had avoided Daventry, and then gradually their old intimacy returned, their old visits to Tearle's were resumed. Not one word had Bryan ever spoken to which John himself could have objected —but the knowledge was always there. Underneath, smouldering fiercely, was the flame ; deliberately she ignored it. And if at times there came a faint pre-monition of danger, she thrust it from her. Was there not always—poor old John ?

She took a cigarette from the case he was holding out to her, and waited while he lit a match.

" How goes the research, Bryan ? "

For a moment his eyes gleamed with the enthusiasm of the scientist ; then he grinned boyishly. And when Bryan Daventry grinned, people he was with forgot he was a brilliantly successful investigator of thirty-five ; they regarded him as a schoolboy who had just been presented with half-a-crown within sight of the tuck-shop.

" It's early days, Grace, to say for certain," he answered. " But I believe honestly and candidly that I've got it. And if so—— " His fist clenched on

the table, and under his breath he whispered again—
" If so—— "

" If so—— " She looked at him with shining eyes.
" Why, you'll have done what no one has done before,
Bryan."

" That's so," he answered gravely. " Yes, that's
so. But it's not so much that I'm thinking of : it's
the suffering thousands who have died of it. Died in
agony, Grace—hideous agony. It's the most awful
disease—cancer. And if one can save 'em in
the future—if—— " Once again his eyes glowed
fiercely.

" And when will you know if you are right ? "

" Not for years—for certain." Quickly, incisively,
his hands moved as he spoke—strong, capable hands
—the hands of a great surgeon. " You see," he was
talking rapidly, and the ash grew longer on her
forgotten cigarette, " one operates. Apparently everything is all right ; the growth is removed. But not
for five, six, possibly ten years, can one be certain
that it will not return. By the old method it always
did—in a few months. Now, by my new way, I know
it will not come back for years : I hope it will not
come back at all. But it's all experiment, experiment,
experiment. One must find cases ; one must operate ;
and then one must see. Because "—his fingers
drummed on the table—" there is a risk—a big risk."

" You mean that it is kill or cure ? "

" More or less. At least, that's what they say."
He laughed shortly. " Old Sir Henry Darlington told

me so this morning. He was very nice about it ; but he evidently regarded it as the enthusiasm of youth. So do Birkett and Longworth." He paused for a moment and stared at the girl. " I'll show 'em, Grace," he continued quietly. " I'll show 'em that it's cure—not kill. And then—— " His voice rang out with a triumphant note ; on his face was the look of the strong man who sees success within his reach, and already tastes the sweets of it in his mind.

The girl touched his hand with one of hers. " I know you will, Bryan," she whispered, and there was a wonderful light in her eyes. " I know it. And oh ! my dear, how proud I'll be of you."

She had spoken without thinking, spoken the thing that was uppermost in her mind. And the smouldering flame seized its opportunity and burst out. The doctor had gone ; it was the man who sat beside her staring into her eyes, with the unmistakable message blazing from his own. She shivered, and tried to look away, but it was too late.

" Don't say it, Bryan, don't say it. For God's sake, don't say it."

" And why not, Grace ? Why shouldn't one say the truth ? You've known it, my dear, all along."

He beckoned to the waitress, and paid the bill. Then, in silence, he helped her on with her coat. Once his hand brushed her neck, and with a sudden, ungovernable rush of joy he felt her shiver at his touch.

" I'm going to take you home," he said quietly.

" There are one or two things I must say to you ; things which should have been said before."

He beckoned a taxi and gave the driver the address. Then he got in, and the car shot out into Shaftesbury Avenue.

" You care, Grace," he said, still in the same quiet tone, and, taking both her hands in his. " Thank God ! I know it : I saw it in your eyes. . . . But I'd just love to hear you say it, my dear . . . once."

" Oh ! Bryan. . . . " Her voice was trembling, so that he could scarcely hear the words. " What's the use, my dear.. . . what's the use."

" I don't care what the use is just at the moment," he answered. " I only know that I'm a man, and you're a woman, and that I've loved you as I never believed I could have loved anyone for years." He was bending towards her as he spoke. " My dear," he whispered hoarsely. " Oh ! my dear."

He caught her in his arms and kissed her ; kissed her eyes, her hair, her mouth. And after a weak, little fluttering attempt to push him away, she wound her arms round his neck, and gave him back kiss for kiss.

It seemed as if they could never stop, but at length, with a little gasp she broke away from his arms and leant back in the corner of the taxi, with closed eyes. He watched her hungrily by the light of the passing lamps, taking in every detail of the exquisite profile. For the time he was mad, past thought, past care, past everything save the unutterable wonder of the woman he had held in his arms.

" It's all wrong, Bryan," she said wearily. " Why did you do it, my dear—why ? "

" As well ask a flower why it comes out in the sun," he answered gravely. " I couldn't help it, Grace ; I just couldn't help it." He took one of her hands, and it lay in his, lifeless and inert. " We've been playing with fire for a long while, dear ; and I've known it. But I couldn't have given up seeing you ; you meant everything to me. You tried once, I know—and that ought to have warned me. But, I suppose, there are some things which are a bit too strong for us." He laughed suddenly, and drew her to him again. " What's it matter, darling, what's anything matter, except that you're you and I'm me." He was whispering close to her ear, hardly conscious of what he said. " I love you, you wonderful woman, adore you, worship you. . . . And I can't think of anything else that counts two straws—not in the whole wide world."

He tried to kiss the averted face, but this time she pushed him away, gently but inexorably.

" John matters, Bryan," she answered quietly. " That's why I don't think you must ever see me again."

" Not see you again ! " With a short, amazed laugh the man looked at her. " After this ! My dear, you don't love John."

" No," she said, thoughtfully. " I don't . . . I

don't think I ever have—not really. It's been a sort
of pity all along. But I'm married to him."

" That difficulty has been got over before now," he
answered grimly. " Grace ! dear girl of mine—you *can't*
tie yourself for life to a receptacle of patent medicines."

" I have done so ; that's the trouble." She looked at
him gravely ; then, with a weary little laugh she turned
and stared out of the window. " Oh ! Bryan, why
did you do it ? " The oft-repeated cry came again
—came with a catch in her voice. " I did so love our
friendship ; our teas together : hearing about your
work and life. It was the only thing that made life
possible. And now—it's over."

" A man and woman like you and I want more than
teas and friendship, Grace." With level eyes the man
was staring at the driver's back : then they fixed
themselves on the cigarette carefully placed behind
his ear. " We deluded ourselves into thinking that
we could cheat fate : we failed. If you like, I failed.
It doesn't matter very much, does it ? All that concerns
us at the moment is what we are going to do now."

" What thousands of others have had to do before
us," she answered wearily. " Grin and bear it, Bryan
—what else ? "

" What else ? " he cried fiercely. " Why everything else. Why should we do as thousands of others
have done ? Why should we make ourselves miserable
because a lot of damned fools say it's the proper thing
to do. Grace—we've only got one life. It's ours to
make or mar. My dear ! it's impossible for us to

leave it like this—utterly, absolutely impossible. We're nearly there now : I've got no time to *make* you feel as I feel—to *make* you see the only solution." He took her hand, and held it in both of his. " Come and have tea with me to-morrow. Let's talk it over, Grace : let's see if we can't find a way out : let's be sure. . . ."

The taxi drew up at the house, and he dropped her hand. " Will you come ? "

For a moment they stood together on the pavement facing one another. Then, very slowly : " I don't know, Bryan : I don't know."

" Will you ring me up ? " Eagerly he pleaded with her, clinging to every second left.

" Perhaps," she answered. " But I've got to think things out—alone."

Then she left him, and the door closed behind her.

" Cold night, guv'nor." The driver's voice roused him from his thoughts.

" Very cold," he answered. " Take me to the Junior Reform, please."

And, peering through the curtains of the house he had just left, stood Grace Marwood, watching the red tail lamp of the taxi till it disappeared round a bend in the road.

3

Dinner was never a very edifying meal in the Marwood household. Grace had long given up the experiment of asking in any guests : in fact, the last time had been four years ago. The remembrance of that occasion still lingered in her memory. A certain flippant stockbroker had been present, who insisted on capping every one of his host's symptoms with those possessed by an aunt of his. In fact, the hypothetical aunt won in a canter : the finishing touch being put on when the stockbroker jovially comforted Marwood with the information that the old girl wasn't dead yet.

And to-night, as she sat opposite her husband. Grace was trying to get her bearings. In silence she had watched him hobble in between two footmen : with weary contempt she had followed the old familiar procedure. First the footstool was adjusted for the leg that had neuritis : then the cushion was put behind his back. Finally one of the men advanced with a purple liquid on a salver, which represented the last brand of patent filth that was being tried. She had grown so used to the whole programme that generally it meant nothing to her ; it was part of her life, and she had accepted it as such. The thought of changing it in any way had simply never occurred to her : it was as much part of John as his face.

But now, as the meal progressed, in silence as usual —(his latest idea was that speech upset the digestion) —she was taking stock from a new standpoint. Her mind went back to the day when they were married eight years ago. She had been twenty-one—her husband ten years older : and under the influence of

the inscrutable aberration which affects people at such
times she had believed she loved him. She had known
he was a little delicate : but he played golf and tennis
and occasionally rode to hounds. And then, a few
months after their marriage, he had had a severe bout
of typhoid fever. From that date things had gradually
grown worse, until about three years later an aunt had
died unexpectedly, leaving him all her money, thus
enabling him to retire from business and become a
professional invalid. Step by step she recalled the
whole process ; relentlessly she asked herself whether
she, herself, was to blame in any way. Supposing,
when she first noticed the way he was drifting, she had
laughed him out of it—and gone on laughing, till for
very shame he had pulled himself together ! But it
had all been so gradual : so impossible to say, " This
ache of yours is twaddle : and if there's anything in
that one. for the love of Heaven take a cold bath and
go and skip in the garden." Besides, to a woman of
Grace's temperament it seemed so inconceivable that
anybody could *want* to be ill. . . .

" My digestive tablet." Her husband's voice
recalled her to the present, and she looked across
at him.

One of the footmen was bearing a small bottle
forward on a tray. He then poured out a wineglassful
of warm water, and with great solemnity John Marwood
consumed his pill, to frown heavily on sipping the
water.

" It is, I suppose," he remarked wearily. " too much

to expect that you would give me water of the right temperature. This is several degrees too hot."

And suddenly Grace laughed. " Why don't you tickle your throat, John, and slip it down like a dog ? You'd get some exercise that way."

" My dear Grace "—he stared at her in pained surprise. " Are you trying to be funny ? "

For a moment she seemed about to speak ; then she changed her mind, and continued her dinner in silence. For the first time in their married life she saw her husband as he really was : only too clearly she realized the cause of her enlightenment. She was still undecided as to what to do when they rose from the table : her mind seemed incapable of grappling with the problem. It was so unexpected, so huge ; it dazed and frightened her. Two facts alone stuck out clear above everything : she loved Bryan Daventry, and she was married to this—this receptacle of patent medicines. . . .

" If you could spare me a few minutes, Grace," he remarked, with his usual expression of studied politeness, " there is something I would like to say to you in my study."

" I will come in shortly. There is something I have to say to you, also."

She watched him totter from the room, supported by the two footmen : then she moved to the fire, and spread out her hands to the blaze. Once or twice she shivered, though the room was warm : then, turning round, she studied her reflection in the long mirror opposite. She looked at herself critically, as she would have looked at another woman : then she summed herself up.

" I am pretty, prettier than nine women out of ten. My figure is good, and so is my complexion. And I might as well be forty-eight with false teeth, as far as John is concerned. Is it worth it ? "

Again she crouched over the fire, striving to read the answer in the flames. Bryan's face danced in front of her, and she pressed the back of her hand to her mouth as if she could still feel his kisses, warm and passionate, on her lips. It was impossible : she couldn't go on ; she would go to him to-morrow, and tell him. . . .

" Mr. Marwood is in his study, madam."

The footman's voice at the door roused her, and she rose to her feet. And as she walked slowly down the passage to her husband's room there was a faint smile on her face.

He was in his usual chair carefully muffled up in a shawl : sudden changes of temperature were very apt to give him a chill. By his side was the inevitable red treatise on diseases, and a jug of hot water : his face bore its invariable expression of resigned misery. For a while she stood on the other side of the fireplace watching him : then she sat down.

" What is it you wish to say ? " she asked.

" I can hardly anticipate that it will be of much interest to you," he remarked. " What little consideration you ever possessed for my health seems to have gone long ago . . . But still, in case anything should happen to me, I feel it right to let you know what occurred this afternoon. Possibly you remember that stabbing pain I mentioned to you last night ? "

" Yes, I do." Her voice was expressionless.

" I am honoured." He took a sip of hot water. " This afternoon when you were out, and I, as usual, was alone—it returned. For half an hour I suffered incredible agony, and I am convinced that something very serious is the matter with me." He paused impressively. " It is not that, however, which I wish to discuss with you : the matter is not likely to interest you sufficiently. It is the question of business, and money, in the event of my death. Would you be good enough to hand me that account-book ? "

But Grace made no effort to rise : her eyes remained steadily fixed on her husband's face.

" How old are you, John ? Forty, isn't it ? "

" I hardly see the relevance of the remark : though I am flattered at your intimate knowledge."

" Forty," she continued. " And we've been married eight years. Eight years—time enough to have had two or three children."

" My dear Grace." He raised a protesting hand. " With my state of health . . . Children . . . "

" What do you think those eight years have meant to me, John ? Living with a man the height of whose ambition is to discover a new pill."

" Really, Grace." Genuine amazement was dawning

on his face. " You are talking most strangely to-night."

" Am I ? " she answered. " I wonder why. The only pity is that I didn't start talking strangely, as you call it, rather sooner in our married life. I'm very much afraid it's too late now."

" Too late for what ? "

" What would you say, John, if I went away and left you ? " She looked at him curiously.

" Went away," he echoed. " Haven't you everything here that you want ? A comfortable house—servants—money. My dear Grace, I think you're mad."

" No, John—I'm sane for the first time. During these last few years, I've watched you slowly become a useless thing. It's been so gradual—the process, that it's been difficult, at any particular moment, to put out a hand to try to stop it . . . Besides, I don't know that I particularly wanted to. You were very happy ; I, as you have just said, had a comfortable house—servants—money. You were just part of the house to me : exactly, John, as I was part of the house to you." She watched the outraged horror which was slowly overspreading her husband's face. " To-night at dinner, for the first time I realized where we stood. I don't want a husband who is part of the house."

" And would it be indiscreet to ask what has caused this sudden illuminating discovery ? "

" Not at all. I was on the point of telling you.

House—servants—money : but can't you think of anything else, John, which a woman wants, besides which all those things count for nothing ? "

The man swallowed twice, and leaned forward, plucking at the arms of the chair. " You mean," he muttered thickly, " that you're in love with another man ? "

" Another is hardly the right word. I've never been in love with you, though, at one time, you might have made me so. But I am in love with a man."

" Who is he ? What is the blackguard's name ? " His voice rose to a shout, and he half rose to his feet.

Grace looked at him unmoved. " Why should you mind, I wonder ? You don't love me yourself : I'm just part of the furniture. You would infinitely sooner read about a new symptom than talk to me."

. " Don't argue," he cried, " don't quibble, damn you. Who is the man ? "

She gave a short laugh. " You're very nearly human to-night, John. It's the only time I've ever seen you behave like a man. But," she went on quietly, " I am not going **to** tell you his name : at least—not at present."

With a stupendous effort Marwood controlled himself and sat back in his chair. " Is it too much to hope," he remarked in his usual voice after a few moments, " that I shall be sufficiently honoured to be told what you propose to do ? "

The girl looked at him thoughtfully. " I haven't

I

made up my mind myself yet," she answered. "The thing has come so suddenly that I don't quite know where I am. In one way, I'm sorry : anything which completely uproots the old familiar landmarks is disturbing. But in another way, John, I'm glad— wonderfully, wonderfully glad." She stared at the fire in silence for a while, and the man watched her covertly. To all appearance he had completely re- covered his self-control : but behind his mask of cynical indifference a volcano of fury and hatred was seething. She had got clean through the joints in his armour : for the first time, in so many words, she had told him that she knew his ill-health was merely a pose. And such was the manner of the man, that it was that fact which now made him boil with rage, far more than the knowledge that she was in love with somebody else. He felt an insane desire to punish her for his failure. . . .

"May I ask," he said at length, "when you made this interesting discovery ? "

"A long, long while ago," she answered quietly. "But it was only this afternoon . . ."

"That things came to a head." Marwood laughed sneeringly. "And then, as befits a dutiful wife, you immediately decided to give your husband the joyful news."

"No. Oh! no, I didn't." She shook her head. "I decided to study you from the new aspect : to try and think of you as a man and not as—well, not as I have thought of you in the past. But it can't be done—not here. Your surroundings are too strong ; you can't break away from them in this house. You had your digestive pill as usual, and I only just averted a discussion on the new symptom. Now, I've got an offer to make to you, John. I want to think of you as a man : I want . . . to give you a fair chance . . . Will you come with me for two months—one month even—to Switzerland, and go in for some winter sports ? Will you make an effort to break away from all this ridiculous twaddle—and live once more, as a man should live ? If you'll do that, and succeed—and I know you will succeed—I'll make you : I promise you that I, on my part, will give up the—the other man. I can't promise that I won't see him again ; but there shall never be anything more between us than there is now—and that is nothing." She turned to her husband . . . " Well ! "

But John Marwood made no answer. He had hardly heard the last part of her words, as with agony unspeakable, the stabbing pain of the afternoon again burned through his body. Rigid, gripping the arms of his chair, he sat staring in front of him, while the torture wracked him and the figure of his wife danced before his eyes.

At last, through clenched teeth he got out two words —" My back." Surely she must see the pain he was in : surely even she must realize that this was no pose, now.

But all Grace Marwood saw was the familar spectacle of her husband giving one of his usual performances.

That was his answer to her offer : and a bitter, contemptuous anger took possession of her.

"So that is your reply, is it ? " she said slowly.
"Another dumb Crambo show. So be it : I will act
accordingly."

Without a second glance at him she turned and left
the room. As she opened the door a gasping cry came
from the man in the chair, but she took no notice :
she had heard those gasping cries before. They were a
very popular piece of business with the actor in
question.

The matter was settled : to-morrow she would go
to tea again with Bryan Daventry ; and then . . .
The sight of the telephone made her pause, and after
a moment's indecision, she took the handle off the
receiver. She would ring him up now, and tell
him.

"Mrs. Marwood speaking . . . Oh ! is that you ?
. . . I'll come to tea to-morrow . . . What . . . now
. . . Oh ! I couldn't ; it's so late . . . " Convention
still pulled, convention would probably have won.
To go to a man's rooms at that hour, even if it was
quite safe . . . And then one of the footmen walked
past her with a bottle of green medicine . . . She
turned to the mouthpiece, her mind made up. "All
right ; in half an hour."

She heard the delighted cry of joy at the other end :
with a faint smile she replaced the receiver.

She paused at the foot of the stairs, as the butler
came out of the dining-room. "Parkins, I want a

taxi in ten minutes." Then with the smile still on her lips she went slowly up to her room.

<h2 style="text-align:center">4</h2>

" Bryan—stop ! " With a breathless little laugh, she pushed him away. " You know you're really a most violent person."

" Do you wonder," he answered, taking off her cloak, " when I actually see you here, in the flesh, in my rooms ? Why, you darling, I simply can't believe it. I'll be waking up in a minute and finding that it's really to-morrow morning, and that you are the elderly charlady, who will infallibly give notice."

He pushed her gently into a huge chair by the fire, and then busied himself getting some forks out of a sideboard.

" I don't want anything to eat, Bryan."

He looked at her with a grave smile. " I don't think, somehow, you've had much dinner to-night. And "—he again busied himself with his preparations —" I have here a bird, a little caviare, and a bottle of Perrier Jouet. If I consume the whole bottle I shall be tight ; if you help me and don't eat—you'll be. *Viola tout.*" He put a finishing touch to the table, and then sat down opposite to her. " Has anything happened ? "

" Not at all unexpected." She gave a short laugh.

" I told him after dinner to-night that I'd fallen in love with someone."

" Ah! You told him that, my dear? Well? "

" I didn't tell him who it was—though he wanted to know."

" Somewhat naturally."

" But he isn't natural, Bryan. That's just the point : there's nothing natural about him." Then, after a little pause : " I made him an offer."

" Yes, dear," His voice was very gentle. " What was it? "

" I told him that if he would come with me to Switzerland for two months, or even one, and take up winter sports—if he'd show himself to be a man and not what he is—I'd give that someone up." She heard his breath come sharply. " I had to, Bryan ; I had to give him the chance."

" And what did he say? "

" He said nothing." She laughed at the recollection. " He decided that that was a suitable moment to give one of his celebrated invalid performances. I'd told him that I'd known for years he was only posing. I suppose he thought it was more important to try and convince me on that point than to bother over such an utterly insignificant thing as my being in love with another man. So I got it all complete—including the shuddering gasp as I opened the door and left him." She paused, her hands locked together on her lap. " It's finished it, Bryan. . . . If he'd gone on raving and cursing as he did to start with, I'd have tried again. I'd have made him come. I'd have given him some chance even if not the one I suggested. But . . . now . . ."

With her breast rising and falling stormily, she stared at the fire, and for a while the man watched her gravely. He could see the whole scene as clearly as if he had been there himself, and as he looked at the girl a great wonder took possession of him that any man could be such an unutterable fool as to refuse her offer.

" So now you've come to me." He rose and sat down on the arm of her chair.

" Yes." She looked up into his face. " Don't you want me ? "

" Want you ? My dear." He bent and kissed the upturned mouth, and for a moment she clung to him.

" You do love me, Bryan—really and truly ? "

" Really and truly," he answered with a little smile. " So much that . . . " He rose abruptly and stood by the fireplace with his back to her. " So much that I'm afraid. You see, I'm only a man, and not a particularly righteous specimen at that."

" Afraid ! What of ? "

He knew she was standing just behind him, and with a sudden gasp he swung round and caught her in his arms.

" I'm afraid because friendship isn't enough, Grace : because you know that it isn't and I know that it isn't. Because I want you immeasurably more than that ; because I want everything you can give me ; because I want you—all of you." He held her at arm's length and stared into the eyes which met his without flinching. " We're neither of us children ; we both of us know exactly what it means. And, my dear, sooner or later, it is the woman who pays. That's what makes me afraid. It's no good hoping that we shall be exceptions to the rule ; everybody has always hoped that, and found they were wrong." Gently he pushed her backwards and forwards, and though his lips were smiling, his eyes were grave and serious. As he had said, they were neither of them children, and he, at any rate, knew exactly where he stood. The trouble is that an exact knowledge of one's proximity to the top of the cliff is not of great value if there's a landslip.

" I ought not to have asked you to come round to-night, my dear," he went on slowly. " But then we don't always do what we ought, little girl . . . not always. And I couldn't help it ; I couldn't help it. When I heard your dear voice at the other end of the line—why, I just went mad." He gave a whimsical laugh, and the girl laughed too.

" Ah ! but did you, my dear ? " she said. " I oved your madness."

" But would you love it, Grace, if it went on ?" he answered soberly. " Would there not come a time when you'd say to me, ' The madness is past ; we must be sane.' And you'd find it was too late ?" His eyes searched her face hungrily, and suddenly he threw back his head and laughed. " What fools we are— what damned fools ! Day after day, night after night, I've imagined this, Grace : thought of it—longed for it. I've seen you sitting in that chair opposite me ; I've held conversations with you. And then I've woken up to reality and done some work." His hands fell to his sides, and he laughed again.

" It is reality, Bryan," said the girl with an adorable smile. " I'm here."

"Do I not know it ? " he cried roughly. He seized her in his arms and rained kisses on her face—mad, passionate kisses that left her gasping and breathless. " That's why I'm such a fool. . . . You're here ; I can see you, touch you. The dream has come true ; and now—I'm afraid."

With a weary little sigh the girl sat down. She felt suddenly tired—tired and hopeless. She knew he was right, and yet . . .

" What are we to do, Bryan ? " Helplessly she appealed to him. " I can't go back to him. It isn't as if he wanted me—he doesn't. He's just utterly selfish. And why should I ? "

" For no reason at all, dear, as far as he's concerned." Even at that moment the complete change of *rôle* appealed to him with cynical humour. " He's absolutely unworthy of the smallest consideration. It's you I'm thinking of . . . "

" But if I'd sooner, Bryan. . . . Surely if I'm prepared to risk it . . . " Her hand was on his arm,

I*

pulling him towards her. " Don't you understand, my dear . . . I—I love you ? "

Blindly he turned towards her and held out his arms. What did it matter ? . . . And at that moment the telephone bell rang.

With a muttered curse, Daventry took off the receiver.

" Speaking. . . . Oh ! it's you, Arbuthnot, is it ? . . . Where from ? " His back was towards the girl, and she did not see the look of amazement which was spreading over his face. She could hear the low metallic voice of the man at the other end, punctuated occasionally by a word or two from Bryan. The speaker seemed to have a lot to say, and idly she wondered who he was . . . Arbuthnot : the name conveyed nothing to her. And then she ceased to bother, and simply lay back, watching the man she loved. What a man he was ; how utterly worth the sacrifice. After all, why should people find out ? Why shouldn't it just be their secret—his and hers ? And perhaps in time she could fix up something— arrange a divorce somehow, and . . .

" Finished your old talk ? " He had put down the receiver, and was standing motionless, still with his back to her. " Then come over here at once—I'm jealous."

After a while he turned round, and with a little cry, the girl rose.

" What is it, Bryan ? What has happened ? "

" How long has your husband had this pain in his

back ? " The question was so completely unexpected that for a moment she could only stare at him speechlessly.

" What do you mean ? " she stammered at length.

" I've just been talking to Doctor Arbuthnot." His voice was devoid of all expression. " He is with your husband now. He tells me that he is suffering from a malignant cancerous growth, and suggests that I am the only man in London who can possibly save his life. He further remarks that it is an admirable opportunity for me to test my new cure."

For what seemed an eternity, there was silence in the room ; then, very slowly, Daventry crossed to the girl. And after a little while he spoke again with a dreadful deliberation.

" I'm going round to see your husband now. Isn't it damned funny ? "

5

In the hall below Grace Marwood waited while Daventry made his examination. She felt dazed and a little stunned by the suddenness of it all ; barely conscious of the presence of the servants who seemed to be ceaselessly going up and down the stairs to her husband's room on different errands. So preoccupied had she been with her thoughts that she had almost forgotten to play her necessary *rôle* of ignorance as Dr. Arbuthnot told her the dreadful news.

" I have telephoned for Doctor Daventry," he murmured. " A specialist, Mrs. Marwood . . . young, but extraordinarily brilliant. Should be here at any moment. . . . Until then, perhaps, it would be better if you did not see your husband. It might upset him, you know. Why not have a glass of wine and a biscuit ? "

At length the worthy doctor had left her alone, only to return in a few minutes and introduce Bryan Daventry. The solemn introduction had seemed in keeping with everything ; she had felt a wild desire to scream with laughter, and only Bryan's quiet, steady eyes had pulled her together. Then the two men had left her alone and gone upstairs to her husband . . .

She glanced at her wrist-watch impatiently. Half an hour. Surely they could have found out in half an hour. Cancer . . . John with cancer . . . John really ill, in agonizing pain. It was impossible—all imagination, as usual. Arbuthnot was an old fool. . . . But why half an hour if it was only imagination ? Bryan wouldn't take half an hour diagnosing a case of imagination. . . . He was far too clever to be deceived, and once he knew, he was far too straightforward not to say what he thought. . . . If it was imagination that is . . . If not . . .

Ah ! if not, what then ? It altered everything at once. John with one of his countless little aches

and pains was one thing ; John with cancer was quite
another. Dimly she tried to realize what it would
mean—how it would affect her life, but her brain
would not respond. It seemed to be whirling in a
series of vicious circles, with a jeering fate grinning at
her through the centre of each.

" You thought to escape, did you ? " it mocked.
" You thought you could take matters into your own
hands ? Well, let's see what you make of this card
I've just dealt you."

Cancer ! And suddenly Grace Marwood passed
her hand over her forehead with a little cry. After
all, he was her husband, and for the last half-hour her
thoughts had principally centred on what this
thing would mean to her—not on what it would mean
to him. . . .

She looked up as a door above opened, and her heart
began to beat a little faster. They had decided—she
could hear their low voices—and in a moment or two
she would be told, one way or the other. Slowly
the two doctors came down the stairs, and crossed the
hall towards her, while she peered at Bryan's
inscrutable face, trying to read what was in his mind.

" Well ! " Her dry lips traced the word rather than
spoke it, and Bryan Daventry pulled forward a chair
for her.

" Sit down, Mrs. Marwood." For a moment their
eyes met ; then he looked away again quickly. " I
am afraid that what Doctor Arbuthnot feared is
quite correct." His voice was very quiet, and he

kept his face half averted from the woman he loved. " Your husband is undoubtedly suffering from a cancerous growth ; though it will be necessary for me to make another examination to-morrow."

" Is he in great pain ? " she whispered.

" Very great, while it lasts ; but it is intermittent," answered Daventry.

" And what—what are you going to do ? " She was still staring at Bryan, but it was Doctor Arbuthnot who answered.

" You probably don't know, Mrs. Marwood," he murmured, " that Doctor Daventry has recently been engaged in the most exhaustive research work into this very disease. And it will be necessary for you and your husband to come to a decision." He glanced inquiringly at Daventry, who remained motionless, staring at the fire. After a slight pause, he turned back to Mrs. Marwood. " A decision, my dear lady, and a grave decision. As you probably are aware, science up-to-date has produced no certain cure for cancer. The growth can be removed with a knife, but in practically all cases it returns again. I may say in all cases when it has gone so far as I fear is the case with your husband. Consequently, speaking humanly, you have your first alternative for certain. An operation ; the gradual return of the growth ; a further operation. And finally the time when another operation is of no avail."

" And what is the second alternative ? " Her words seemed to come from a great distance as she asked the question to which she already knew the answer.

Doctor Arbuthnot cleared his throat, and again glanced at Daventry. " The second alternative is this. Doctor Daventry in his research work believes that he has discovered a cure for this dreadful disease, which will prevent its return in the course of a few years. In other words, he believes that one operation by his process would be sufficient. But the process has not yet been put to the test of time. It may be that he is wrong, that the growth will return. . . . "

" In which case my husband would be no worse off than under the first alternative," said Grace Marwood, still in the same detached voice. She felt as if she was acting in a play.

" Yes, but there is another thing," began Doctor Arbuthnot, slowly rubbing his hands together. " Perhaps Dr. Daventry——"

At the direct request, Bryan Daventry swung round, and stared at the woman.

" The other thing, Mrs. Marwood, is this. By my method your husband might die at once." Arbuthnot had turned away and was studying an old print on the wall ; for the moment he was forgotten. " He might die at once," repeated Daventry slowly.

" That is the second alternative. . . . "

Her breath coming quickly, her knuckles gleaming white on the arms of her chair, Grace Marwood stared at Bryan's face. It was the sort of situation which happened in books—impossibly unreal—grotesquely

absurd. And once again the feeling that she was
acting in some dreadful play came over her. Bryan's
eyes were still fixed on her ; the ticking of the hall
clock sounded incredibly loud.

" He might die at once," she repeated foolishly.
" Perhaps it would be better—I mean——" she added
hurriedly as she saw him stiffen and grow rigid—" I
mean even that would be better than years of horrible
suffering."

But still she stared at him fascinated, and he stared
back, while the worthy Doctor Arbuthnot passed on
to another print.

" Supposing my operation was successful," Bryan
Daventry was speaking again—speaking mechanically,
" your husband would require the most constant
and unremitting attention for many years to
come. He would have to leave England and live in
a warmer, drier climate . . . the South of France,
perhaps, or some place like that. He would, in fact,
be an invalid, and an invalid in reality," he added as
an afterthought.

She glanced at Doctor Arbuthnot—he was at the
other end of the hall—then she stood up suddenly.

" Bryan," she whispered. " Bryan, what does it
mean—to me—to you and I ? "

" It means," he answered slowly, " the most devilish
temptation that a human being can well be subjected
to. Because—Grace," and for a moment his hand
gripped her arm, " no one *can* ever find out."

" Well, have you explained everything to Mrs.

Marwood ? " Bryan's hand dropped to his side as Arbuthnot approached. " It is a risk, of course, my dear young lady," continued the doctor, swinging his pince-nez between his fingers, " a great risk. But as an old practitioner, who has been forced in the course of many years to see much of the dreadful agony which goes with this hideous scourge, I would venture to suggest to you that the risk is worth while. To see a dearly loved one in the throes of the most fearful pain, to realize that no medical skill can alleviate that pain, is a very terrible thing. And that, Mrs. Marwood, is what it must come to under the old methods—my methods. Doctor Daventry is of the younger school, and, in medicine as in other things, youth will be served. Anything, anything is better than the future which I can offer your husband—even death at once." He paused, and laid a kindly hand on her arm.

" Then it is your advice, Doctor Arbuthnot," she said steadily, " that my husband should put himself in Doctor Daventry's hands ? "

" Yes," answered the old doctor gravely. " That is my advice."

" I will tell him what you say." Her voice came still steady, but her eyes avoided Bryan Daventry. " Shall I go to him now ? "

" Certainly. But don't over-excite him. Daventry and I will come round again to-morrow."

With a slight inclination of her head, she left the two men and passed up the stairs. And it was as they heard the door of John Marwood's room open and close that Arbuthnot turned to his companion.

" A fine girl," he remarked. " And a dreadful tragedy. But, my young friend—it's *your* chance."

" Precisely," murmured Daventry. " Precisely. It's my chance. Shall we say eleven o'clock to-morrow morning for our further examination ? "

6

Her husband was propped up in bed as Grace entered his room. For a moment she stayed close to the door, watching his profile ; then she crossed to his side and stood looking down at him.

" Have they told you ? " He opened his eyes as he spoke.

" Yes, John. . . . I'm sorry." Even as she said it the pitiful inadequacy of the words mocked her.

" You are more than kind," he murmured. " I trust that my trifling ailment has not interfered in any way with your plans this evening—or curtailed your enjoyment."

His wife bit her lip and turned away. It was going to be hard ; everything had always been hard with John. He seemed to take a delight in making it so. But in that one brief look at his face before he had spoken the die had been cast, the decision made. She hardly realized it herself yet ; the events of the past two hours were still too fresh. But one thing she did realize with an awful horror, which left her tongue-tied—for a time downstairs she had actually contemplated—murder. Not exactly that, of course. Not murder, but an accident . . . one of the alternatives. . . . And Bryan had contemplated it too. She, an ordinary normal woman ; and—murder.

She shuddered a little, and as quickly as possible, so as not to disturb him, she put some coal on the fire. Murder. . . . The word danced at her out of the flames. . . . Murder. To kill her husband, or to connive at his death, so that she might be free to marry the murderer. She shuddered again, then she rose and stood at the foot of the bed. Thank God ! the madness was past ; the only possible course was plain to see. Whatever was best for her husband must be done ; if necessary, another opinion must be taken, and . . .

" Have they told you the alternatives ? " John Marwood's harsh voice broke in upon her train of thought.

" Yes, John," she answered gently. " They told me just before I came up."

" And can you detach your thoughts sufficiently from the fortunate man who has obtained your affection to give your opinion on them ? " He closed his eyes wearily and lay back on his pillows.

" I want you to understand one thing quite clearly," returned his wife, still in the same gentle voice. " The fact that you have cancer completely alters everything. Had I known earlier in the evening I should never have

spoken to you about it. . . . As it is, I want you to
try and forget what I said, if you can. It was—oh !
I was irritated, because I thought you were shamming."

The man laughed—a little malevolent laugh.
" What a dreadful shock it must have been to you
when you found I wasn't. But whatever the cause,
my dear Grace, of your interesting confession, the
fact remains that you have confessed. And it is a
source of great grief to me that we shall apparently
have to leave London and go and live abroad for some
years. It is dreadful to think of you being parted
from him." He raised a feebly protesting hand.
" Would it be asking too much of you not to shake the
bed ? "

" You propose, then, to let Doctor Daventry try
his new cure ? " she asked slowly.

" That is my intention at present," returned her
husband. " What do you think about it ? "

For a moment she hesitated ; then : " I think we
ought to get another opinion."

" May I ask why ? I am fairly well conversant with
the subject of cancer, and what that fool Arbuthnot
says is quite correct. There is no cure known for it at
present, and to continue suffering this agony for the
rest of one's life is not an alluring picture. Whereas
Daventry—if he is successful—will cure me of the
pain, though still leaving me an invalid for some
years."

" I quite understand the attraction of the idea,"
Grace could not forbear the thrust. " But there's

another thing, John. Doctor Daventry's cure may do as you say, but it may prove—fatal, almost at once."

He raised himself on one elbow, and his face went white. " He told me there was very little fear of that, and, Grace "—the man's voice was trembling— " he said that he had every hope that it would prove successful. . . . Why—why—you see, it will be his first case, and it's very important to him that it should prove a cure. So he's bound to take extra care, isn't he ? I mean . . . " His voice tailed off, and he sank back, frightened and shaking.

She watched him contemptuously. What a miserable specimen he was. And then a wave of pity came over her. After all, cancer might make anyone a coward.

" I'm sure he'll be successful," she said reassuringly. " He told me this afternoon that he felt absolutely confident that he'd discovered the cure."

It was out before she had realized what she was saying. Had he noticed it ? Had he noticed the slip ? Why, oh, why had she not said this evening ? She had only meant to comfort him, cheer him up— and, without thinking, if he put two and two together, she had told him the name of the man she loved.

The shaking of his hand had ceased ; he was staring at her from his pillows intently.

" You met Doctor Daventry this afternoon ? " he asked slowly.

" I did ; full of his new discovery." Her tone was light, a shade too light ; and suddenly John Marwood laughed.

" How interesting," he murmured. " How very interesting. And where did you meet Doctor Daventry ? "

" At tea." She had recovered herself ; at all costs she must rid his mind of this suspicion. " Lady Grantley had quite a crowd."

But the suspicions of a suspicious nature are not allayed so easily, and though John Marwood said no more, she was conscious during the remaining two minutes she stayed with him that he was watching her covertly the whole time. Bryan's name was not mentioned again—nor was her meeting with him alluded to ; but as she bent over her husband and kissed him—a thing she had not done for months, and which he suffered resignedly—her uneasiness returned in full force. She felt instinctively that he knew. Then when she reached her own room she felt inclined to laugh at her fears. After all, why on earth should he put such a construction on her words ? It might be as well, however, to warn Bryan when she saw him to-morrow. . . . John had a habit of asking disconcerting questions.

He had, and he had no intention of waiting till the next day to do so. He waited just long enough to hear his wife's door close ; then he reached out a languid hand and picked up the telephone by his bed. With many moans and expressions of pain, which he

periodically indulged in even when alone, he rang up
Lady Grantley's house.

" It is Mr. Marwood speaking," he said to the
butler who answered him. " Did Mrs. Marwood
leave her vanity bag behind to-day when she had tea
with her ladyship ? She did not have tea, you say ?
Really. I must have misunderstood Doctor Daventry.
He told me he thought he'd seen it there. What ?
Doctor Daventry was not there either ? Oh, my
mistake. Sorry to have disturbed you."

He replaced the telephone, and lay back on his
pillows. So it was Daventry, after all, was it ? And
they thought themselves damned clever, did they ?
And they didn't see that they'd played right into his
hands ? Oh, no. They couldn't see that they'd
given him a weapon which made him safe . . . Safe
. . . And if by any chance any accident did occur. . . .
He chuckled horribly, almost resigned to such a thing
happening, so wonderful was his dream of revenge.
Only he must catch them red-handed, must have an
absolute certainty to go on. Nothing less than that
would be sufficient.

And as he lay gloating in anticipation, suddenly
the pain began again. Stab—stab—stab ; the red-
hot skewers ran through him, while he writhed and
moaned, biting at the sheets in his agony.

It was half an hour later that the impassive footman,
whom he hated, found him whimpering like a little
child.

" Your medicine, sir," he remarked, supremely

unconcerned at the spectacle. "Also the washing
bill you wished to see. And I feel sure you will be
glad to hear that the kitchen clock has been put right."

Without another glance at the figure in the bed, he
left the room, closing the door noiselessly. And it
was only as he stood in the passage outside that his
face became convulsed with a dreadful fury. But in
a moment it had gone; it was just the deferential,
well-drilled man-servant who joined the rest of the
staff in the servants' hall.

"Your call, Simpson," said his partner, lighting a
cigarette from the stump of an old one.

The impassive footman glanced at his cards. "I
go one heart," he remarked quietly.

"'Ow's the old swine to-night?" demanded
another player.

"Mr. Marwood seems much as usual," returned
Simpson. "One heart it is. You go down, partner."

The man who had asked the question snorted, but
he said nothing more. They often used to remark
on the fact in the servants' hall that Simpson seemed
different—somehow.

"Keeps 'isself to 'isself," as the cook had summed
it up on one occasion. And so it had been allowed
to remain.

7

It was at half-past eleven the following morning
that Doctor Arbuthnot descended the stairs in search

of Grace Marwood. Daventry was still with her husband in his room, though the further examination had been finished some quarter of an hour previously.

"I must be going, Mrs. Marwood." The old doctor patted her hand and smiled. "Between ourselves I wasn't really wanted at all this morning. Merely professional etiquette——"

"And what have you finally decided, Doctor Arbuthnot ? "

"To let Doctor Daventry operate. Your husband won't hear of anything else. Seems more cheerful this morning." He smiled at her, and once more patted her hand. "You must keep him like that, my dear young lady. Keep him cheerful and smiling. . . . Worth ten years of life to smile. . . . Well, I must be off. Daventry will tell you everything when he comes down."

The worthy man bustled away, leaving Grace in a thoughtful mood. It wasn't like John to be cheerful : since she'd known him he never had been. And, like an idiot, she had forgotten to mention anything about Lady Grantley to Bryan before he went up to her husband. For a moment or two she thought of going upstairs and interrupting them ; then it struck her that seeing her in the room with Bryan might recall suspicions to her husband's mind. That for a while he had suspected, she was positive ; but ever since she had left his room the preceding night she had been endeavouring, more or less successfully, to persuade herself that she had reassured his mind. And that morning, when she had gone in to see him, he had certainly seemed quite pleasant and normal— as far, that is, as John Marwood ever succeeded in being anything of the sort. He had restrained his paroxysm of silent laughter till the door had closed behind her. . . .

She looked up as a step sounded in the passage above, and the next moment Bryan Daventry was coming towards her down the stairs.

" Has Arbuthnot gone ? " He stood in front of her, looking into her eyes.

" Yes." She nodded gravely. " He said you would tell me everything. Will you come in here ? "

In silence he followed her into the sitting-room and closed the door ; then in silence he stood by the mantelpiece looking down at her.

" Bryan," she said abruptly, " I was mad last night."

" So was I. May I smoke ? "

" Of course. Do you realize, Bryan, that for a moment—I played with the idea of—of murder ? "

" So did I." He gave a short, hard laugh. " I played with it—or, rather, it played with me—all through the night."

" And now ? " She breathed the question half fearfully.

" Why now, my dear, your charming husband will have the pleasure of being my first case. And everything which medical skill and careful nursing can perform, will be devoted to prolonging his damned life, and restoring him to perfect health."

He laughed again, harshly and bitterly. "It's not entirely altruism, Grace ; I don't flatter myself on that point. But there are things one can't do, I suppose. And to put it on the lowest and most selfish motive, such a foundation for our life together—afterwards— would not prove a source of abiding happiness." He took a few steps up and down the room, while the woman watched him from her chair by the fire.

"Tell me, Bryan : did he ask you anything about Lady Grantley this morning ? "

He stopped in his walk. "Lady Grantley ! " he echoed in surprise. "No. Why on earth should he ? I hardly know the woman."

Grace Marwood gave a sigh of relief. "Thank Heavens ! But don't forget if by any chance he should, you had tea there yesterday. . . . And we discussed your new cure for cancer."

Briefly she told him of her slip the night before, and he nodded comprehendingly.

"I've got it, dear," he said, as she finished. "With a nature like this, you've got to be mighty careful. Though I must say he seemed positively genial this morning." He took a few steps forward and stood by her chair, while his fingers played absently with her hair. "Oh ! Grace, my darling," he whispered, "what a dirty trick of Fate. What a dirty trick."

Swiftly he bent and kissed her neck, where the little

soft tendrils of hair left the smooth whiteness of her skin, and she shivered under his touch.

" Will it really mean the South of France, Bryan ? " she asked slowly.

" Yes, darling."   His voice was grave.   " Or some warm spot like that."

" And shall I never see you ? "

His hands clenched by his side, and the veins stood out on his forehead.

" My God ! " he muttered ; " you must see me. I can't imagine life with you blotted out completely. I shall come over and see how he's getting on, every now and then—and touch your hand, Grace, and hear your voice and look into your eyes. And then I shall come back again to blankness and work ; while you stay out there with blankness and him. . . . A real pukka invalid at last. . . . The goal obtained. . . . Ordered to be one by a live doctor. . . . Why, the blighter is gloating over the prospect already."

For a while they fell silent, staring at the fire ; then very gently she took one of his hands in her own.

" You must write to me, Bryan ; tell me how things go with you. I couldn't go on without that."

" Write."   He echoed the word scornfully.   " Write. Oh, yes ! I'll write. Send you bits of paper with letters and words scrawled on them. . . . A wonderful substitute for you—the flesh and blood of you—your whole glorious body. What's the good of a letter when there's nothing else to follow—except another letter, and then another ? "

Abruptly he dropped her hand, and strode to the window, where he stood with his back to her, staring across the street outside. Faintly the roar of distant Piccadilly came into the quiet room ; the monotonous, deadening sound which forms the eternal accompaniment to London's comedies and tragedies. The human units may laugh or cry, may be born to strut their allotted span and disappear unnoticed whence they came, but the buses still run past Hyde Park Corner. . . .

" I think I'll go, Grace." Slowly he turned and faced her. " I'm not very sure of myself to-day. The operation will take place to-morrow, here. I'll make all the necessary arrangements about nurses, and Arbuthnot will give the anæsthetic. Only light food for dinner to-night, and nothing to-morrow morning."

" Very well." A little pale, but quite composed, she rose as he spoke. " There's only one thing, Bryan, I want you to know. Out of the madness last night has come sanity, but the possible alternative still remains. You have said so yourself—before we knew anything about John. Should he die, I shall know that you did everything in your power to make the operation a success. You understand that."

" He mustn't die ; he won't die." Roughly he took her in his arms. " Don't you see, Grace. I daren't let him die—I daren't."

" But you're only human, Bryan."

" I don't care—I may be. But John Marwood
—*must* not die. . . . Not after what we've—said, and
thought. . . ."

For a while he held her at arm's length, devouring
her hungrily with his eyes ; then with a smothered
cry he drew her to him, and covered her face with
kisses. " My darling," he whispered again and again
—" My darling."

And at that moment the door opened and John
Marwood entered.

" A most entertaining spectacle," he murmured.
" Would it be indiscreet to ask if this is your normal
method of procedure, Doctor Daventry ? "

He was clad in his dressing-gown and as he closed
the door with ostentatious deliberation, Bryan
Daventry had a fleeting glimpse of a dark, impassive
face peering over Marwood's shoulder from the hall
beyond. It was the footman who had been at hand
during his examination that morning, and in that
one brief second, before the door closed, the thing
which dominated his mind was not the master, but
the man. For there was a strange, inscrutable look
on the footman's face—a look of mingled mockery
and scorn. And it seemed to Daventry that the
object of the look was not himself, but the malevolent
hobbling figure in the dressing-gown.

" I repeat, Dr. Daventry," gasped the harsh voice,
as the sick man sank into a chair, " is this your usual
method of conducting your cases ? "

With a slight frown the young doctor thrust his

hands into his pockets and stared at his patient ; the situation was undeniably awkward.

" No, Mr. Marwood," he remarked at length, " it is not my usual procedure."

" Indeed," murmured the other. " Most gratifying ! Then might I be permitted to ask why am I thus honoured ? "

Daventry glanced at Grace ; she was staring at the fire, one foot tapping ceaselessly on the fender. Then with a slight shrug of his shoulders, he turned back to Marwood.

" The reason, I should imagine, is fairly clear," he remarked gravely. " I love your wife."

" How kind of you." Marwood gave a grating chuckle. " And judging by the—shall we say— amorous position I found you in, one might almost be led to suppose that my wife loves you ? "

His cold eyes searched his wife's face, and after a moment she nodded.

" I told you yesterday, John," she said quietly, " that I was in love with a man."

" Only neglecting to mention his name," he returned. " But I may say this has hardly come as a surprise after what I found out last night. After your departure my dear Grace, I took the precaution of ringing up Lady Grantley. And, to my horror and surprise, I found that not only had you not been to tea there yesterday, but that Doctor Daventry as well had not honoured her with his presence. Wherefore, by a process of inductive reasoning, partially interrupted by a bout of intense agony, I came to the conclusion that you had lied to me. Why lie on such a matter, unless there is something to conceal? And then, remembering our interesting and harmonious chat after dinner, I put two and two together. One is glad to have such indisputable confirmation that the answer is true."

Hunched up and malignant, John Marwood sat in his chair, while his venomous eyes rested first on the doctor and then on his wife.

" You neither of you seem very loquacious," he snarled.

" You seem to be supplying that end of the business," said Daventry calmly.

" Don't talk to me like that, damn you," shrieked the other, his voice shaking with rage. " Have you got no shame whatever, you scoundrel, coming into a man's house and making love to his wife, when he is at death's door upstairs."

" If you don't stop exciting yourself, you'll have another bout of pain," said the doctor, still in the same calm voice, and the threat had the desired effect.

With a great effort John Marwood controlled himself, though the seething volcano of hatred in his mind still showed on his face.

" If I did, it would probably afford you endless amusement," he sneered.

" Endless," agreed Daventry. " And now, in view of what has occurred, it might be as well to come to the point. As a form of entertainment, this conversation bores me. I have told you I love your wife ; she has told you she loves me. But I wish you to understand quite clearly, Mr. Marwood, that there has never been anything more between us than what you saw to-day."

The invalid gave a grating laugh, but Daventry continued unmoved. " In one way, I am glad you found out ; it absolves me at once from the necessity of operating on you. I therefore throw up the case, and either you or I can invent some good reason to palm off on Doctor Arbuthnot."

He paused, fascinated against his will by the hideous silent laughter of the man in the chair.

" So you intend to throw up the case, Doctor Daventry, do you ? " chuckled the other. " Refuse to operate, do you ? "

" Somewhat naturally, I assume that you would prefer I did not," replied Daventry slowly. " And anyway, I would prefer not to."

" Do you count ? " asked John Marwood suavely. " Do your wishes matter vastly ? "

" They matter everything, Mr. Marwood," snapped the doctor. " On every ground I throw up the case and refuse to operate."

" Then, Doctor Daventry," said the other slowly, " I shall institute divorce proceedings against you forthwith. There's no good laughing, because neither you nor my wife will find it a laughing matter. I don't say that I should get my divorce, but—well,

K

you won't forget, will you, that I took the precaution of having a witness this morning. And I don't think it would do you much good professionally, Doctor Daventry ; and I don't think it would do my wife much good socially, Doctor Daventry. In fact," his voice rose to a hoarse snarl, " I'll drag you both in the mud, and then I'll laugh at you."

" You won't laugh for long, Mr. Marwood," answered Daventry, his face a little white. " You'll be dead."

" I'll laugh long enough to see you hounded out of your profession. I'll laugh long enough to see everybody's door closed against my wife."

" You inhuman devil," said Daventry slowly. " Your mind is more diseased than your body."

" Perhaps it is," sneered the other. " At any rate, I don't go round to other men's houses professionally, and then seduce their wives." For a second he cowered back as if afraid Daventry would strike him ; then, a little more calmly, he continued. " So you had better decide—and decide at once. Either you operate to-morrow, or the world will have another tit-bit of scandal to digest over its meals."

With his hands still in his pockets, Bryan Daventry walked over to the window. Once more the roar of the traffic came plainly to his ears—a contrast to the dead silence of the room behind. He heard the sudden rustle of Grace's dress as she moved, then absently he stared at a man opposite who was busy polishing the outside of a window. He was sitting on the ledge in one of the wooden flower stands beloved of London houses, and the doctor idly wondered what would happen if the outside gave way. The earth would fall on to the pavement, but would the man? And if he did, would he still continue to whistle that damned tune from the Alhambra?

"Why are you so anxious that I should operate, Mr. Marwood, in view of what you know?" His voice sounded singularly lifeless to his ears.

"Because I consider you are the best man for the purpose."

Once again there was silence in the room. The window polisher was standing up to his work now, and two errand boys were staring at him enraptured.

"I suppose you have remembered what I told you," continued Daventry, "that there is a chance of my cure proving fatal?"

"I hope not, Doctor Daventry, for both our sakes—and my wife's." The voice was soft and menacing, and Daventry swung round on his heel.

"What do you mean?" he said quickly.

"Why," murmured the other, "I merely alluded to a very natural precaution on my part. Should anything happen to me—which, in the hands of a man of your skill, I do not anticipate for a moment—I shall leave a letter to be opened at my death. I shall, of course, make no accusation in it; I shall merely state—with the witness's signature attached—what I happened unfortunately to see this morning. And if people are uncharitable enough to draw their own conclusions——"

" Stop ! " thundered the doctor. " That settles it.   Under no circumstances whatever will I undertake the operation under such conditions."

" Really."   John Marwood smiled gently.   " Then I will tell my lawyers to institute proceedings at once."

" But, John, think."   For the first time Grace Marwood intervened, and her husband with studied politeness listened to her.   " Such a bargain is wicked —unfair.   It's a new cure—untried ;   and Doctor Daventry told you last night that there was the chance of its proving fatal.   The bare chance . . . against absolute recovery.   You can't—you simply can't— make such a condition."

" Nevertheless, I do.   Doctor Daventry need not accept it unless he wishes."

" In other words," said Bryan in a hard voice, " it's heads I win, tails you lose, Mr. Marwood."

" More or less, more or less," agreed Marwood. " With one slight modification.   In the happy event of the operation being brilliantly successful, we both win, my dear Daventry—in fact, we all three win. I become completely cured ;   you lay the foundation of a still more brilliant reputation ;   Grace continues her social career in complete safety.   It is," he murmured, " a form of insurance to produce, if possible, additional   care—when   under   the   anæsthetic. Accidents will happen—and they mustn't—not this time." His cold eyes fixed themselves on the young doctor. " You see, I am in a very difficult position. The one man who would benefit most by my death is the one man in whose hands I must place my life. Do you blame me for taking—er—precautions ? "

For a long while Daventry stared at him in silence, and if John Marwood had expected a furious outburst at his insult he was disappointed. For Daventry's thoughts were not in the room ; they were centred round a fantastic, ghastly, mental struggle waged through the sleepless hours of the past night. And it seemed to him that a Fate—inexorable but just—had confronted him. It was retribution, and only the success of his skill could wipe out his sin. The challenge was thrown down ; so be it ; he would accept the challenge. He could not do less.

" Very well, Mr. Marwood," he answered slowly. " I agree. I will operate to-morrow as I arranged."

Without another word he left the room, and as he closed the door, his patient's harsh, grating chuckle came to his ears.

" Your coat, sir."

He turned to find the impassive footman holding his overcoat in readiness.

" Might I ask if you are operating to-morrow, sir ? "

" I am," said Daventry briefly.

" I trust you will be successful, sir."

Bryan Daventry looked at him quickly, and for a moment the eyes of the two men met. And behind the footman's steady glance there lurked the ghost of a smile.

8

To say that John Marwood felt pleased with himself would be totally inadequate. For the remainder of the day he literally hugged his cleverness to his bosom ; he turned it over and over in his mind ; he reviewed it from every conceivable angle. To have combined a subtle revenge with the maximum chance of his own complete cure struck him as being the work of a genius. The fools ! The treacherous fools ! And when the operation had proved successful, he wouldn't give them away publicly—that would finish things far too quickly. He'd just hold his knowledge over their heads, and every now and then he'd give the wheel another little turn so as to keep them on the rack. He even thought out a few of the remarks he could say to his wife, as he sat in his invalid chair on the sunny promenade at Nice or Cannes ; biting, sarcastic little sneers which would make her writhe . . . And at intervals her lover would come out to examine him, and he could watch the two of them together as a cat watches a mouse—gloatingly. Because he'd got them ; *got them ;* GOT THEM ; and as he realized it he shook both his fists in the air, and the sweat glistened on his forehead with the strength of his passion.

A faint twinge of pain sobered him down ; he must

be careful—just at present—not to excite himself. Afterwards it would be different—after he was cured. But until then he wanted no return of that vile agony. Besides, there was one more thing that had to be done before the operation took place—in case anything should happen. He refused to allow himself to consider it as anything but the barest possibility—everybody said Daventry was the most brilliant of the younger surgeons—but just in case of accidents it had to be done. Besides, in every way it was the most subtle touch in his whole scheme, and from the artistic point of view it was inconceivable that it should be omitted. He'd have to get that impassive brute of a footman to do his share of it, so tact would be necessary. It was a pity he hadn't always been quite so polite to him as he might have been.

For a quarter of an hour the silence of the room was only broken by the scratching of a pen on paper. The first effort he tore up in disgust—it failed in pungency ; but the second proved more satisfactory, and when he had read it through and digested it, he rang the bell by his side.

" Ah, Simpson," he said as the door opened, " I am sorry to have to disturb you at this unusual hour, but the circumstances are peculiar."

The footman's eyebrows went up at such an unheard-of speech, and his shoulders shook slightly. Then, with exactly the right touch of deference, he stepped to the side of the bed. " Not at all, sir," he murmured. " What can I do for you ? "

" It's a terrible thing, Simpson," continued Marwood in a low, sad voice, " to have to discuss with anyone ; but it is made easier in your case, because you saw the occurrence. I allude—to what happened—this morning. What we both of us saw when—when I went into the sitting-room downstairs."

" A most regrettable incident, sir," said Simpson sympathetically.

" One finds it difficult to know what to do," remarked Marwood, staring at the fire. " Very difficult. I am an invalid and, of course, Mrs. Marwood is young ; but still——" He sighed heavily.

" Such an incident should not go unpunished, sir," returned Simpson firmly.

" I agree, Simpson ; I agree." Apparently the fool was going to be easy. " But what can I do ? My hands are tied. They made a bargain with me— me, a man with cancer. Unless I consented to their— acquaintance continuing, Doctor Daventry refused to operate. And he's the only man in London who can cure me. Simpson, I am powerless in his hands."

For a moment the footman seemed to have some difficulty in speaking. Then—" Monstrous, sir," he murmured. " Atrocious."

" Unless I condone their sin, he leaves me to a lingering death of agony. What can I do ? " Weakly he stretched out his hands. " And what is worse, Simpson, is that there is a chance of the cure proving fatal ; as you may know, it's a new and untried one. Supposing it did prove fatal—and it is so easy for a

mistake to occur in such matters." He looked mean-
ingly at the footman, who inclined his head slowly.

" Undoubtedly, sir," he remarked. " It is a very
awkward position for you to be in."

" No one to turn to—not a soul," said John Marwood,
piteously. " Deserted even by my wife. It's not
fair, is it ? Not a square deal. And so I've written
a letter, Simpson, which I want you to witness ; and
I shall send it to my lawyer to be opened in the event
of my death." He glanced covertly at the man
standing beside him, but his face was expressionless.
" You don't mind doing that for me, do you ? "

" Far from it, sir. I shall be delighted."

And John Marwood's fists clenched ecstatically
under the bedclothes.

" I'll read you what I've written, Simpson," he
continued after a moment. " It's not very long :

'I, John Marwood, suffering from cancer, from which terrible
malady I am to be operated on to-morrow morning by Doctor
Bryan Daventry, who will carry out his new cure for the first time,
write these words, which will only be revealed in the event of my
death. On going downstairs this morning, I discovered my wife,
Grace Marwood, in the arms of Bryan Daventry, who had just
concluded a professional visit to the house. They admitted their
love for one another, and openly boasted to me of their misconduct
in the past. Further, Doctor Daventry threatened to throw up the
case and refuse to operate unless I condoned their guilty relations
in the future—thereby condemning me to a lingering death or a
shameful alternative. But more was to come. There is in his new
cure, he admits, the possibility of a fatal result almost at once ;
from the expression on his face as he said it, I read the sinister
intention at the back of his mind. I believe the operation will
prove fatal—*in my case.*
    K*

' And so, standing, as I fear, at the threshold of eternity, I put these facts on paper, for people to draw their own conclusions.

' JOHN MARWOOD.' "

He glanced at the man beside him, but the footman's face was as impassive as ever ; then he looked back at the paper in his hand.

" Under that, Simpson, I have added the following, which, if you will, and if you think it just, I will ask you to sign :

" ' I '—let me see, what is your Christian name ?— ' Charles,' you say—' I, Charles Simpson, footman in the employ of John Marwood, Esq., hereby state that on the morning of November 25th, 1919, I saw Grace Marwood in the arms of Doctor Daventry, who had just concluded a professional visit to my employer.' "

" If you will sign that, Simpson, I will write a covering letter to my lawyer, and then seal up that statement."

" Certainly, sir," answered Simpson. " A very just accusation."

And John Marwood might not have permitted himself the luxury of a sardonic smile had he seen the look on the footman's face as he signed. But since his back was turned away from the bed, his employer could hardly have been expected to.

" Thank you, Simpson." He glanced at the signature, and then, just before he folded the paper up, he glanced at it again.

" Your writing seems vaguely familiar to me," he

remarked jovially. " And very good writing it is too. Well, there it is—with the covering letter. Will you post it for me this afternoon, Simpson ? "

" Certainly, sir. Is there anything else you require, sir ? "

" No, thank you. Oh! except one thing. Forty-eight, you said, I think. You're wrong, Simpson ; sixty in future."

" I thank you, sir," murmured the footman from the door.

He went out, closing it without a sound. And it was only as he got to the top of the stairs that he paused and listened. For the bed in John Marwood's room was shaking as a bed will shake if the occupant is convulsed with laughter.

9

It was in the same sitting-room in which the hideous bargain had been made the previous day that Grace Marwood waited for the result of the operation. Since Bryan had left the morning before she had only seen her husband once, and then only for a few minutes, with a nurse present the whole time.

She had remained in her own room, shunning the servants as far as possible. That the whole household knew by now she was fully aware—especially as she had never particularly liked Simpson. But as the day passed by she came to the conclusion that they must be a particularly good brand. Keenly alert though she was for the faintest trace of veiled insolence, she could detect nothing. Her maid was a little more solicitous for her comfort, perhaps, but otherwise absolutely as usual; Parkins, the butler; Mrs. Johnson, the cook—in none of them could she see the slightest difference. And after a while she ceased to worry; what did such a trifle as the opinions of servants matter compared to the other things at stake?

Whatever happened, the future seemed to hold no hope. At best—or was it at worst?—a vista of dreary years tied to a professional invalid who knew her secret and who could be trusted to remind her of the fact every day. And if not that—she drew a deep breath— if her husband did die! What then? For Bryan, professional ruin—or, at the very least, the rest of his life spent under a cloud of ominous blackness. For herself—social ruin.

Almost she wished that he had stuck to his original refusal; at any rate, that would have settled the matter definitely. And there could have been no suspicion then of the far more dreadful accusation which, however unfounded, would be bound to get about, if—there was a fatal result. Resolutely she refused to think of it; Bryan, with his genius, would succeed—must succeed.

She had had one glimpse of him as he passed through the hall an hour ago, and he had seemed to her like a man in a dream. Doctor Arbuthnot had been with him, and another doctor who, she gathered, had come

more or less as a spectator. And then the door upstairs had closed, and for an hour she had been waiting.
Would they never finish ?

Once she had crept to the foot of the stairs to listen,
but everything was silent. At that moment Bryan
was operating ; at that moment the wheel of Fate was
turning—turning one way or the other. But which ?
With a shudder she went back to the sitting-room.
Would they never finish ?

Suddenly she stiffened and sat upright ; a door
above had opened, and someone was coming down the
stairs. It was a man's step, and she waited tensely
as he crossed the hall.

It was Doctor Arbuthnot, and he stood for a moment
by the door, smiling at her.

" A most successful operation, my dear Mrs. Marwood," he announced. " Your husband has stood it
wonderfully, and——"

She rose to her feet, holding to the arm of her chair
for support, and suddenly the old doctor's kindly face
became blurred and indistinct. There was a roaring
in her ears and then a merciful oblivion. And Doctor
Arbuthnot, catching her as she fell, turned as Bryan
Daventry and the other doctor entered the room.

" Fainted," he said briefly. " The news proved too
much. Just help me lift her on to that sofa."

For a few moments they bent over her ; then, as the
colour began to return to her cheeks, Bryan Daventry
stepped back and stood watching her from near the
fireplace.

" Just rest a little, Mrs. Marwood," Doctor Arbuthnot smiled reassuringly. " I broke the good news too abruptly, I'm afraid, and you fainted."

She slowly opened her eyes and stared round the room. What had he said—" stood it wonderfully ? " So the wheel had turned ; Fate had decided. And at that moment her eyes and Bryan's met and held. Then he looked away, and she lay back once more.

" A most brilliant operation, Daventry." The doctor she did not know was speaking. " You are to be congratulated. A great step in medical science."

" Thank you," answered Bryan, and his voice was dull and lifeless. " He stood it well. And in ten years or so we shall know for certain."

The woman stirred restlessly. Ten years ! Oh ! God—and then the others after that. . . .

" I am much obliged to you for letting me witness it," continued the other. " And it will be interesting to know from time to time how Mr. Marwood progresses."

" Most," assented Bryan. " I'll let you know, Birkett—keep you posted with the latest bulletins." He held out his hand abruptly. " Good-bye. Glad you managed to come, in spite of the short notice."

" Glad you asked me," returned the other cordially. With a slight bow to Mrs. Marwood he left the room, and Doctor Arbuthnot glanced at Bryan Daventry curiously.

" Difficult fellow to get hold of is Birkett," he said. " Usually too busy to eat."

" I made a particular point of his coming," said Daventry shortly. " Rang him up late last night. Don't you bother to wait, Arbuthnot. I'm going to have another look at the patient when he's quite out of the chloroform."

" Right." With a smile he held out his hand to Mrs. Marwood. " Don't move ; lie still a bit longer. And in a short while you'll have your husband out of bed and free to travel to some nice warm climate. I envy you, my dear young lady, envy you. My old bones like an English winter less and less each year."

With a cheerful wave to Daventry he fussed out of the room, and it was not until they heard the front door close behind him that Grace Marwood sat up on the sofa and stared at Bryan dully.

" Ten years—of hell. And not over then. I don't think I can, Bryan."

" You must, my dear ; and so must I." He gave a little mirthless laugh. " It's the penalty we've got to pay." Then, contemptuously—" He reminded me of the letter he had sent his lawyers this morning, before I began."

" I think that's what sticks in my throat more than anything," said the girl slowly. " He thinks he threatened you into operating—and operating successfully. And he'll never let me forget it."

" What does it matter what he thinks ? " answered Daventry wearily. " At any rate, you are safe now. Of the mentality of a man who would drive such a bargain the less said the better ; but that he was in a position to do so is an indisputable fact. He knew I wouldn't let you suffer—if there was the faintest possibility of avoiding it." Mechanically he lit a cigarette. " Well, I took him at his word, and he's not going to die—though I brought Birkett round in case of complications. My debt to him—our debt to him—is absolutely sponged out. As far as a human being may say such a thing, I have given him back his life. And if, Grace," his voice grew hard, " in the days to come he grows too vile, and you can't stand him—well, my dear, send for me, and I'll come. There is a limit to the demands one human being may make on another."

For a while he stood in front of her, watching her gravely ; then, very gently, he raised her to her feet.

" My dear, dear woman," he whispered, and, bending forward, he kissed her on the lips. For a moment she clung to him, then, with a little smile, he raised both her hands to his lips. " It's a funny world," he said, slowly, " damned funny. Take care of yourself, my darling."

Abruptly he turned away, and long after the door had closed behind him she stood where he had left her. Then at last, with a pitiful little moan, she sank down by the sofa and covered her face with her hands. And the inexorable turning of the wheel through the dreary future creaked mockingly through her brain.

For two hours she crouched there motionless ; then

with slow, lagging steps she passed through the hall and up the stairs to her husband's room.

10

It was a week before the hospital nurse could be dispensed with—a wasted week to John Marwood. Only on rare occasions had he seen his wife alone— and never the doctor. Whenever Daventry had been the nurse had remained in the room, which had necessitated his bottling up his verbal arrows, or so disguising them that they had lost half their sting.

He had tried congratulating Daventry once on the success of the operation, in a way which only just veiled the innuendo underneath, but the result had not been a success.

The cold, frozen stare which had greeted the remark on the part of the nurse, who cordially loathed her patient, and the contemptuous indifference of the doctor himself, had stung him to the boiling point of fury. But he could wait : there was plenty of time yet to make his wife and her lover feel the lash. It was typical of the man that he always thought of Daventry as her lover, though at the bottom of his mind he knew he was not.

With his wife he had been a little more successful. He had had the satisfaction of seeing her flinch and change colour at his sneers, but she had deigned no answer, and had finally left the room in silence. But it didn't matter : there was plenty of time—years yet—to revenge himself on the guilty pair.

The nurse left in the morning, and it was in the afternoon, after a light lunch, that life began to look really good to John Marwood. That cursed, thin-lipped woman would badger him no longer ; he was free : free to enjoy himself. . . . He had written the preceding day to his lawyer, requesting him to return the sealed letter, as the necessity for it no longer existed, and he was expecting to get it back by the next delivery. A wise precaution—to wait till the nurse had gone, undoubtedly : she looked the sort of woman who would read anything. . . . He hadn't quite made up his mind yet whether he would destroy it or not. There didn't seem to be much object in keeping it, and yet it was rather a pity to do away with such a literary gem, especially with Simpson's signed statement underneath. A useful document to possess : he particularly liked that phrase, " at the threshold of eternity." No : on mature consideration he would keep it. Quite possibly it would come in handy later on.

A knock came at the door, and a footman brought in the mail. Yes : there was a letter right enough from his lawyer's firm, and he picked it out and put it on one side to deal with later. Then, with a sudden change of expression he picked it up again : it struck him that it seemed very thin to contain any enclosure. In fact, he realized at once that it didn't, and hurriedly slit open the envelope.

" Dear Sir," it ran . . .

" In the absence of our Mr. Gatehouse on a short holiday we
beg to say in reply to yours of yesterday's date that we are unable
to find any trace of the sealed letter to which you refer."

And he had addressed it to Gatehouse, care of his
firm, so that in case he was away it would be opened
by them.

" Tell Simpson to come to me," he said querulously
to the footman who was making up the fire.

" Very good, sir." The man departed, and John
Marwood again read the brief, typewritten letter.
" Unable to find any trace." What did the fool
mean ?

" Simpson," he cried agitatedly, as the impassive
footman came into the room, " you remember that
letter I gave you to send to my lawyer the day before
I was operated on ? "

" Perfectly, sir." A quick change came over his
face, as if the question was a little unexpected, and
necessitated a change of plan.

" Well, I've just had a letter saying they never
had it." In his excitement he sat up in bed, and as
his eyes fell on the footman his jaw dropped foolishly.
" Wh—what on earth are you doing, Simpson ? " he
stammered.

" Locking the door, Mr. Marwood," returned
Simpson imperturbably, " in order to ensure that no
one will interrupt our little conversation. . . . "

" But I—I don't understand. Who is going to
interrupt us ? And, damn you, who told you to sit

down ? " John Marwood was rapidly losing his temper. If this impertinent fellow thought he was going to presume, he'd soon find his error. His presence was no longer in the least degree necessary : in fact, in many ways it might be a good thing to get rid of him at once. And then, with a sudden, unspeakable rage, he saw that this impassive, insufferable servant had drawn from his pocket the very letter which he had been told to send to the lawyer over a week ago. He sat there, lolling in his chair, holding it loosely between his fingers, and on his face there hovered a faint, mocking smile.

"Is it too much to hope," said Marwood icily, "that I may be honoured with some small explanation ? "

"Far from it, John Marwood," returned the other. "It is in order that you may have an explanation in full that I have locked the door."

The invalid's eyes narrowed. To be called John Marwood—by one of his footmen ! What was it— blackmail ? He became uneasily aware that some of the statements in his death-bed accusation were, to put it mildly, somewhat exaggerated. But this man couldn't know that : anyway, he couldn't prove it.

"In the first place," continued Simpson impassively, "shall we consider this interesting effusion ? Is it too much to say that it is an abominable tissue of vile and malicious lies from start to finish, which by reason of the time when it was written would have carried conviction in the event of your death ? "

" You impertinent scoundrel," spluttered Marwood. " Give me that letter at once."

Simpson laughed. " Always ready to learn, John Marwood, I continued to listen outside the door of the sitting-room that day, after you had left the vantage point of the key-hole and gone in. And so I happen to know what really occurred. This—" he twiddled the letter between his fingers and thumb, " hardly seems to be exactly—shall we say—accurate. You seem to be finding it a little difficult to speak, so while you compose yourself—for I have a little more to say to you, John Marwood—I think I will take the precaution of removing that hand-bell from your reach. And I may say," he continued, as he resumed his seat, " that if you shout, I shall gag you."

The man in bed stared at him with dilated eyes : was he mad—or dreaming ?

" In the first place," said Simpson, leaning forward and speaking in his usual dispassionate voice, " do you really think that I'm a footman by trade ? "

" I—I—— " stammered Marwood, " I've never thought about it."

" Do you remember, John Marwood, in the days when you had a business, a certain confidential clerk to whom, for some reason or other, you took a dislike ? "

" My God ! " muttered the invalid weakly. " You're . . . "

" Beginning to come back, is it ? Yes—I'm Henry Firebrace : whom you sacked without a character, because in the vile meanness of your petty bullying soul you knew he despised and loathed you. You faked up a reason—anything was good enough, and you sacked him, at a time when clerks were a drug on the market, and his wife was having her first child. He tramped all over London, John Marwood, looking, begging for work—but no one wanted clerks, certainly not those without a character. And he couldn't get work." The speaker's dark eyes glowed sombrely. " No work, John Marwood—no money. And his wife was having her first child. Do you know what happened ? The child was born dead, and the mother died two days later. . . . "

A log hissed and spluttered in the grate, while the man in bed stared fascinated at the speaker. Henry Firebrace ! Now that he knew, he marvelled he had never recognized him before, great though the change was.

" He made one appeal to you, John Marwood, if you remember. Told you the reason of his appeal. . . . Went—down—on—his—knees. . . . And you laughed in his face, and told him that yours was a business company, and not a babies' crèche." The man in the chair swallowed twice : then in the same level voice he continued :

" For a while after his wife had died, Henry Fire-brace went mad. And while he was mad he committed a burglary, and was caught by the police and sent to prison. When he came out the war had just started, and the thought of it appealed to him. So Henry

Firebrace died, and Charles Simpson enlisted, and in the ordinary course of affairs was called on to kill a German every now and then. . . . And one night he started to think, John Marwood. The Germans whom he killed had never done him any harm : many of them, doubtless, were quite decent, pleasant fellows. So if he killed them, was there any logical reason why in the fullness of time he shouldn't—provided he came through all right—kill the man who had done him such grievous harm ? "

" One is war : the other is murder," said Marwood thickly.

" True : but this thinker was not concerned with such niceties. All he could bother with was the thought that he would infinitely sooner put a bayonet into the stomach of the man he hated, than into that of a complete stranger, even though he was a German. So he played with the idea, John Marwood : and the more he played with it—the more he liked it." The footman's eyes, hard now and merciless, were fixed on the trembling man in bed.

" In due course he was demobilized, and having found out where you lived, he applied for a post as your footman. He heard you were an invalid, and if he had found that in truth you were—that you were, in reality, a sick man—he might even at the eleventh hour have stayed his hand, and foregone his revenge. Instead, he found that you were even viler and more utterly inhuman than you had been in the past, and that your peculiar faculty for inspiring hatred in those around you had grown with the years. So he decided to bide his time. . . . "

With a trembling hand Marwood wiped the sweat from his forehead.

" He liked to gloat over you, John Marwood, and say to himself, ' Some day I will do to him what in the past he did to me.' And not one single word you spoke, not one single act you did, ever tended to inspire in him one vestige of pity. He saw you for what you are—utterly and infinitely despicable. And then came the day when they found you had cancer." He paused and smiled slowly. " Once again he decided to give you a chance : cancer is a sufficient punishment in itself. Once again the brief twinge of mercy was killed at birth—even as his child was born dead, John Marwood—by the interview he overheard in the sitting-room. And then—this letter." He held it up in front of the other's face, and this time he laughed gently. " This letter . . . which you so trustingly gave him to post. Had you died, John Marwood, under the operation, it would have been handed direct to Doctor Daventry—even as it will be handed to him after your death—now."

With a strangled scream Marwood started up, only to be hurled back again on his pillows by the impassive footman.

" He didn't want you to die," continued Simpson. " He told Doctor Arbuthnot that he trusted the operation would be successful. And it was, John Marwood, wonderfully so. So successful that for the past week, from what he knows of your mentality, you have been gloating over the future in front of you. A revenge such as you love is yours for the asking—so you have been thinking : and in that dark, fetid mind of yours you have been planning every detail of it. . . . And now, you wretched brute, it's going to be snatched away from you." With his face blazing with implacable hatred he rose and stood over the cowering man. " For you're going to die, John Marwood ; even as my wife died : and as you die just remember that your wife will be able to find happiness at last with the man she loves—and that he has been started on the road to fame by you."

His hands were on Marwood's throat, and as the terrified man's mouth opened in a plea for mercy, the footman slipped in a gag. Then he released him and stood back watching the agonized terror in the rolling eyes. After a moment he turned away and took a bottle off the shelf. He filled a wine glass standing on the table by the bed, and then once more he bent over the other man.

" A little prussic acid, John Marwood," he murmured, and deftly holding his hand steady, he poured the contents of the glass into the other's mouth. His eyes bored into his victim's brain as he carefully caught a few drops that were spilled on his handkerchief. Then, with a quick wrench, he extracted the gag. . . .

For a moment or two he watched the writhing, convulsed man : then, as impassively as ever, he took

three or four of the bottles off the shelf and placed
them on the table.

And before he softly turned the key in the door and
left the room, the body of John Marwood had ceased
to writhe.   Prussic acid is rapid in its action. . . .

II

It was two hours later, in the middle of tea, that a
violent peal on the bell of John Marwood's room
disturbed the assembled servants.

" He seems to be becoming convalescent," murmured
Simpson.

" Go up and see, will you ? " ordered Mr. Parkins.
" Our period of peace is over, I suppose."

Simpson rose and walked to the door, only to come
back in a moment or two looking a little
agitated.

" It's Mrs. Marwood, Mr. Parkins.   I think something nas happened.   You'd better come."

Majestically the butler rose and followed the footman
—only to pause and turn white at what he heard.

" Dead, madam ? "   It was Simpson who was
speaking.   " Impossible.   Why, when I left Mr. Marwood. . . . "   He ran up the stairs quickly.

" Ring up Doctor Daventry at once, Parkins," said
Grace Marwood.   " Oh ! it's dreadful. . . . "   She
sank into a chair, half fainting.

" Doctor Daventry will be round at once, madam,"
said the butler, in a shaking voice, and as he spoke
Simpson came down the stairs.

" I fear, madam, there is no doubt what has
happened," he murmured gently. " By some extraordinary error, Mr. Marwood must have taken a dose
of prussic acid in mistake for his tonic. Both bottles
are on the table by his bed : but the glass smells
strongly of the poison."

The appearance of her maid cut short any further
conversations, and the butler and Simpson retired
once more to the servants' hall to discuss the sudden
tragedy.

" Undoubtedly prussic acid," said Simpson. " The
smell is unmistakable : the effect almost instantaneous.
And if he drank the whole glass it was enough to kill
ten men."

" What was it doing there at all ? " demanded the
butler.

Simpson shrugged his shoulders. " Something to
do with Doctor Daventry's treatment, I expect. It's
labelled ' poison,' and marked ' for external application
only.' "

" Well," declaimed Mrs. Thomson, " it don't seem
right to speak ill of the dead, and 'im not cold—but
for all that, I says ' Good riddance.' And I don't
mind who 'ears me, neither. Lor ! Mr. Simpson, you
'ave a nerve, you 'ave. Going on with your tea, an'
all. An' just seen 'im dead."

Simpson smiled. " We got used to it in France,

Mrs. Thomson, you know. A little more sugar this time, please."

" What was he doing when you left him ? " said the butler after a while.

" Taking his tonic—as far as I could see," remarked Simpson, helping himself to jam.

" The person I'm sorry for is that there young doctor," remarked Mr. Parkins, sententiously. " After being so successful—for this to happen."

" Quite, Mr. Parkins : quite," agreed Simpson. " However, these accidents will happen."

" You're quite right, Simpson," remarked the butler, reminiscently. " They will. Why, when I was with Lord Nairn. . . . "

But the providential arrival of one of the footmen saved them from the remainder of the oft-told harrowing details.

" The doctor wants to see you, Simpson. Up in the bedroom."

As impassively as ever, Simpson left the room.

" I understand you saw Mr. Marwood last ? " Bryan Daventry was standing at the foot of the bed as he entered.

" I did, sir—to the best of my belief." He glanced at the figure in the bed over which the bedclothes had been completely pulled.

" What was he doing ? "

" Preparing to take his tonic, sir, I think. I heard the sound of bottles clinking as I left the room."

" How came this bottle of prussic acid on the table beside the bed ? "

" I really couldn't say, sir. A most unfortunate tragedy." His steady, inscrutable eyes met those of the doctor, and after a while he felt in his pocket and produced a paper. " This might interest you, sir," he murmured. " I found it on the floor when I came up after Mrs. Marwood had discovered her husband's death."

Casually, Bryan Daventry glanced at it : then, as he read, his face grew black with rage. It was John Marwood's " death-bed " accusation.

" The infernal blackguard," he muttered.

" Precisely, sir," remarked the footman. " An infernal blackguard."

" Do you object if I burn that ? " said the doctor slowly.

" If you don't, sir, I shall."

For a moment or two Daventry studied the paper in his hand : then he stared at the footman. " It looks as if something had been cut off at the bottom," he remarked slowly.

" Now you mention it, sir, so it does," agreed Simpson. " Shall I put it in the fire ? "

In silence they watched it burn : then the footman stabbed the ashes with a poker till nothing but a fine dust was left.

" I don't quite understand you, my friend," said Daventry, thoughtfully.

" Indeed, sir," murmured the footman.

" Have you always been a footman ? "

" Always is a long time, sir," remarked Simpson, quietly. " Might I ask if you have definitely decided on the cause of Mr. Marwood's death ? "

" Yes, my friend, I have. Mr. Marwood died as the result of a dose of prussic acid administered——" he paused, and—was it his imagination, or was there, indeed, the ghost of a smile lurking again behind those expressionless eyes—" administered inadvertently, by himself."

" In mistake for his tonic," murmured the footman.

" In mistake for his tonic," agreed the doctor.

Simpson moved towards the door, and it was just as he was opening it that he spoke once more. And this time his voice was a little different.

" An infernal blackguard is dead, Doctor Daventry. It may be of interest to you and Mrs. Marwood to know that your secret has died with him."

He left the room : and for a long while Bryan Daventry stood frowning at the closed door. Then, with a last look at the motionless figure in the bed, he too, went out. . . . And dimly through the window came the roar of the traffic from distant Piccadilly.

THE END.